Night Music

A Novel

Night Music

Copyright 2017 © Deanna Lynn Sletten

Paperback Edition

ISBN – 13: 978-1-941212-33-2
ISBN – 10: 1-941212-33-6

Editor: Samantha Stroh Bailey of Perfect Pen Communications
Cover Designer: Deborah Bradseth of Tugboat Design

Night Music

A Novel

Deanna Lynn Sletten

Novels by Deanna Lynn Sletten

One Wrong Turn

Finding Libbie

Maggie's Turn

As the Snow Fell

Walking Sam

Destination Wedding

Summer of the Loon

Sara's Promise

Memories

Widow, Virgin, Whore

Kiss a Cowboy

A Kiss for Colt

Kissing Carly

Outlaw Heroes

Prologue

March 29, 1969

Joseph Russo crouched in a pit surrounded by sandbags, his M-16 standing at attention beside him. It was 02:00 and all of Firebase Jack was on red alert. Two hours earlier, the rangers out in the field had called in a warning: a large number of North Vietnamese soldiers were heading their way. Charlie was coming; it was only a matter of when.

Three other men occupied the small sandbagged area where Joe sat. Clint stood nearest to the 155 artillery weapon, casually smoking a cigarette with his own M-16 slung over his shoulder. He was a red leg, an artillery man who operated one of the several 155s on the base. Roger, a tall, slender man with light blond hair, stood across from Joe. He was prepared but didn't look all that concerned. However, Tony, a short, wiry guy who everyone called "spaghetti," was smoking and pacing in a circle, clutching his weapon in his hand.

"They're coming," Tony said, stopping to stare Joe dead in the eyes. "I can feel it. They're so close, I can smell them."

Clint snorted as he crushed his cigarette out under his heavy boot. "Spaghetti, get a grip," he said in his smooth Arkansas drawl. "All you smell is yourself after a week without a shower."

Roger laughed. "Smell them. That's funny."

Tony narrowed his eyes. "I can. If you'd ever been down one of their rat-hole tunnels, you'd be able to smell them too. It's the sweat, man. The smell of sweat and fear."

Joe watched as Tony continued to pace in his tight circle. Tony was in the middle of his second tour. He'd been a tunnel rat during his first tour, and part of this one. That was where his nickname "spaghetti" had originated. He was thin and limber and able to twist and contort his body in the narrowest of places like a string of spaghetti. Unfortunately, his nerves had become frayed after months of slipping through Viet Cong tunnels in search of the enemy. Sending him to Firebase Jack was supposed to be easier on him. From what Joe had observed, Tony's nerves still got the best of him.

Despite Tony's jittery disposition, he and Joe had clicked as friends. They were both Italians from New York and they shared the same background. They'd grown up in rough neighborhoods with tough dads. Joe, with his never-ending patience and calm demeanor, was the only guy on the base who could tolerate Tony's endless, frantic energy.

Joe gazed up into the clear night sky. The stars glittered so bright he could make out the constellations. It was hot, despite the sun having gone down hours ago, and the air was thick with humidity. Sweat rolled down his neck and back. He'd spread out his poncho beneath him, but the damp ground seeped through. Nothing ever dried out in this godforsaken place.

He cocked his head and listened to the night sounds around him, crickets humming in the tall elephant grass beyond the base's perimeter and nocturnal birds chirping their strange songs.

Night music. All was safe as long as the night music played on.

"Relax, Tony," Joe said calmly. "As long as we can hear the night music, we're okay."

Tony stopped a second and listened as he sniffed the air. The nightly sounds seemed to pacify him for a moment, but then he continued pacing in his small circle.

Joe reached inside his shirt, pulled out a worn envelope, and unfolded it. He slipped out one of the four letters inside and carefully opened it. The handwritten words filled the page in perfectly shaped cursive letters. *A girl's writing*, he thought. Clear, with a touch of flowery script. He read the letter as he had dozens of times before.

Grand Falls is so small that you can't walk down the street without waving or saying hello to at least ten people. The shops sit in a perfect line down Main Street with the bakery's scent wafting out onto the street, inviting you in for a tasty treat while the gift and candle shops tempt you with their latest wares through their big, shiny windows.

Joe sighed. Were there really towns like that anymore? He sifted through the letters again and found the small photo of the girl who'd written it. It looked like a high school or college picture. In it, a lovely young woman with long, straight, dark hair and amazing amber-brown eyes stared back at him. She had the fresh-scrubbed look of a small-town girl, not the overly made-up type he was used to back home in the Bronx. He imagined that this girl wore nicely tailored clothes, low-heeled shoes, and listened to soft rock on the radio. She probably went to the movies every Saturday night with her friends then stopped for a Coke and maybe a piece of pie at the local café afterward. She was an all-American girl, and it made him smile just looking at her.

"There he goes again," Clint said. "Joe's getting all goo goo eyed over his girlfriend's picture."

Joe glanced up. "She's not my girlfriend. We're just pen pals."

"Yeah, man. Just keep saying that, but we ain't buying it," Roger said, smirking.

Joe ignored him. He knew the guys liked teasing him, but he didn't care. He enjoyed the letters from Charlotte. Her first letter had been in a packet sent from an organization that wrote to soldiers. Joe never got mail, so when the company clerk asked who wanted a letter, he'd been excited to take it. From there, he and Charlotte had started writing regularly. He knew little about her except what she looked like from her picture and what she told him about her town. She'd said her brother had died in Vietnam a year earlier and she wanted to know more about what it was like to be there. Joe never gave much detail—he didn't want to share the horrors of war with a young woman—and hoped her letters would keep coming. He liked the idea of living in the same small, friendly town your entire life where everyone knew your name. It was the exact opposite of where he'd grown up—people came and went and no one talked to you.

"Do you think charming small towns still exist?" he asked no one in particular. "You know, like Mayberry from *The Andy Griffith Show*."

Clint grinned. "I wouldn't mind believing that Hooterville from *Petticoat Junction* actually exists."

Joe chuckled.

Roger shrugged. "I grew up in a small town in Wisconsin where everyone knew my name. I couldn't wait to get out of there."

"Well, you picked a great place to move, coming here," Clint said.

"Like I had a choice," Roger said.

"Shh! Listen!" Tony called out to their group.

Everyone sat silent, as did the men in the other pits around them. The crickets and birds had stopped chirping. The silence was deafening.

An explosion shattered the silence. A claymore at the outer perimeter of the firebase had gone off.

Charlie was here.

Everyone went into action. Joe quickly stuffed the letters and picture back inside his pocket and reached for his weapon. Another claymore blew, then another. Gunfire erupted as more claymores blasted, and then out of nowhere, mortars exploded at a rapid pace. It took Joe a moment to realize which side was shooting them.

"Where the hell did they get so many mortars from?" Clint screamed over the noise.

No one had time to answer.

Joe pulled himself out of the sandbagged area and assessed the situation. Most of the men on the base had M-16s and M-60s, but he thought he heard the distinctive deeper sound of AK-47s within the base.

The back! Crap! Joe remembered how lightly guarded that area was. The North Vietnamese Army must have slipped in through there.

"This way, Tony!" Joe yelled over the noise.

Tony followed as they ran toward the back area. Sure enough, there were NVA soldiers streaming inside, shooting at anything that moved.

Joe and Tony shot back, picking them off one after another. Roger joined them, and soon there were several other men at their side warding off the tide of enemy soldiers pouring in.

"They just keep coming!" Roger shouted. "What the hell?" He pulled a grenade from his belt and ripped the pin out.

As he threw it in the direction of the incoming soldiers, Joe and the rest of the men turned and ducked. The blast was deafening, but it did the job. The heavy stream of NVA slowed down.

Overhead, two Cobras flew over the base, taking turns shooting up the outside perimeter with their mini guns. Joe looked up and smiled. "The good guys have arrived."

"Head back to the pit," Roger told Joe. "No one's guarding Clint. Tony and I have this covered."

Joe started to run back to the pit when suddenly a sharp, searing pain hit his left leg. He crumpled to the ground. Looking down, he saw blood gushing out from below his knee.

Tony and Roger were there in an instant. Tony fired past Joe and an NVA fell to the ground. The twosome grabbed Joe under each arm and carried him back to the sandbagged area as Roger screamed for a medic.

"I'm fine," Joe said as his friends set him down against the sandbags. Joe knew he wasn't fine. His leg looked torn to shreds and he hadn't been able to stand on it. Strangely enough, he felt nothing. No pain at all.

"Stay here!" Roger ordered. "If you see one of those damned NVA, shoot him!"

By now the Cobras had run out of ammunition and the red legs had taken over firing their 155s out into the base's perimeter. As if in a dream, Joe watched as Clint expertly manned his weapon. He gazed up and saw the most amazing sight: a Spooky gunship had arrived and took over where the Cobras had left off. White and red rain seemed to be falling from it, lighting up the inky night sky.

"Will you look at that?" Clint asked. He'd stopped shooting and was also staring up at the magnificent airship. "That'll teach Charlie."

A large, square man jumped into the pit, startling Joe.

"Don't shoot me. I'm the medic." He got right to work on Joe's leg, cutting his pant leg off to get a better look, then placing a tourniquet on the lower part of his thigh. "How ya feeling, soldier?"

"Fine. Dizzy. Kind of dazed," Joe said. He stared at the burly medic and wondered why he couldn't remember the guy's name.

"You've lost a lot of blood, so that's bound to make you dizzy," the guy said. "Just keep still and enjoy the light show. We'll get you evacuated as soon as the party is over."

"Evacuated? Can't you just wrap it up?" Joe asked.

The medic chuckled. "Sorry, guy, but you need more than a Band-Aid. But look on the bright side—you just got your ticket home."

Chapter One

September 1970

Charlotte Parsons slipped out of her 1964 Pontiac GTO and smoothed down her plaid skirt before picking up a pile of books. It was her first day of college, and she was both nervous and excited. It had felt like this day would never come, and now, here she was.

"How do I look?" Patty Hartman asked as she stepped out of the passenger side.

Char smiled. Patty was one of her two closest friends who she'd known since kindergarten. She was always worried about her appearance. With her auburn hair and creamy white skin, Patty was a very pretty girl, especially with her rich brown eyes. She was a little plump—her words—but she knew exactly how to dress to accentuate her best features.

"You look amazing, as always," Char's other friend, Jenny Burke, said as she exited the back seat. "I'm sure all the boys will love you." Jenny was not as tall as her friends, but slender, and her light hair and blue eyes were her best features.

"But do I look fat in this dress?" Patty asked. "Do I look old enough or like a kid playing a grown up?"

"Old enough for what?" Char asked, laughing softly. She brushed back her long, dark hair and closed the car door. Walking around to where the other two were, they all stood and stared at the school grounds spread out before them.

They were attending their hometown college, Grand Falls University. It sat on the edge of town, right on the banks of the Illinois river. Lush green lawns stretched out around the large campus that held up to five thousand students. The buildings were gothic style, built in the 1920s, which made them appear even more commanding and impressive.

"Old enough to attract a junior or senior," Patty said, breaking the silence. "I don't want to go to college forever to find a guy."

The trio began walking across the parking lot toward the buildings. Throngs of students carrying stacks of books were everywhere. The first day was usually a crazy rush for freshmen who hadn't yet learned the campus's layout. Char knew the school well, though. She'd not only been here many times with her boyfriend, Deacon Masterson, but had walked the campus earlier this summer to make sure she knew exactly where her classes were.

"You know, Patty," Jenny interjected, "some of us are actually coming to school to learn, not to meet men. I want to graduate so I have a degree and can support myself."

Patty visibly shivered. "Don't even say that! I don't plan on working a day of my life. That's what men are for."

Jenny rolled her eyes. "How very 1950s of you."

Char laughed. "I can't wait to start classes. I love learning."

"Easy for you to say," Patty said. "You already have a cute boyfriend who's a senior. Now it's my turn."

Char couldn't deny that. She and Deke had been dating for almost a year, and it was going pretty well. She'd known him nearly her entire life because he'd been her brother Jeremy's best friend since they were five. Deke had never looked at her twice until she turned eighteen last year. Their casual friendship had grown into a sweet romance.

The girls stopped in front of the main building. "This is it," Char said. "I go to the English building from here."

"Me, too," Jenny said.

Patty sighed dramatically. "I have science first. I'll see you both at lunch."

Char and Jenny headed inside the building, found their classroom, and took seats near the back. The room was small with tall windows across one wall. The desks were old and scarred from years of use. None of this bothered Char in the least. She was excited to be in English class. The entire year of freshman English was devoted to writing a thesis paper and reading the classics. For most students, that was torture, but for Char, it was heaven. She enjoyed reading, and especially loved to write. She'd worked on the high school newspaper, and she hoped eventually to be on the college paper, as well. Her parents thought she was focusing on an English degree to become a teacher, but she secretly dreamed of becoming a writer.

As the other students filled the room, Char glanced around to see if she recognized anyone. Some of the kids from her high school were attending this university, while several had gone to schools as far away as Northern California and Florida. Char had never even considered leaving for college. She liked their small town and the people in it, and, truth be told, she wouldn't have been brave enough to leave anyway.

Just as the class filled up, Jenny nudged her.

"Look at that guy coming in. Is he a student?" Jenny asked.

Char saw a man wearing faded army fatigues and a black T-shirt with a pack on his back. His face looked young except for a few light creases on his forehead—worry lines— and strands of gray running through his black hair. What stood out the most, though, was the cane he used to walk, his left leg moving stiffly. He ignored the stares that came his way as he found one of the last open seats near the back of the room and slowly lowered himself into the chair.

"He must be a student," Char whispered to Jenny.

"But he has gray hair."

"He must be a vet," Char said quietly. "He's wearing fatigues. I don't recognize him, though. He's not someone who went to our high school."

It wasn't unusual to see Vietnam veterans at the college. Some of the local boys who'd served had come back home to attend college. If Char's brother, Jeremy, had survived, he'd have gone to school here, too. The mere thought of him tore at Char's heart.

"He looks old enough to be teaching this class, not taking it," Jenny said.

Char studied the man. He had olive skin, a strong jaw, and nice cheekbones. His hair was thick and wavy and slightly long, but combed neatly. Most of the guys at the college had long hair, some even in ponytails. But not this guy. His strong facial features wouldn't look right with long hair.

As Char studied him, the man glanced up and looked right at her. She turned away quickly, feeling her face flush at being caught. But before she'd turned away, she'd seen his gray eyes. And he'd smiled, a small, kind smile.

The professor walked in and began speaking, so Char's

attention turned to him. But she couldn't help but feel the eyes of the stranger on her throughout the class.

* * *

That evening, Char sat on the steps of her parents' house, waiting for Deke to pick her up. The front yard consisted of two rectangular sections of perfectly mowed lawn with a sidewalk down the middle. A three-foot-high white picket fence surrounded the yard, and flower gardens and rose beds bloomed in front of the white-railed porch that ran the full width of the house. It was a typical small-town, middle-class home in a nice, quiet neighborhood where everyone mowed their lawns on Saturdays and women tended flower beds regularly. Char's mother belonged to the local flower club, as did most of the women on the block. No one in the neighborhood would ever consider letting weeds overrun their prize flowerbeds. Char found it amusing but admitted that their efforts did bring charm to their neighborhood.

The sky was painted in pink and red streaks as the sun dipped over the horizon. She had already eaten dinner with her parents and now was going with Deke to a movie at the drive-in. Every Tuesday and Thursday during the school year the theater ran discounted movies for the returning college students. Tonight, the movie was *M*A*S*H*, which they'd already seen earlier in the year when it had first come out. Deke had enjoyed it though, so Char didn't mind seeing it again.

As Char waited, she thought back on her first day of school. She had a full schedule; all her classes were for her general education requirements. She loved English and history, didn't mind algebra or social studies but wasn't a big fan of science. English was the only class she knew anyone in. All throughout her school years, she'd known everyone in her classes. It felt odd now not knowing everyone.

And then there was the guy with the cane.

He was in her English and history classes. He stood out because it was so obvious he was a veteran by the way he dressed and the use of the cane. Their college had a huge anti-war presence; Deke was the president of their Students for a Democratic Society chapter. Even though the national SDS had gone under, many colleges still had active chapters. For that reason, many of the Vietnam vets who attended the school tried not to stand out. But this guy didn't seem to care. Was he flaunting his service, or did he simply not realize his fatigues gave him away?

"Hi."

A deep voice startled her out of her thoughts. She looked up, and there he stood. The very man she'd been thinking about.

"Hi," she said after recovering from the shock of seeing him there. It was as if she'd conjured him up.

He gave her a small smile. "Sorry if I startled you. I was walking by and saw you sitting there. I didn't realize you hadn't noticed me."

Char stood, not sure if she should walk to the gate or stay where she was. She didn't want to be rude, but she also didn't know this guy. He seemed nice enough, and had a friendly smile. Still she was hesitant. "I was just spacing out, I guess," she said.

"Yeah. I do that sometimes too." He raised his hand to shake. "I'm Joe, by the way. We have the same English and history classes."

Looking at his outstretched hand, Char had no choice but to draw nearer and shake it. "I'm Charlotte. But everyone calls me Char."

"Hi, Char." He smiled warmly.

Char noticed that his gray eyes had silvery flecks in them. She'd never seen eyes like his before. "Did you walk all the way from the college?" she asked, her eyes unconsciously drifting to his cane.

He nodded. "Yeah. It's only a few blocks. Don't let this thing fool you," he said, lifting the wooden cane. "I get around pretty good in spite of it."

Char felt her face grow warm at being caught staring at it. "Sorry."

"No need. It's obvious, right?"

"Do you live near here?" Char asked, wanting to change the subject. She was unnerved by his straightforward manner. She'd been taught better than to point out a person's disability, yet she'd done it without thinking. She wasn't usually that comfortable to speak so bluntly with someone she'd just met.

"I live over at Mrs. Bennington's Boarding House."

"Oh. She's nice. You'll like it there," Char said. Mrs. Bennington was a widow who'd opened her large home to earn extra money. Her son had died years before in the Korean War and her husband had passed away too.

"Yes, she is. She keeps leaving homemade cookies in my room. I think she wants to fatten me up." Joe chuckled.

"Yeah, that's how she is."

Silence fell between them just as night settled in. Char fished for something to say. "Do you have family around here?"

He shook his head. "No, I don't. I'm from New York. I'm surprised you haven't mentioned my Bronx accent. Everyone I've met has made a point to ask about it."

Char had heard it but thought it was rude to point it out. "I noticed. I just thought that you might have moved here because of relatives."

"Nope. I'd heard this was a great place to live. After leaving Nam, I figured a nice quiet town might be just the thing for me."

Char studied him, wanting to ask where he'd been stationed in Vietnam and what it had been like. He'd brought it up, after all, so it gave her an opening. But she couldn't make herself ask. She barely knew him. "Who told you about this town? Someone from here?"

Joe nodded and looked into her eyes. "A really sweet girl told me, so it had to be true."

Char tilted her head and stared at him, wondering who that girl could have been. His sweet smile caused a chill of delight to run up her spine. It surprised her.

Before either could say another word, Deke pulled up in his car and hit the horn, making both Joe and Char jump.

"Hey, baby. You ready to go?" Deke called out. He drove a 1965 white Pontiac Firebird Convertible with a candy apple red interior. The top was down.

Both Joe and Char turned to look at him a moment before she came to her senses and spoke.

"Hey, Deke. I'm ready." She opened the gate and walked through as Joe moved aside to let her pass.

"Who's your friend?" Deke said, eyeing Joe.

She hesitated. She knew Deke wasn't generally polite to Vietnam veterans. "This is Joe. He started school today, too. We have English together. He lives down the street at Mrs. Bennington's Boarding House."

Joe stepped over and opened the passenger door for Char. Stunned, she gaped at him then hurriedly slipped inside.

He carefully closed the door. "And history, too," he said with a grin.

"Yes. History, too," Char repeated.

"See you tomorrow," Joe said to Char. Then he nodded at Deke and made his way down the sidewalk.

Deke's eyes narrowed as he watched Joe walk away, but then he turned and smiled at Char. "Ready to go?"

"Yeah." She was relieved Deke hadn't made a big deal about Joe. As they drove away from the house, Char's mind wasn't on the beautiful September evening or "Three Dog Night" playing on the stereo. Her thoughts were on Joe's gray eyes with the silver flecks and his warm smile.

* * *

Joe slowly walked along the sidewalk toward the boarding house, his rucksack full of books growing heavier with each step. He'd had months to recuperate after he'd been shot in Nam, and had also gone through physical therapy to help him learn to walk properly with his cane. His thigh bone had been shattered and he'd lost most of the muscle from the knee down. He was thankful to still have his leg, but sometimes it was frustrating how slowly he moved. He urged himself to go a little faster, wanting to get to his room and drop the heavy pack off his back.

His thoughts turned to Char as he walked. She was even more beautiful than her picture, and just as sweet as he'd thought she'd be. He'd been astonished this morning when he'd walked into his first class of the day and saw her sitting there. Since he'd believed she was already in college when she wrote to him two years before, he'd figured she'd be a junior or senior by now and their paths wouldn't cross. Seeing her sitting in English had been a wonderful surprise.

He'd meant to tell her tonight who he was when he'd stopped at her gate, but their conversation never gave him an opening.

He hadn't wanted to blurt out, "Hey, I'm the guy you were writing to in Vietnam." He was afraid that would scare her. If he could have eased it into the conversation, it would have been better. But then her boyfriend drove up in his fancy car and he'd lost his chance.

Joe made it to the boarding house and turned onto the flower-lined sidewalk that led up to the porch. Mrs. Bennington's house was an old Victorian with a wrap-around porch, a large formal dining room and parlor, and had three floors plus an attic. Besides Joe, four other people rented rooms from her, two on the second floor and two on the third. Each floor had a bathroom that they shared. Joe's room, however, was all the way up in the attic.

When Joe had first come to look at the available room, he'd noticed the steps leading up to a fourth floor. "What's up there?" he'd asked Mrs. Bennington.

"Oh, that's just the attic. There's a large room, but I rarely rent it. It has a tall ceiling with open beams and small dormer windows, but most people don't want to be up there."

A tall ceiling with open beams sounded wonderful to Joe. "Can I see it?" he'd asked.

Mrs. Bennington had looked surprised. "It's an awful lot of stairs for you to walk up every day," she'd said, glancing at his cane.

Joe had smiled. "Please?"

She'd shown him the room and Joe had fallen in love with the open space. He took it, foregoing adding meals to his rent so he could afford the larger room. He figured he could always buy a cheap meal at a café or the student union.

As Joe walked into the house, Mrs. Bennington greeted him from the parlor.

"Good evening, Joe. Have you eaten?"

He grinned. Even though he wasn't paying for meals, Mrs. Bennington still worried if he'd been fed. "Yes, ma'am, I have. I'm going up to bed."

"Well, if you get hungry, there's chocolate cake on the counter in the kitchen and milk in the fridge. Good night."

"Good night," he said, then headed up the stairs.

As he put his pack down in his room and lay on his bed, Joe thought again about Char. He'd see her every day for the next few months. At some point, he'd have a chance to tell her who he was.

Chapter Two

The movie flickered on the screen high above them as the speaker crackled from the window. Deke had raised the top of the car against the evening chill, allowing them privacy. Despite the bucket seats, Deke had his arm looped around Char and was kissing her neck. She wriggled away, sitting straight up in her seat.

"Come on, Deke. Let's watch the movie."

He hesitated a moment, then moved from her neck to her lips.

"Deke!"

"Ah, come on, baby," Deke said, still holding her close. "We hardly get any time alone anymore." He attempted another kiss as he ran his hand down to her waist to pull her closer.

"Not now, okay?" Char pulled away again and Deke finally gave up and fell back into his own seat.

"What's the matter, Char? You've been upset since I picked you up." He pushed his hair back from his face. He'd recently grown his blond hair longer as well as his side-burns and was also sporting a goatee. He was a handsome man with high cheekbones and a strong jawline. But it was his intense eyes that drew people, especially women, to him. They were a deep blue and seemed to stare right into your soul.

"Nothing's the matter," she insisted. "I thought you wanted to watch the movie."

Deke grinned at her. "I do. But I'd rather watch you." He took her hand. "We haven't been together, I mean really together, in a while. I was hoping we could sneak away tonight and be alone."

Char sighed. Ever since she and Deke had first made love a few weeks ago, it had become all he wanted to do when they were together. She enjoyed being with him but didn't feel like being intimate tonight. Her mind was elsewhere.

"I'm sorry. I'm just tired. It was a long day and I have a lot on my mind," she said.

Deke eyed her a moment. "Did that guy, that *soldier boy*, upset you? You've been distracted since we left your house."

Char shook her head. "No, he didn't. He just said hi, nothing more."

"Are you sure? Those damned vets are all alike. They come home and flaunt how tough they are because they killed a bunch of women and children. They're murderers, every one of them."

Char winced. She hated it when Deke talked like that. "Don't say that. Jeremy wasn't a murderer."

He immediately looked apologetic. "Oh, no, sweetie. You know I didn't mean Jeremy. Your brother had a heart of gold and didn't belong over there. He should have stayed home and gone to college. We're going to end this war and stop the bloodshed. And he should have been here, with me and his family, to see it end."

Char didn't look up. All she could think of was the last time she'd seen her big brother. He'd stood so proud in his uniform before shipping out to Vietnam. He'd been such a kind soul, but he'd said he wanted to do his duty then come home and move on with his life. He never got that chance. Within three months, he was dead.

Deke moved closer and slipped his arm lovingly around her shoulders. "Char, sweetie. I'm sorry. I didn't mean to upset you. You know I loved your brother. He was my best friend since kindergarten. I miss him as much as you do. When I talk about vets, I never mean him. He was special."

Char nodded. She was proud of Deke for his ability to stand up and speak his mind against the war, but she wasn't sure she believed in everything he said. She'd been confused since Jeremy's death. All her beliefs about duty and pride of country had flown out the window. She wanted desperately to understand why U.S. men, boys really, were dying so far away from home.

"Hey? Let's get out of here and do something else, okay?" Deke said, clearly trying to smooth things over.

"I want to go home," Char said. She didn't know why she was upset. She just was. Despite what she'd told Deke, her encounter with Joe had unnerved her. He'd seemed so familiar, yet she couldn't pinpoint why.

"Please stay out a little while longer. Hey, you're a big college girl now. Let's head over to the student union and have some coffee and hang out. I'll buy you a piece of pie." He smiled at her.

Char couldn't resist one of Deke's smiles. He was very charming when he wanted to be. "Okay. For a little while, I guess."

* * *

Char's first week of college went quickly and by Friday night, she was deep into schoolwork. She'd seen Joe every day in her

English and history classes but had been too busy to talk to him. When their eyes met, he'd just nodded and gone about his business. A couple of evenings, she saw him walking past her house on his way home. He was always alone, and Char felt bad for him. He seemed like a nice guy, but she knew it would be difficult for him to make friends at the college. Being a vet made him a pariah among the college crowd. She hated that it was true, but it was.

Char wondered if that would have happened to Jeremy. Ever since the My Lai Massacre, students had become even more outraged over the Vietnam War, and that anger had turned toward the soldiers, too, not just the politicians. It was hard for her to believe that people would have been hostile toward her brother, but now she'd never know. Because of that, though, she felt a little sorry for Joe.

Char took her book out to the front porch swing to sit and enjoy the evening as the sun hung low in the sky. She'd finished helping her mother make dinner and set the table, and was now just waiting for it to be ready. Opening the novel—required reading for English—she sighed with delight. It was *For Whom the Bell Tolls* by Ernest Hemingway. Char had already read all the works by Hemingway on her own in high school, but she was thrilled to have a chance to re-read it and discuss it with the class.

"Hi, again," a voice said not far from her.

Char jumped in her seat and almost dropped her book. There was Joe, standing at the bottom of the porch steps. *How on earth did he sneak up on me with a cane?*

"I'm sorry," he said. "I startled you again. I didn't mean to. I saw you were up here, reading, and your gate was open, so I just walked up."

Char looked over at the open gate. She guessed Joe had

taken that as an invitation to come in. "It's okay. I hadn't heard you come up."

"Sorry," he said again, looking sheepish. He wore his usual fatigues with a dark sweater, and had an army coat on over it, the baggie type with large pockets. His pack was on his back and looked heavy.

"Are you just now going home?" she asked. She'd been home since four o'clock. There were no evening classes on Friday, so it seemed odd he'd be going home this late.

"Yeah. I stayed at the school library to study. I like working in there."

Char watched as Joe shifted his stance a bit, as if his bag was getting the best of him. "Do you want to sit a minute? Your bag looks heavy." She moved over on the swing, making room for him.

"Thanks." Joe walked up the steps carefully and slid the pack off. It hit the porch floor with a thud. He slowly sat down on the swing, keeping his left leg straight as if he couldn't bend it.

"So, people actually have these. I've always wanted to sit on a porch swing," he said, turning to grin at Char.

"You've never sat on a porch swing? A lot of porches have them. Mrs. Bennington has one on hers," Char said.

"I know. I saw it. I just haven't had a chance to sit on it."

Char cocked her head. "Didn't anyone have a porch swing where you grew up?"

Joe laughed. "No, they didn't. We had stoops. Neighbors sat on the stoops at night to try to catch a cool breeze. Moms would sit together and take turns yelling at their kids to get out of the street when a car passed by. Most of the kids played ball or rode bikes in the street."

Char smiled at the image he'd created. "Was your mom one of the moms who yelled at the kids?"

His smile faded. "No. My mom died when I was very young."

"Oh, I'm sorry. I shouldn't have asked."

"No, it's okay. My dad did enough yelling for two parents, when he cared enough to notice what we were doing," Joe said.

"We? Do you have a brother or sister?"

Joe nodded. "A brother. He's two years younger than I am. My mom died when he was born."

"That's so sad. Your poor dad, having to raise two boys alone." Char's heart went out to Joe, thinking of him growing up without a mother's love.

"Oh, it wasn't as bleak as all that. I had aunts and uncles and a slew of cousins in the neighborhood, too," Joe said. "I think I was related to everyone in our building."

"Well, that's good." Char studied him a moment. "Can I ask you a question?"

"Sure."

"How old are you?"

Joe's brows rose. "What?"

"Well, I mean, I know it's a strange question, but you look older than most of the students attending college and, well…" Char stopped. She felt stupid for asking. "Forget it. I shouldn't have asked."

He gave her a slow smile. "I'm twenty-one."

"Really?"

Joe frowned. "Why? How old do I look?"

She felt her face grow warm. "Sorry. I didn't mean to imply you look old. It's just, well…"

"Are you going to start stammering again?" Joe teased.

"No. I just noticed that you have gray in your hair," she blurted out. The minute she said it, though, she was sorry. Again.

Joe ran his hand through his hair, looking thoughtful. "Oh,

yeah. This. When I had it shorter in the service, the gray didn't show. I didn't have any gray hair when I went into the army. I guess it's a by-product of living in hell for a few months."

Char winced. "I shouldn't have said anything. It was a stupid question."

He shook his head. "No, it wasn't. I've known guys who came home from Nam almost completely gray. It happens."

She was at a loss for words. How thoughtless of her to have brought it up. They sat there as night settled in, swinging the chair ever so slightly back and forth while listening as the crickets and frogs began their nightly serenade.

"It's so peaceful here," Joe said softly. "I love the sounds of the night."

Char relaxed. "I do too. The crickets and frogs have a tune all their own."

"Night music," Joe said.

Char looked at him quizzically. "What did you call it?"

"Night music," he repeated. "In Nam, as long as we could hear the sounds of the night, we knew all was safe. It's a comforting sound."

Char's mind began to spin. She'd heard that phrase before, but she couldn't remember where. It was related to Vietnam, though. She eyed Joe suspiciously. "Why did you come here? You have no family, no friends. Why here? Why in the middle of Illinois where you've never been before?"

Joe stared at her with his silvery gray eyes. "Because a beautiful girl told me all about this wonderful town and how peaceful it was and how everyone said hello when they passed you on the street. I had to see if such a place existed, and if it did, I wanted to live here." He pulled something out of the breast pocket of his jacket and handed it to Char.

She took it and gasped. It was a picture of her.

"You were the girl who told me about this town. I came because of your letters," Joe said gently. "I hope that doesn't creep you out. I didn't come here to bother you. I came here to go to school and enjoy a quiet life."

Char gaped at him in disbelief. "You're Joseph Russo? The soldier I wrote to in Vietnam?"

He nodded. "Yes. I so enjoyed your letters. They brightened my day. No one wrote to me while I was in-country, so I jumped at the chance to get one of the letters that a volunteer wrote. And I felt fortunate it was from you. You gave me something to look forward to."

Char stood suddenly, backing away from Joe. Glancing nervously between him and the front door, she asked, "Why didn't you tell me when we first met?"

Joe sat up straight in the swing. "I meant to, but I didn't have a chance until now. I didn't come here to scare you or bother you. I promise. I actually thought I'd never run into you. I thought you were a college student and you'd be ahead of me in school by the time I came here. You can imagine how surprised I was to see you in English class that first day. But I was happy about it, too."

Char lowered her voice. "I lied about my age so I could join the group of college girls who wrote letters. I wanted so badly to learn about the Vietnam War from a soldier's perspective. I was so devastated by my brother's death, I had to do something. I needed to try to understand."

"I know. You said that in your letters. I'm afraid I wasn't able to tell you very much. The army frowns on that. And to tell the truth, I really didn't want to share the horror stories of Vietnam with a beautiful girl. Reading about your life in this delightful town was what I enjoyed."

She stood there another minute, weighing his words. He seemed harmless. And, truth be told, she'd been the one to initiate the letters, not him. She took a deep breath and let it out slowly, then tentatively sat back down on the edge of the swing.

"I'm sorry I reacted that way," she said. "It did kind of freak me out. I never expected to meet you in person." She looked through the window at her father sitting in his chair, reading the newspaper. Her gaze returned to Joe. "Could you please not mention my writing to you in Vietnam to anyone in town, especially my parents? They'd be upset if they knew I'd been writing to a soldier I didn't know when I was only sixteen."

"It's our little secret," Joe assured her.

Char relaxed. The more she thought about it, the more she realized that he'd have no one to tell anyway. It wasn't like Joe would have any reason to talk to her parents.

"Can I have my picture back?" he asked.

She looked down at the photo in her hand. She supposed it wouldn't hurt if Joe had it. After all, she'd sent it to him. "Sure. Here."

"Thanks." He slid it back into his pocket. "I should be leaving. I'm glad I finally got the chance to tell you. I feel better about it now."

Char stood. "I'm glad you told me, too. Maybe we can talk more sometime. I'd still like to hear stories about Vietnam and what it was like."

Joe nodded as he leaned on his cane. "Maybe."

The front door squeaked open, making Char jump.

"Hey, sweetie. Dinner's ready," Char's father said, sticking his head out the screen door.

Char placed her hand over her thumping heart. "Okay, Dad. I'll be right there."

Ronald Parsons glanced over at Joe. He stepped out onto the porch. "Well, now. I didn't know you had company, Charlotte."

"Oh, um, yeah," she said, wishing now that Joe hadn't stayed so long. "This is Joe Russo. He just stopped by on his way home. He's in a couple of my college classes and lives at Mrs. Bennington's."

"It's nice to meet you, Joe," Ronald said, offering his hand. Char watched as the two men shook and saw her father give Joe the once-over. Ronald was still wearing his typical work clothes—gray trousers and a white, button-down shirt. His dark hair was neatly cut and combed back. There was just a sprinkling of silver at the temples. What Char loved most about her father was his kind face and easy disposition. He always had a teasing glint in his brown eyes. Normally, she'd be happy to introduce him to friends, but tonight she wanted to get Joe out of here, fast.

"It's nice to meet you, too, Mr. Parsons," Joe said.

"I see you're wearing fatigues. Are you a veteran or do you just like the Army Surplus store?" Ronald grinned.

"A veteran, sir," Joe said. "I was in Vietnam."

Ronald's expression grew serious. "Well, good for you, son. It's refreshing to meet a young man who's served his country in this day when men are burning their draft cards."

"Dad," Char said disapprovingly.

"Oh, now dear," her father said. "I know all the arguments. Believe me, I've heard Deke express them often enough. But you know I'm old-fashioned. I believe in a man serving when his country calls him."

Char looked over at Joe. "Dad served in World War II."

"And I'm very proud of it," Ronald said.

She smiled at her dad. It was hard to be angry with him.

"Joe was just leaving," she said, then turned back to Joe. "Thanks for stopping by. I'll see you in class on Monday."

Joe grinned. "Yeah. I'll be on my way."

"What's the hurry?" Ronald asked. "Have you eaten dinner yet, son? You're certainly welcome to join us."

Char froze. She couldn't believe her ears. "Ah, Dad. I'm sure Joe has already eaten."

"Well." Joe glanced at Char. "Actually, I haven't."

She stared hard at him, but Joe seemed to be ignoring her.

"Then come on inside," Ronald said, waving him in.

"But, Dad. Maybe there isn't enough food for company," Char said.

"Oh, I wouldn't worry about that," Ronald said. "Your mom always makes more than the three of us can eat in one sitting. Come on in, Joe. Do you drink? I'll get you a beer."

Char's dad walked inside and she stood there with Joe, feeling anxious.

"I don't have to go in if you don't want me to," he said. "You can make my excuses for me."

Char bit her lip. She didn't want to make a scene. "No, it's fine. Come on in."

Joe lifted his pack, and followed her inside.

Chapter Three

When Joe entered the house, Ronald already had a beer in hand for him. Char's mom, Ellen, came into the living room as he set down his rucksack and slipped his coat off in the entryway. She was the same height as Char, with brown hair touching her shoulders. She wore hunter green slacks with a matching tunic top and an apron tied at the waist. Joe thought she looked exactly like the TV moms he'd envisioned lived in this town. His only memory of his own mother was from an old black and white photo that sat on the shelf over the television. He'd been too young when she'd died to remember her. The sight of Char's mom looking so perfect warmed his heart.

"I hear we have company for dinner." She smiled at Joe as she took his coat and hung it in the closet.

Char made the introductions, and Joe thanked her mother for inviting him for dinner.

"It smells wonderful," he said, accepting the beer from Ronald. He'd actually taken the time to pour it in a glass. Joe took a sip, savoring the rich flavor. This was not cheap beer from a can. He was sure it was expensive and came in a bottle.

"Char, why don't you set a place at the table for Joe and I'll bring the food out?" Ellen said as she headed for the kitchen.

Char glanced at Joe one last time before following her mother.

Joe surveyed the room. The Parsons had a nice home. The living room was large with a bay window on one wall and a brick fireplace on the other. Family photos lined the mantel. The carpet was gold shag and the furniture was in varying earth tone shades. Everything was neat and tidy. Compared to the cramped apartment he'd grown up in that was never clean and had lumpy, torn furniture, this looked like a page out of a magazine.

Ronald led him through a large archway into the dining room where a table for eight was set for the four of them. A tall hutch full of china sat against one wall and the kitchen door was to the left. There was also a pass-through bar between the dining room and kitchen with three tall bar stools lined up in front of it.

Ronald stood at the head of the table and motioned for Joe to sit at his right. Ellen and Char came in with steaming platters and bowls of food, setting them down on the table before they sat across from Joe. Ronald said grace then they began passing the food around.

The meal looked and smelled delicious. Joe took huge portions of everything: roast, mashed potatoes and gravy, and green beans. There was also a platter of raw vegetables from which he liberally served himself.

"You must be hungry, Joe." Ellen grinned at him.

Joe looked sheepish. "Sorry. I haven't had a home-cooked meal like this in a long time. It all tastes so good."

"I'm just teasing you," she said. "Eat as much as you like."

"Isn't Mrs. Bennington feeding you enough at her boarding house?" Ronald asked. "I hear she's an excellent cook."

"I'm sure her meals are delicious," Joe said. "But I chose not to pay extra for meals. I'm on a tight budget, and I wasn't sure if I'd be able to make it to dinner on time every night anyway."

"Where do you eat?" Ellen asked, looking concerned.

"I've been picking up a sandwich or bowl of soup at the café or grabbing something at the student union. It's inexpensive and easy." Joe chuckled. "Mrs. Bennington has been spoiling me, though. She leaves cookies out for me and is always offering me leftovers. The other night she left a huge piece of banana bread in my room. I think she's afraid I'm not eating."

"She's a sweet lady," Ellen said. "She lost her son in the Korean War, and her husband died a while back. She enjoys looking after her guests. They're like family to her."

Joe nodded as he ate more roast. He listened as Ronald talked about his day at his hardware store then asked his daughter how school was. She mentioned she had a paper due on Monday for English, and she was looking forward to writing it.

"Our Char fancies herself a writer," Ronald said with a twinkle in his eyes. "She wants us to believe she's majoring in English to become a teacher, but Ellen and I both know she wants to write the next great American novel."

"Dad!" Char admonished him. "Joe doesn't want to hear any of this."

Joe looked up at Char. "Is that true? Are you interested in becoming a writer?"

She nervously moved her food around her plate with her fork before meeting his gaze. "I like to write, but there are all types of writing. I could write for a newspaper or magazine. I never said I wanted to write a novel."

"If you're going to do something, then you should think big," Ronald said.

His words brought a smile to Char's lips.

"What about you, Joe?" Ellen asked. "What's your major?"

"I haven't declared a major yet," Joe said. "But I'm considering political science with a minor in English. I enjoy writing and reading too. Like Char."

Their eyes met again across the table. Joe noticed how her amber-brown eyes glittered in the dining room light.

"Isn't Deke majoring in political science?" Ronald asked Char. When she nodded, he continued. "What will he use it for? Does he plan on going into politics? He certainly talks like a politician."

Ellen swatted her husband on the arm. "Ron! Stop teasing Char in front of Joe."

Ronald chuckled. "Sorry, dear. You know I like to kid you."

"I'm just going to ignore you, Dad." Char grinned. "But to answer your question, Deke plans on teaching political science at the college level. He has no intention on entering politics."

Joe continued eating as he listened to their good-natured family banter. It was nice being around a family that obviously cared about one another.

"So, Joe. What do you think about all this anti-war rhetoric in our colleges these days?" Ronald asked. "I would assume with you having served, you'd be against it."

Joe hesitated, considering his answer. He didn't want to get into a discussion about the pros and cons of the Vietnam War, but he wanted to be honest. "Well, sir. I guess it's their right to protest the war. That's what soldiers are fighting for, isn't it? Our freedom to express ourselves."

Ronald stared at Joe, surprise written on his face.

For a moment, Joe worried he'd said the wrong thing. But then Ronald broke out into a hearty laugh. "Very good answer, son. Very diplomatic."

Joe glanced over at Char and thought he saw her sigh with relief.

After they'd finished eating, Ellen suggested they have dessert in the living room. Joe followed Ronald out there while Char and her mother cleared the table.

"Excuse my directness," Ronald said as he sat in his recliner. "But from your accent, I assume you're a long way from home."

"Yes, sir. I'm from New York."

"Do you have family around here?"

Joe shook his head. "No, sir."

"Really? How did you find our little town and college?"

Char walked into the room with two plates of chocolate cake and Joe saw her eyes grow wide at hearing her father's question.

"Dad, you're interrogating poor Joe. Students come from all over the country to attend our college." She handed Joe one of the plates then gave her dad the other.

"I don't mind," Joe said, smiling up at her. "I searched for colleges that had excellent programs for my intended major then narrowed it down to ones that were affordable. Grand Falls State University kept coming up at the top of my list. Plus, I wanted to live in a smaller town after having grown up in a big, crowded city. This one seemed to suit me."

Ellen came in with a tray of coffee cups and a piece of cake for Char. "How are you liking our little town so far?" she asked Joe as she passed around the coffee.

"I like it a lot. The people are nice, and the college is exactly as I'd hoped it would be. I'm glad I came here."

Char sat quietly eating her piece of cake. She looked relieved that he had kept his promise and didn't mention that her letters were the reason he'd chosen Grand Falls.

"This cake is delicious," Joe told Ellen.

"Thank you."

They sat in silence, eating their dessert. That's when a photo on the mantel caught Joe's eye. He set his empty plate on the coffee table and stood, walking over to the fireplace. A young man in an army dress uniform stared back at him. His dark hair was much like Char's and he had her warm, brown eyes. "Is this your son, Jeremy?"

All three looked up at once.

"Char told me her older brother was in Vietnam," Joe said, suddenly regretting having brought it up. He saw a sad look cross both Ellen and Ronald's faces.

Ronald nodded. "Yes, that's our son."

Joe looked at the photo once more before turning back to them. "He looks like a nice, young man," he said quietly.

"Thank you. He was," Ronald said. He stood and walked over to Joe. "He was a good boy, always willing to lend a hand and help a friend. He went into the army even though he could have easily deferred by going to college. We're very proud of him."

Joe nodded. He wished he hadn't said anything. Jeremy's memory obviously caused pain for all three of them. He'd noticed that Char, too, had dropped her eyes to the floor after he'd mentioned her brother.

"Can I ask you a question?" Ronald asked Joe.

"Of course."

Ronald met his wife's eyes first, and there seemed to be a mutual agreement between them. He returned his attention to Joe. "Our Jeremy was in Vietnam for only three months before he was killed. I've pondered that often. I thought you might know if that's unusual for him to be killed so soon after arriving there. His letters sounded positive, like there wasn't too much action around his camp and he was safe. But then, he was gone."

Joe took a breath. He didn't know how to explain the horror of Vietnam without it being graphic and disturbing. "Do you know how he died?"

"We were told he accidently tripped a landmine while on patrol with five other soldiers. It killed our son, and wounded two of the other men," Ronald said.

Joe nodded solemnly. "I'm afraid that happens often. Men go out on patrol daily, and sometimes all it takes is to veer even a small step from the point man's trail and a mine is triggered. Every step could be your last. I'm sure Jeremy was as careful as any soldier, but unfortunately in the wrong place at the wrong time."

Ronald nodded, looking as if he were trying to come to terms with Joe's words. Joe glanced over at Char, who also seemed deep in thought.

"So, you're saying that soldiers die this way often?" Ronald asked.

"Yes, sir. I'm sorry to say, but they do. Your son being there three months or nine months wouldn't have made a difference. I've seen even the most experienced soldier trip a landmine without ever seeing it."

"That's so sad," Ellen said. She looked up into Joe's eyes as if searching for answers. "I worry that Jeremy suffered."

Joe's heart clenched. He'd watched men die slowly and in agony after losing limbs from landmines. "I'm sure he died quickly, ma'am," he lied.

Ellen nodded and stared down at her hands. Joe caught Char's gaze. Her eyes were watery.

"I'm sure your son was a good soldier. He gave the ultimate sacrifice for his country. You should be very proud of him," Joe said.

Ronald nodded. "We are." He gently patted Joe on the back. "Thank you, son, for talking to us about it. There's so little we know about this war. It's very different from the war I fought in. Your words have brought us a little peace of mind."

After a moment of respectful silence, Joe said, "I should probably be going. Thank you for the delicious meal. It's the best I've had since coming here."

"You're very welcome," Ellen told him. "I hope you'll come over again sometime."

Joe smiled. "I'd like that."

Ronald eyed Joe curiously. "Son? I was wondering. Will you be working while you attend school?"

Joe saw Char's eyebrows shoot up at her father's question. "Well, actually, yes, sir. I was going to walk around town tomorrow and see if anyone had part-time work available. I could use the extra money."

Ronald's face broke out in a wide grin. "How would you like to work at my hardware store? I need a good hand around there, and you could work after school and on Saturdays. We'll schedule around your classes."

"But Dad, I work there on Saturdays," Char protested.

"Yes, I know, dear. But I could really use some extra help. Besides, you've been talking about taking over the bookkeeping for your mother. If I hire Joe, you could spend more time on Saturdays doing the books instead of working the register."

Char gaped at her father. Joe wasn't sure if he should accept.

"It's awfully nice of you to offer me a job, sir," he said. "But I don't want to cause any trouble."

"It won't cause any trouble at all," Ronald said. "And it will be nice having someone younger than forty in the shop for a change." He winked at Char. "Other than you, of course, dear.

But Harvey, my other employee, is sixty and I'm getting up there too. You'll be a breath of fresh air around there."

"I think it's a wonderful idea," Ellen chimed in. "And Charlotte, if you take over the bookkeeping, it will free up some time for me."

Joe looked at Char and their eyes met. He didn't want to upset her or push his way into her life. He hoped she realized that. Yet, he really needed the money. But not if it made Char uncomfortable. "Only if you don't mind," he told her.

"Sure. Why not?" Char shrugged. "Maybe I'll have more Saturdays off then, too."

"See, Joe? There's no problem," Ronald said. "Can you start tomorrow?"

"Okay. That'll be fine," Joe said.

"Wonderful. Come around nine. I'll get your sizes and we'll give you a couple of white shirts with the store logo and a pair of slacks to wear for work. How does that sound?"

"It sounds too good to be true. Thank you, sir," Joe said, shaking Ronald's hand.

"And no more of this 'sir' business. Call me Ronald, okay?"

"I'll try," he said as he pulled on his coat and slipped his pack on his back.

Joe said his goodbyes and Char piped up, "I'll walk outside with you." The two made their way out the front door into the night.

She followed Joe to the gate where he stopped and turned to face her. "Are you sure it's okay that I work at your father's store? I don't want to make you feel uncomfortable."

"It's fine. I was just surprised Dad asked. It seems my parents took an instant liking to you."

"They're nice people," he said.

She nodded.

"You should go back inside. It's chilly out here," Joe said.

Char hesitated, then spoke. "I wanted to thank you for what you said in there, about Jeremy. I realize you didn't know him, but your words seemed to comfort my parents. I appreciate that. It's been really hard on them, trying to come to terms with his death even though they supported his decision to go. It's been hard on all of us."

"You're welcome. I only spoke the truth. But if it gave your parents some closure, then I'm happy I could do it."

"You're a nice guy, Joe."

He grinned. "I know."

Laughter sprang from her lips. "And humble, too. I guess I'll see you tomorrow."

He walked outside the gate and turned one last time to face her. "Yeah. I'll see you tomorrow." Then he headed slowly down the sidewalk toward home.

* * *

Char stood at the gate and watched Joe walk away. It was dark out, but the sky was clear and the stars twinkled high above her. All was quiet, except for the chirping of the crickets and the croaking of the frogs around the neighborhood.

"Night music," Char said softly. The words made her smile.

Chapter Four

Char was already at the register ringing up a purchase for a customer when Joe walked into the hardware store the next morning.

"Hi, Joe. Dad's in back. I'll take you there in a minute," she told him as she bagged the elderly woman's purchase.

"Who's this young man? I don't think we've met," Mrs. Davis, the customer, asked Char.

She introduced Joe to her. "He'll be working here part-time," Char explained.

"It's nice to meet you, Joe. Enjoy your new job," Mrs. Davis said. She waved as she left the shop.

"She seems nice," Joe said.

"Yeah. Most people around here are. Mrs. Davis was my fifth-grade teacher. Come on, I'll show you to the back room." She walked down one of the five aisles that made up the store. The store wasn't wide, but it was long. The building sat on the corner of the block so one side wall held large, plate-glass windows where they displayed larger items like lawn mowers and snow scoops.

They found Ronald in the back room at his cluttered desk

which sat among boxes of inventory.

"Hello, Joe," Ronald greeted him. "Come on over. I think I have a new white shirt that will fit you."

Char left them and headed to the front again where she took the feather duster from under the counter and began dusting off shelves. As she worked, she thought about Joe and the letters she'd sent him in Vietnam. They must have sounded silly to him, the musings of a young girl, compared to what he was experiencing over there. Yet, he'd come to live in the town she'd described to him because of her letters. It seemed so strange that they were virtual strangers, but they had known each other because of a war half-a-world away. And now he was here, working in her father's store. Fate or coincidence? She wasn't sure.

Joe and her father came up to the front of the store a little while later.

"Charlotte. Will you show Joe how to use the register and where things are around the counter?" her dad asked. "I still have some items to check in from yesterday's shipment."

"Sure, Dad." She walked toward the counter with Joe following behind her. She could hear the click of his cane on the linoleum floor.

"Will it bother your leg standing and walking around the store all day?" Char asked.

"No more than it's already bothered," he said with a chuckle.

Char frowned. "Does it hurt all the time?"

"No. It aches sometimes, but that's only when I've been walking a lot. Otherwise, it's okay."

She glanced down at his fatigues.

"Is there a problem?" he asked.

She quickly raised her eyes. "No. It's just that I see you wearing your army pants all the time and I've wondered why. I mean, it's none of my business or anything, but…" She blushed. "Forget I said anything."

Joe grinned. "You do get flustered, don't you? Two pairs of fatigues are all the pants I have. I had two pairs of jeans when I went into the army, but I slimmed down so they don't fit anymore. I can't afford to buy new clothes right now."

Char felt terrible. She hadn't thought that he wouldn't have enough money to buy clothes when he came out of the service. "Like I said, forget I asked. And feel free to tell me it's none of my business if I ask any personal questions in the future, okay?"

"I really don't mind," he told her, then gave her a sweet smile. "You can ask me anything, anytime."

Char looked into his silvery gray eyes and knew he wasn't teasing her. She didn't understand why she was so nervous around him, especially since he'd been nothing but polite and kind. "Well, let's show you how to work the register."

Char spent the morning by Joe's side as he learned how to ring up customer sales and helped people find merchandise. He had an easy way about him and customers took to him immediately. Once, when he had to climb a ladder to get a can of car wax off a shelf, Char had tried to intervene, but Joe merely shook his head. "Don't worry. I'm fine," he'd told her. She realized that although he needed the cane to aid him with walking, he was completely capable of doing anything anyone else could do.

As she walked with him around the store to see all the merchandise, they passed a closed door in the back corner.

"Is that another storage room?" Joe pointed to the door.

Char shook her head. "No. That leads upstairs to the living quarters. We always keep it locked."

"Living quarters?"

"Yes. There's a two-bedroom apartment upstairs. It's a pretty good size since it's the full length of the store."

"Doesn't your dad rent it out?" Joe asked.

"No. He and Mom used to live up there when they were first married. But now, we use it for storage. Dad keeps saying he's going to turn it into his office, but he never has. I think he likes his cluttered mess in the back room." She laughed. "Plus, there's only the inside entrance, so whoever rented it would have access to the store. Dad doesn't like that idea very much. There's an old fire escape on the back of the building but no outdoor stairs."

Joe nodded as they continued their walk around the store.

Right at noon, the bell on the door jingled and Deke walked in. Char and Joe were both behind the counter, having just rung up another sale. Deke's smile faded when he saw Joe.

"Can I steal you away for lunch?" he asked Char.

"Sure," she said, taking off her apron and placing it under the counter. She turned to Joe. "If you need help, get Dad from the back room."

"I'm sure I'll be fine," Joe said.

"Okay. See you in a bit." She hurried around the counter and over to Deke's side. "Ready?"

Deke eyed Joe, then placed his arm around Char's waist and kissed her softly on the lips. "Yep. Let's go."

The kiss took Char by surprise. Deke usually wasn't affectionate in public. But she didn't give it too much thought.

As they walked out into the warm autumn day, Deke's hand fell from her waist and curled around her hand. He smiled down at her. "Where do you want to eat?"

"The café is fine. Then we don't have to walk far."

They strolled along the sidewalk, passing Berkoff's Bakery and Annie's Gifts before arriving at the Corner Café. Across the street was the town square with an expanse of lush green lawn and an old-fashioned white gazebo in the center. The trees were tipped with the beginnings of fall colors—yellow, orange, and red. Grand Falls was founded in 1896 and the town square had been built almost immediately as a place for residents to gather. All the yearly celebrations from the Fourth of July through the Christmas festival were celebrated on that space as they had been since the very beginning.

"I just love fall," Char exclaimed as she and Deke entered the café and chose a booth with a view of the park. "The colors, the crisp air. It's all so magical."

"Sounds like you're having a good day," Deke said. He took menus from the stand on the table and handed her one, too. They ordered burgers, fries, and Cokes from the new waitress who'd just started college this year like Char. After the waitress had left, Deke sat back in the booth and crossed his arms. "So, when did G.I. Joe start working at the store?"

Char's good mood dampened. "His name is just Joe, and he started today."

"How'd he get the job? Did he just walk in off the street and ask?"

"No. My dad offered it to him last night."

Deke frowned. "Last night? How did that come about?"

She sighed. She already knew Deke wasn't going to like her answer. "Joe stopped by the house last night to say hello. I was sitting on the porch, and he was just being friendly. When Dad came outside, he invited him in for dinner."

"Really? They don't even know the guy and they invite him in for dinner? What's that about?"

"Don't make a big deal of it, okay?" she said, growing irritated.

The waitress brought their Cokes and left. Char wished that Deke would let the whole thing go. She'd had such a good morning; she didn't want to ruin it by sparring with him. Unfortunately, he had much more to say on the subject.

Deke leaned forward on the table. "I will make a big deal about this guy, this baby killer, hanging around your house all the time. You don't know anything about him. He could be dangerous."

The words "baby killer" made Char cringe. She wasn't sure if the Vietnam War was right or wrong, but she hated when Deke called returning soldiers terrible names. "He's not dangerous, and he's not hanging out at my house all the time." She tried to keep her voice down despite her rising anger. "It was just one of those things. You know how my dad respects men who've served. He was just being nice by inviting Joe to dinner." She paused, thinking about her brother and how much her parents missed him. "Losing Jeremy has been hard, Deke. My dad wanted to talk with someone who's been to Vietnam. He and Joe seemed to click."

Deke ran his hand through his hair and tightened his jaw. "I know how hard losing Jeremy has been. I lost my best friend, remember? I was practically a part of your family, growing up, and I've been dating you for a year, but I don't see your father wanting to bond with me. Instead, he brings in this stranger off the street."

"Please, let's not fight." Char sighed, her anger dissipating. "Joe's a nice guy my dad hired. That's it."

Their food came and she took a bite of her burger, but she wasn't hungry anymore. Deke hadn't said another word, but she could tell he was still angry. He could be moody at times, but that was only one side of him. Deke could be sweet, thoughtful, and loving, too. Yet, it was times like this when she felt uncomfortable, because she didn't know how to pull him out of his dark place.

He was halfway through his meal when Deke stopped and glanced up at her, his expression softening. "I'm sorry. You're right. I shouldn't have made a big deal about it. I guess I'm just a little jealous that your dad took to this guy so quickly and barely says two words to me. And I'm also overly protective of you. I'll cool it, okay?"

"Thank you," she said, relieved he'd gotten over it so quickly. "You know, my parents like you too. They always have. But my dad doesn't agree with some of the ideas you believe in, so it's difficult for him to talk with you."

Deke snorted. "Of course he doesn't agree with me. What parent does? I'm telling the truth and the older generation doesn't want to open their eyes and see the war for what it really is. A killing field. Murder. It's an illegal war, for Christ's sake. We've never declared war on North Vietnam, but we still send tens of thousands of men to fight against them." He stopped to take a breath and when his eyes met Char's, he hit his forehead with his hand and chuckled.

"Point taken," he said. "I admit, I do tend to go on and on."

"And that's what I love about you," she said softly. "You're passionate about what you believe in. You never waver. I wish I had one-tenth of your confidence in what you believe."

He smiled and reached across the table for her hands. "And I love how honest you are about being unsure. You'll find what you believe in, and when you do, you'll be as strong in your convictions as I am."

Char gazed up into Deke's deep blue eyes. She loved his strength, his certainty about his causes, and his intelligence.

Even though she'd known him as a boy, one who'd teased her occasionally and pulled her ponytail, she'd never thought twice about him. He was just Jeremy's annoying best friend. But shortly after her brother's death, she'd seen the strong man he'd become, and looked up to him for answers when she floundered in her beliefs. He was so certain of everything, while she was still finding her way. It was that strength, that certainty, and of course those powerful blue eyes, that had drawn her to him.

"Why don't you come over for lunch after church tomorrow?" she asked. "It will give you a chance to spend time with my parents. We'll talk about safe things, like the weather and how good my mom's pot roast is."

He grinned. "Your mom does make a good pot roast. Sure, why not? I'll try not to drive your dad crazy with my views."

They left the café and walked the short distance to the hardware store.

"Want to go out tonight? Maybe head over to the union for a while and hang out with the gang? Or, we could go to a movie. Whatever you'd like," Deke said.

"Yeah. That sounds fun." They stopped in front of the store and Deke bent down and kissed the tip of her nose. "See you later."

Char entered the store and smiled brightly at Joe, who was standing behind the counter. "Were you busy while I was gone?"

"Not too much," he said. "I rang up a couple of items. Your dad went home for lunch a few minutes ago."

"Okay." She put her purse under the counter and tied on her apron. Glancing around, she noticed that Joe was leaning heavily on his cane. "You know, we could set a stool back here so you can sit when there isn't much going on," she offered.

"Do you sit when you work?" he asked.

"No. I'm usually running around the store helping people."

"Then I don't need to sit either," he said.

Char cocked her head. Joe had politely put her in her place. "Sorry. I was just trying to be nice."

He smiled. "You don't have to try. You are nice. But I don't need to be catered to. Just treat me like anyone else who works here."

"Fine. I won't be thoughtful anymore, and if you don't work as hard as I do, then you're fired."

"Fine."

"Fine."

They stared at each other and after a few seconds, both broke out laughing.

As they worked together the rest of the afternoon, Char found that she was happy her dad had hired Joe.

* * *

After the store closed at five o'clock, Joe walked the few blocks to the boarding house. Mrs. Bennington greeted him as he entered.

"How was your first day at work?" she asked kindly. She'd been setting the dining room table for dinner and wore a full apron over her flowered dress.

"It went well," he said, smiling.

"Wonderful. Mr. Parsons is such a nice man. They're a good family. It's a shame about their son, Jeremy. He had a bright future and he was a handsome boy, as well. Such a shame." She shook her head sadly but then straightened up and returned her attention to Joe. "How about some dinner tonight? I can always set another place."

"Thank you for offering, Mrs. B, but I think I'll go up to my room and change. I don't want to get my new work shirt dirty. I'll probably go out later for a bite."

She grinned at him. "Mrs. B? I like that. Bennington is such a long name, isn't it? Mrs. B makes me sound younger. Hip, like you kids say nowadays."

"I'm glad you like it." Joe chuckled. "You are hip. And you make some very righteous cookies."

She laughed and waved her hand through the air. "You don't have to flatter me to get free cookies. My kitchen is always open to you, dear." She bustled back to her work and Joe headed for the stairs.

He walked up the two flights before coming to the door of the narrow staircase that led up to his attic room. He wouldn't have admitted it to anyone, but his leg ached and his back felt tight after being on his feet all day. He ascended the stairs which opened to his big, airy living space. Although the ceiling was slanted on both sides, the middle was high, and exposed beams ran across the space. A large, round, stained-glass window sat high on the wall straight ahead of him. He loved how the sunlight shone through the window every morning, filling the room with a kaleidoscope of color. To his right was the door to his tiny bathroom that held the basics and a shower stall. Joe didn't mind that the bathroom was small. He loved the room because of its openness. He would have felt trapped and confined in one of the smaller bedrooms downstairs. In Vietnam, he'd spent many nights lying under the stars, listening for the slightest noise that didn't belong among the night sounds. Despite the underlying fear that was always present, he'd enjoyed the open air to the small, stuffy tents. Since coming stateside, he'd had trouble sleeping in enclosed places. When he'd seen the attic room, he'd known immediately it would be perfect.

He limped past the worn sofa that sat in the middle of the room to the bathroom to fill a glass with water and then sat down heavily on the bed. Placing the water glass on the nightstand, he opened the drawer and pulled out a bottle of pills he'd gotten from the VA hospital. They were muscle relaxants that he took only when necessary. Joe didn't like taking drugs of any kind, but on days his leg and back ached this much, he was relieved to have them.

After swallowing one pill, he stretched out his left leg and gently kneaded the calf. The doctor had told him it was good to use his leg as much as possible, and that he might even regain a little muscle tissue if he did. So far, all the walking to and from the college only seemed to hurt, not help, but he was determined to keep using his leg. He knew it would never be the same again, but he wasn't going to give up on it either.

Sitting back against the pillows, Joe closed his eyes. He thought about how thankful he was for the little things that made his life whole. He appreciated Mrs. B's warmth and concern, and her delicious homemade cookies. He enjoyed walking the hallways of the old college buildings and the walkways outside that snaked between massive oaks and stark-white birch trees. He was happy he'd decided to come to Grand Falls to attend college. The town was everything he'd imagined, and it made him smile just thinking about its eccentric charm. He loved the one-hundred-year-old brick buildings, the delicious smell of the bakery as he passed by, and the town square. He was looking forward to the fall festival in October, and seeing the kids trick-or-treating up and down the neighborhoods on Halloween. He imagined the downtown decorated in lights for Christmas, and couldn't wait to see it. It was a far cry from his upbringing in a crowded tenement with an angry father and a delinquent younger brother, and so very welcome to a boy who hadn't experienced much joy or happiness in his life.

And then there was Charlotte.

In his wildest dreams, he couldn't have imagined how lovely she'd be in person. And the fact that he'd not only been able to meet her, but was now working side-by-side with her, only made his life so much richer.

He thought about how much he'd enjoyed following her around the store as she talked about everything from faucets to snowplows. She'd worn brown slacks with a pumpkin-colored sweater that had reminded him of the fall colors outdoors. Her long, dark brown hair had gleamed under the store's bright lights, and her amber-brown eyes had glittered when she smiled. She wore very little make-up and looked fresh and young and naturally beautiful. It amazed him every time he'd looked up and seen her standing there. How had he been so lucky to be able to spend the day with the girl he'd dreamt about for almost a year in Vietnam? He felt as if the gods had truly blessed him.

Except there was Deke.

Joe wondered how a bright girl like Char could possibly have any interest in a guy as arrogant and condescending as Deke.

Then again, she certainly wouldn't fall for a simple guy like him, either.

After dozing a while on the bed, Joe awoke with hunger pains. The aching in his leg had subsided, and his back felt better too. It would be very easy for him to hide away in his room for the night, but he knew that he shouldn't. Being alone all the time wasn't good for him, as the army psychologist had kept reminding him while he recuperated in the hospital. Returning soldiers often isolated themselves, feeling more comfortable alone than with people who didn't understand their experiences. It was too easy to live inside your head, but it wasn't healthy.

That was why Joe had been studying in the library at night instead of shutting himself up in his room. And that was why he made himself get up now, change out of his work clothes and into his fatigues and a sweater, and head out for a bite to eat. He grabbed his copy of *For Whom the Bell Tolls* and slipped it into his jacket pocket. He would go to the student union and splurge on a burger. He could read while he ate, so he wouldn't feel uncomfortable sitting alone in a room full of people.

Chapter Five

Char sat at a table in the student union with Patty, listening to Deke speak animatedly about accelerating the anti-war movement at their campus. Char knew that Patty had only come along to get the attention of Deke's friend, Justin. He was tall, blond, and handsome, and planned on going to law school after he graduated next spring. The body-hugging sweater and short skirt Patty had worn were all for Justin. But no matter how many times she crossed her legs or flipped back her long, auburn hair, he took no notice of her. Char held back a grin. She knew that once Deke started speaking so passionately about ending the Vietnam War, he drew all the attention. Even a short skirt wasn't going to pull eyes away from Deke.

"I'm bored." Patty exhaled a long, drawn-out sigh. "I don't know why I bothered coming along."

"You came to keep me company, remember?" Char said. She returned her gaze to Deke, who stood across the room with a crowd gathered around him. "Just listen to him speak. Isn't he brilliant?"

Patty rolled her eyes. "Of course you think he is. But you already have your intelligent, handsome guy. It's my turn now."

Char smiled as she continued listening.

"The day of the peaceful march or protest is over," Deke said, catching the eye of each person in the group around him. "It's time to think big! It's time to let the government know we're serious. SDS has disbanded nationally and at many colleges. The national leaders have started taking real action. So now, we must also."

"How?" Justin asked. "We were at the huge march on Washington last November. Nearly 250,000 people came. It doesn't get any bigger than that."

"And what did it get us?" Deke asked, staring intently at Justin. "The war escalated despite the march. Then there were the dreadful shootings of students by police at Kent State and Jackson State U. Our message is being ignored and innocent protestors are being attacked. It's time to fight back. The peaceful protest is getting us nowhere. I agree with the Weathermen Underground. It's time to show some muscle."

Char grew uncomfortable at the mention of the Weathermen Underground. It was a radical group that had formed the year before by a few of the leaders of the national SDS group. They had declared war against the United States, and had since taken credit for several bombings across the country. Recently, Deke had started talking about changing the tactics of the local SDS group and joining the revolution. That was another word that made Char squirm. Revolution wasn't protesting—it was war.

From the corner of her eye, Char saw Joe walk into the crowded union and make his way to an empty table in the corner. He sat slowly, setting his cane against the wall. When he looked up, their eyes met, and both smiled.

"Who's that?" Patty asked, nudging Char. "I think I've seen him around campus."

"That's Joe. He's in a couple of my classes. My dad just hired him at the store, too," Char said.

Across the room, Joe lifted his book to show Char what he was doing. She nodded and grinned.

"Hey, he's staring this way," Patty said. "You know, he's kind of cute, if you can get past the gray in his hair. And the cane. Why does he walk with a cane?"

Char turned to Patty. "He was wounded in Vietnam."

"Oh, well, there's some honor in that, isn't there? I mean, I know that goes against what Deke believes, but it's honorable, right? Yeah, he's cute. You should introduce me."

Char bristled involuntarily. She didn't understand why, but she hated the thought of unleashing Patty on Joe. Patty was her good friend, but sometimes she was just too boy crazy for her own good.

"He's not really your type," Char said. "I'll be right back." She made her way through the maze of tables and chairs before reaching Joe.

"Hi." She smiled down at him. "Going to do a little light reading?"

"Light, yeah," he said, grinning. "Thought I'd grab a bite and read a little while." He waved to the chair next to him. "Want to join me?"

Char sat down, cutting her eyes to Deke to make sure he was too engrossed in his speech to notice where she was. She returned her attention to Joe. "Are you enjoying Hemingway?"

"Sure. What's not to enjoy? Intrigue, drama, action, even sex." He waggled his brows and his gray eyes twinkled. "But I already knew what I was getting into. I read it in high school."

"Oh, sure," she said, a little unnerved by the sex comment and his sparkling eyes. "Me, too. I mean, I read it in high school, but it wasn't required reading."

"It wasn't required at my high school either, but I like to read. I read all the classics I could get my hands on," Joe said.

"I've read all the classics too. So, what do you think of the book the second time around?"

"I don't think I fully appreciated it the first time I read it. Now, I find it even more interesting. You know, after having experienced war first-hand. It puts a whole new perspective on the story for me," Joe said.

Char hadn't considered that. She wondered in what way it made a difference for him. She wished she could ask him outright but thought better of it. Tonight wasn't the right time to get into a discussion about war with Deke only a few feet away spouting anti-war messages.

As if understanding why she'd suddenly become silent, Joe nodded toward Deke. "He's quite the speaker, isn't he?"

"Yes, he is," she said. "Even if you don't agree with what he's saying, he seems to be able to draw people in."

Joe leaned on the table, his head closer to hers. "Do you believe in what he's saying?"

Char opened her mouth to respond, then closed it again. Did she? Sometimes. Not always. "He makes some good points," she finally said. "I'd better get back to my friend. Enjoy your book." She stood and moved quickly through the throngs of people. As she sat down at her table again, she caught Deke's eye. Her heart beat quicker. He didn't look upset, just concerned, but he kept speaking without hesitation to the group gathered around him.

Char sighed and tried to listen, but her mind was on Joe's question. *Do you believe in what he's saying?* It bothered her that she didn't know the answer.

* * *

Joe ordered a burger and a beer and leaned back in his chair, listening to Deke expound the merits of bringing the war home as a way to stop it. He shook his head slowly. Inciting violence in order to end a war made no sense to him. Like other Americans, he'd read about the bombings of government buildings and ROTC facilities on college campuses by anti-war revolutionaries. Joe didn't believe in violence for any reason, and it was bad enough he'd seen the worst of mankind in war. He didn't mind a peaceful protest, but he didn't want anything to do with a violent anti-war movement.

The waitress brought his food and he opened his book, trying to concentrate on another war from another time as he ate. But it was slow going. He found himself constantly glancing up to stare at Char. She looked bored, sitting at a table with another girl. Joe wondered why a man who was lucky enough to be out with Char would waste his time trying to persuade a group of students to fight instead of spending his time with her.

"Idiot," he said under his breath.

"Excuse me," a tentative voice said from beside the table.

Joe's eyes shot up. He saw two young men with crew cuts, wearing red ROTC T-shirts, looking down at him. "Hello."

The men moved closer. "Hi," the spokesman said. "I'm Mark and this is Jim. We're juniors in the ROTC program here and we wondered if we could talk with you a moment."

Joe nodded. "Sure. Sit down."

The men promptly sat and Mark spoke again. "We're sorry to bother you, but we've seen you around campus and this seemed like a good chance to talk."

Joe's brows rose. "About what?"

Mark turned to Jim, and both men looked hesitant. Joe noticed that the two couldn't have been any more different than night and day. Mark was tall and broad-shouldered with brown hair and eyes, his skin very tan. Jim was shorter and stockier with shocking red hair, hazel eyes, and fair skin. Although they were probably the same age as Joe, he thought they looked young.

Mark finally spoke up. "We were wondering if you'd share some information with us about your experience in Vietnam. In a year, we'll both be graduating and then we'll be going into the army. We just wondered what it was really like there."

Jim nodded enthusiastically.

Joe sighed. He'd seen a few ROTC graduates come and go in Vietnam. They came in as officers but weren't really prepared for what to expect. Some learned to handle it quickly while others fumbled through.

"I don't like talking about the war," Joe told them.

Both men looked disappointed. "That's what other Vietnam vets have said, too," Mark said. "But how are we supposed to know what to expect if no one will talk about it? All we hear is what the news tells us. We want the truth."

Joe understood how they felt. Even after basic training, no one prepared him for what he would see in Vietnam. But the last thing he wanted to do was talk about the horror of that war with these two strangers. "The truth is, it's hotter than hell and twice as humid, the rainy season is miserable, and you'll feel wet all the time. Keep your boots as dry as possible, bring extra socks, and try not to get killed."

Both men stared at him as if wondering if he was serious.

Mark spoke up again in a reverent tone. "Did you kill people?"

Joe's jaw tightened. That's all everyone wanted to know. The worst part of war. "My job was to protect the artillery men so they weren't killed. I did my job."

Mark glanced down at Joe's stiff leg. "But you were hurt, so you must have been in a firefight. You must have shot at the enemy then."

"I did what I had to do to stay alive," Joe said in a clipped manner. "It's not something I like talking about."

"I can't wait to kill Charlie," Jim said, looking flushed with excitement.

Joe winced. "I'm sure you'll get your chance. Now, if you don't mind, I'd like to get back to my book."

Jim and Mark looked crestfallen. "Sorry, man. We didn't mean to bother you, really. Or insult you. We just thought you'd understand where we're coming from."

Joe's expression softened. "I do. But nothing I say will prepare you for that war. The best you can do is train well and be ready for anything. Once you're there, instinct will kick in."

Both men nodded then stood up, each shaking Joe's hand.

"Thanks. I hope we can consider you a friend," Mark said.

"Yeah. Sure," Joe said. He watched them walk toward the door, but not before they each glanced Deke's way and glared at him. Joe grinned. He knew several men who would do more than glare at Deke. Personally, he didn't care what Deke's opinions were. He had the right to talk about revolution. As long as Joe didn't have to fight in it, he couldn't care less.

Joe opened his book again, but before looking at the pages, he sneaked another glimpse of Char. Her head was close to her friend and they were talking, but she stopped for just a second to look up, meet his eye, and smile, before returning to her conversation.

Joe's heart warmed as he dropped his eyes back to Hemingway's words.

* * *

"He keeps staring at you," Patty whispered to Char, their heads close. "What's going on between you two?"

Char feigned ignorance. "He's not staring at me. We're right in his line of vision. He can't help but look at us."

Patty frowned. "You're holding out on me. First you said he wasn't my type then you went over and talked to him. It's like you want him for yourself."

Char rolled her eyes. "Don't be silly. Joe and I are just friends. Nothing more. You're the one who said you want to meet an older guy and be set for life. Joe's not that guy. He's a freshman, just like us, and he doesn't have a cent to his name. That's not what you're looking for."

"Well, you're right about that." She sighed. "I wish Justin would pay attention to me. He's going to be a lawyer. That's perfect," Patty said, sliding her eyes in Justin's direction.

"Why don't you ask him to drive you home?" Char suggested. "That way he can get to know you better."

Patty's eyes lit up. "Can you ask him for me? He might do it if you ask."

"Sure."

Deke's group broke apart and he came over to the table with Justin and Craig tagging behind. Deke slipped into the chair beside Char and draped his arm over her shoulders.

"Sorry about that," he said. "I invite you out and then turn it into an SDS meeting."

"It's okay," Char said. "I enjoy listening to you speak."

Deke pressed a kiss to her cheek. "I'm the luckiest guy in this school." He glanced across the room to where Joe sat then back at Char. "I saw you talking with soldier boy over there."

"We were talking about Hemingway. We're reading *For Whom the Bell Tolls* in English class," Char said casually.

"Hmm." Deke took one more look Joe's way and then said, "Hey, let's blow this place. Why don't you and I go somewhere quiet?"

Char hesitated. She knew when Deke said, "somewhere quiet," he meant back to the small house he and two other college guys rented. It was never quiet there, and not very private when the guys watched her and Deke head for his bedroom. She didn't feel like going there tonight.

"Honestly, Deke, I think I'll just go home. I'm tired and I have to get up early for church tomorrow."

Deke looked disappointed, but he was good about not pressuring her.

"And remember," she added. "You're coming over for lunch tomorrow."

"I won't forget. Come on. I'll walk you to your car," he said, getting up.

Patty elbowed her and Char remembered what she'd promised to do.

"Oh, Justin? Would you mind dropping Patty off at her home?" Char asked. "I'm so tired and it's out of the way. She lives the same direction as you do."

"Ah, sure," Justin said, looking anything but sure. He turned to Patty. "Ready to go?"

She stood quickly and gave him a big smile. "Yes. Thanks, Justin." They headed for the door and before they left, Patty turned and winked conspiratorially at Char.

Deke chuckled. "Playing matchmaker?"

"Just helping a friend," she said, letting Deke help her on with her coat. She appreciated his manners even though it wasn't thought of as cool anymore.

They walked together to the door, his hand gently touching the small of her back. As they passed Joe's table, Deke stopped.

"I hope you and your ROTC buddies weren't planning a takeover of the college," Deke said to Joe.

Joe stared Deke directly in the eyes. "No more than you're planning a revolution."

Deke stood there a beat, looking unsure, then grinned at Joe and headed out the door with Char.

Chapter Six

When Char arrived home that night, it was past ten and her father was sitting alone in the living room, watching a John Wayne movie on television.

"Have a nice time tonight, dear?" he asked.

"I guess." Char hung her coat in the closet. She walked closer to her father's chair and stared at the cowboy movie on the set. "Is Mom already in bed?"

"Yeah. She was tired and went up a little while ago."

"So, it's just you and The Duke?" she teased.

Ronald chuckled. "You know your old man can't resist a good cowboy movie. It's almost over."

She leaned over and kissed her dad on the cheek. "I'm going to bed. Good night."

"Good night, dear. Sleep well."

Char walked to the stairs and headed up. The bathroom was at the top and to her right was Jeremy's bedroom. Her room and her parents' bedroom were further down the hall. She stopped and stared at her brother's closed door. Tentatively, she moved toward it and slowly turned the knob. Opening the door, she was hit by a stale odor. She reached in and snapped on the light, and immediately all the memories of the past came rushing over her.

Jeremy's room had been kept exactly the same since the day he'd left for boot camp. His twin bed was made neatly with a navy comforter, and an afghan their grandmother had crocheted for him was folded neatly at the foot of the bed. On the night-stand was an old milk glass lamp and an alarm clock. Books sat on the shelf below. Jeremy had been an avid reader like Char, and they had often exchanged books between them, starting with their *Nancy Drew* and *Hardy Boys* collections when they were younger. Those mysteries had long ago been packed away, but Char remembered them as if it were yesterday.

She entered the room and slowly looked around at the shelves above the bed and the top of his dresser. Jeremy had played baseball and basketball all through high school. Trophies and medals lined his shelves and team photos from high school stood beside them. On his dresser, his high school yearbooks were stacked in a neat pile. One of Char's last memories of Jeremy was him sitting on his bed, paging through his yearbooks. She'd come in his room and had quietly sat down beside him, watching as he pointed out pictures. At the time, she'd wondered what he was thinking and if he was scared to go into the service. But she didn't ask. She just sat there with her brother and listened as he spoke about all his friends.

She'd give anything to hear his voice one more time.

Now, Char sat gingerly on his bed and picked up a stuffed bear that laid on his pillow. His high school girlfriend, Donna, had given it to him for Valentine's Day. The little heart tag with his name on it still hung from the bear's ear. He and Donna had broken up months before he'd left for the army and he hadn't had a serious girlfriend when he'd left. The thought that Jeremy would never come home, find his soulmate, and marry broke Char's heart.

"Hey, Kitten. You okay?" Ronald asked softly from the doorway.

Char turned her eyes to her father and sighed. "Just remembering," she said.

He walked into the bedroom and looked around. "I know. I do this sometimes, too. It's heartbreaking, yet, in some way, it's comforting too."

"Do you believe in this war, Dad?" she asked. "You lost a son to it. Wouldn't that make you hate it?"

"Ah, Char." Ronald went to the bed and sat down next to his daughter. "Everyone hates war. All wars, not just this one. But Jeremy believed in doing what his country asked of him. And I do, too. I served in World War II without question. I understand it was a different type of war than Vietnam is, but it's still an honor to serve. And Jeremy did the honorable thing."

Char leaned on her father as he placed his arm around her shoulders. "I know he did, Dad. But it's hard. With so many people saying that the war is wrong, it's difficult for me not to think that Jeremy's death was senseless. I hate feeling that way."

Ronald pulled away and looked down into Char's eyes. "I know this is a difficult time, dear. And I know that Deacon thinks the opposite of what I do. But I have to believe that my son died for a good reason. If I believed his death had been for nothing, and that his service to his country had been worthless, I couldn't live with his loss. It would be too much to bear."

Tears filled Char's eyes. She hugged her father. "I have to believe that, too." They pulled away a moment later, both wiping their eyes. "But Dad? I also think the war has to end. The thought of so many boys dying each day is too much for me, or my generation, to bear."

Ronald gave her a tired smile. "I understand. And you've a right to your opinion."

They sat a while longer, gazing around the room.

"Do you think Mom will keep Jeremy's room like this forever?" Char finally asked, not sure if she'd ever want it to change.

"I think she'll keep it this way for as long as we all need it," Ronald said. "I'm not sure how long that will take."

Char nodded, and they both stood to leave. Char returned the bear to its spot and gently smoothed the bedcover. Then they closed the door quietly behind them.

* * *

After church the next day, Char helped her mother fix lunch. She peeled the potatoes and carrots while Ellen prepared the roast beef and they placed it all in the roasting pan to cook. Ellen had made an apple pie the night before and Char whipped up cream to use on it later. Char was just setting the table when the doorbell rang at one o'clock.

"I'll get it," she called out, wanting to speak to Deke privately before he came in. After her talk with her father last night, she wanted to make sure that Deke didn't mention the war today. She pulled opened the door, and there stood Joe.

"Hi, Char." He smiled.

Char's mouth dropped open a moment before she clamped it shut. "Uh, hi, Joe. Come on in."

"Hey, Joe," Ronald called out from his chair in the living room. "Are you a baseball fan? The Cubs are playing the Pirates."

"Sure. I'll be right there," Joe said. He turned back to Char. "You look surprised to see me."

"Um, yeah, a little. No one told me you were coming."

His expression turned serious. "Should I leave?"

"No, of course not," she said. "Give me your coat and I'll hang it up."

Joe leaned his cane against the wall and pulled off his coat, handing it to Char. "Thanks," he said as he picked up his cane again.

"Go on in and sit with Dad. Lunch will be ready soon," Char told him. She hung up his coat and headed straight for the kitchen.

"Mom? Did you know Joe was invited to lunch today?" she asked.

"Of course, I did, dear. Your father told me last night he'd invited him over."

"But when I told you I'd invited Deke, you never said anything."

Ellen looked at her, confused. "Why would I? Can't we have both men here for lunch?"

"Mom. You know all about Deke's politics. And he doesn't approve of my spending time with Joe, either," Char said, growing more nervous by the minute.

Her mother looked concerned. "Why doesn't Deke like Joe?"

Char sighed. "Oh, Mom. It's complicated."

"Isn't it always complicated when Deke's involved?" Ellen said with a grin.

"Mom!" Char was so wound up, she thought for sure she'd snap at any moment. "I'll be right back," she told her mother and made a beeline for the front door again.

Deke was just pulling up in his car when she stepped outside. Char walked briskly down the sidewalk toward him.

"Well, how did I get so lucky to be greeted at my car by the prettiest girl on the block?" Deke asked, beaming. He walked over to Char and wrapped his arm around her shoulders, giving her a quick kiss. "What's the matter? You're stiff as a board."

Char took a deep breath. "Dad invited Joe over for lunch."

Deke's smile faded. "Why?"

"Because Dad and he get along well. I didn't know he was coming until he was at the door. Maybe you should come for lunch another time."

"Did your dad tell you to tell me that?" Deke frowned.

"Of course not. But I know you don't like Joe. I thought you wouldn't want to stay for lunch if he was here," Char said, hoping Deke would agree.

A slow smile spread over Deke's face. "I don't mind if Joe's here. Maybe we'll have a lot to talk about." He kissed the tip of her nose and started heading toward the door with his arm around her.

"Deke, you can't bring up Vietnam or anything to do with the war today. Please. I want my parents to see what a great guy you are when you aren't talking politics."

"Your parents have known me since I was a kid. I think they already know I can be a nice guy," Deke told her. "Don't worry, sweetie. I won't try to make anyone angry. Okay?"

They were already at the door so Char had no other choice but to agree. "Okay." But as they walked inside, she could feel the tension rising inside her.

* * *

So far, so good, Char thought as they all sat down to lunch. When Deke had entered the house, he'd politely shaken both her father and Joe's hands then sat down to watch the game with them. Char had reluctantly left them to set another place at the table. Thankfully, lunch was ready soon after that.

They sat down at the large table with her parents at either end, she and Deke on one side, and Joe on the other. After saying grace, they began passing the food around and filling their plates.

"How are your parents, Deacon?" Ellen asked after everyone was served. "I haven't seen your mother in a while."

"They're doing fine, thank you, Mrs. Parsons," Deke said. "Dad works long hours at his accounting firm and Mom keeps busy with her clubs and volunteer work. I'll tell them you asked about them the next time I'm over there."

Char knew that Deke saw very little of his parents these days. When they did get together, they argued about what they called his "radical" politics. His father earned a nice living and paid for Deke's college tuition and living expenses. Deke earned a little money at the part-time job he had in the college's administration office, but he'd never be able to support himself without his parents' help.

Ellen turned to Joe. "Did you enjoy working at the store this weekend?" she asked.

"I did. Charlotte's a very good teacher." Joe winked at Char.

Ellen chuckled. "Char has been running around that store since she was a toddler. She knows it like the back of her hand."

"Joe. What are you majoring in?" Deke asked.

Char froze with her fork midway to her mouth.

"I haven't declared a major yet, but I'm leaning toward political science with an English literature minor," Joe responded.

"Really? That's interesting," Deke said, staring down his nose at Joe.

"This roast is delicious, Mom," Char said, interrupting what was sure to be the start of an argument. "It turned out perfectly."

"Yes, Mrs. Parsons." Joe turned his attention to Ellen. "The whole meal is delicious."

Ellen beamed. "Thank you, Joe."

None of this deterred Deke. "Why political science, Joe? You're not thinking of going into politics, are you?" he asked, sneering.

"Are you?" Joe shot back, staring at him. "Char tells me that's your major."

Deke glared at him for a beat, then sat back in his chair. "I'm just surprised it would interest you."

Joe shrugged. "I'm interested in how our government works. Just as I'm interested in literature. I haven't figured out yet how it will all fit together, but I will, eventually."

"What do you think of President Nixon bombing Cambodia and Laos?" Deke asked.

Ronald's eyes darted up and Ellen shifted in her seat.

"Deke, not now," Char said softly, nudging him.

"I just figured as someone who's been to Vietnam, and who's interested in politics, Joe would have an opinion on the illegal bombing of those two countries," Deke said.

Joe shrugged. "Who am I to question the president on his decisions? Maybe he's aware of something we aren't."

Deke snorted. "Who are you to question his actions? Why, I think you'd be very interested, considering our government sent you there to kill North Vietnamese citizens. You must have an opinion on whether we should be bombing their neighbors, as well."

Char watched as her father drew himself up in his seat and set down his fork and knife. He looked irritated. "Deacon. The table isn't the proper place for a discussion about war. Let's just enjoy our meal."

Deke turned toward Ronald. "Excuse me, sir, but don't you think that the table is the perfect place for a discussion about the war? In fact, I think people all over the United States should be talking about why we're killing people in a foreign country in an illegal war. Maybe then all Americans would realize we don't belong there, murdering helpless women and children."

"That's enough, Deacon," Ronald insisted, his face growing red.

"I see," Deke said, glancing around the table. "I guess Joe can't speak for himself."

Joe locked his sights on Deke, his gray eyes flashing. Char could tell he was struggling to keep his anger in check. She wouldn't be surprised, if at any second, he jumped across the table and wrung Deke's neck.

"I wasn't sent to Vietnam to kill," Joe said. "I was sent there to protect my fellow soldiers and work beside the ARVN as they struggled to fight against their enemy."

"Right. So, you're telling me that you didn't kill anyone while you were there?" Deke taunted.

"I did what my government asked me to do," Joe said steadily.

"And did your government ask you to murder old men, women, and children?" Deke's voice rose. "Because that's what's going on there and you know it. Civilians are killed every day. Murdered, by U.S. soldiers just like you."

"Stop it now, Deacon!" Ronald said, his voice a low growl. "There will be no more talk like that."

Deke spun on Ronald. "Like what? The truth? Not only are our boys being sent off to be slaughtered, but they are told to kill first and ask questions later. Look at the My Lai Massacre. And the bombing and napalming of villages and towns. People like him," he pointed at Joe, "are murdering civilians every day and no one is stopping them."

"Enough!" Ronald slammed his fist on the table so hard the plates and silverware rattled. All eyes darted to the head of the table.

"I will not have you maligning a veteran of our armed services at my table, under my roof! Is that understood?" Ronald bellowed.

In the ensuing silence, a small voice spoke up from the other end of the table. "My son wasn't a murderer," Ellen said as one lone tear rolled down her cheek.

Char's heart constricted as she watched her mother.

"I never meant Jeremy, Mrs. Parsons," Deke said quietly, looking chastised.

Ellen dropped her head in her hands.

"Do you see what you've done?" Ronald asked angrily. "Are you proud of yourself for making Charlotte's mother cry?"

Deke stood. "I'm sorry. I overstepped. I'll be leaving now."

No one said a word, so Deke took his leave, with Char following him out into the living room.

"Why did you have to do that?" she asked, incensed. "Why couldn't you have just let it go this one time?"

He retrieved his coat from the hall closet and looked down at Char. "I'm sorry I upset your mother. But I can't compromise my beliefs just to please everyone. I won't give up until the killing stops and every man is back home where he belongs."

"Not even for me, Deke? Don't I mean anything to you?"

"You mean everything to me, Char. You know that. But my principles are who I am. I can't pretend otherwise." He tried to give her a kiss on the cheek, but Char turned away. Looking hurt, Deke walked out the door, closing it softly.

Chapter Seven

Char returned to the dining room where only Joe remained, looking uncomfortable.

"Where are Mom and Dad?" she asked, sitting in her seat across from him.

"Your mom went into the kitchen. I think she was crying. Ronald went to check on her."

Char sighed. "I'm sorry about the way Deke spoke to you. There is no excuse for it. He gets so wrapped up in how he feels about the war that he doesn't realize he's insulting anyone."

Joe gave her a small smile. "Oh, I think he knows what he's saying."

Char's brows rose, surprised, but then she also broke out in a grin. "I guess he does."

"He's pretty intense, but I can take it," Joe said. "I'm just sorry he upset your mother."

"Me, too."

They sat there in silence a moment. The food was cold by now and despite it having been a delicious meal, clearly neither of them felt like eating anymore.

"Maybe I should leave," Joe said, standing up.

"Please don't go," Char said quickly, then realized how desperate she'd sounded. "I mean, if you leave, Mom and Dad will feel even worse. Stay and have dessert. Mom made an apple pie and we have whipped cream and ice cream to go with it."

Joe hesitated only a second, then sat back down. "I've never been one to decline homemade apple pie." Their eyes met and they both smiled.

Char relaxed for the first time since lunch had started. She knew that Joe's easy manner was the reason for that.

Ronald and Ellen returned to the dining room.

"I'm so sorry about leaving in the middle of lunch," Ellen told Joe. "I'm glad you stayed. Let me heat up these dishes so you can have some more." She began to pick up the meat platter, but Joe stopped her.

"To be honest, Mrs. Parsons, I'm too full to eat another bite. Well, except for the apple pie Char was raving about. I'd love to have a slice of that."

Ellen looked relieved that everything was back to normal. "Then let's have some pie," she said, cheerfully. "Char, will you help me clear the table and get the dessert plates?"

Char did as her mother asked and when her parents weren't looking, she mouthed, "Thank you" to Joe. He nodded and smiled at her.

* * *

After dessert, Joe thanked the Parsons for inviting him and praised Ellen's meal once more. As Joe headed to the closet for his coat, Ronald placed a hand on his shoulder.

"You're always welcome here, Joe. Please forgive the drama at the table today. It wasn't a typical Sunday lunch, believe me."

"No apology necessary, sir," Joe said. "I'll see you Tuesday afternoon."

They had figured out a weekly schedule for Joe so he could work two days a week plus Saturdays. Joe's school day was shorter on Tuesdays and Thursdays so he could work one o'clock to five.

"I'll walk you out," Char offered, grabbing a sweater from the closet and following Joe outside. It was a perfect fall day with sunshine and a cool breeze. "I needed some fresh air."

"Want to walk for a bit?" he asked.

"Sure."

As they walked side by side, Joe snuck a glance at Char. She was still wearing the skirt and sweater he presumed she'd worn to church but had on a pair of flats. He figured she'd changed out of heels and into flats when she got home to be comfortable while helping to cook lunch. He liked that about her. She could run around in jeans and sneakers as easily as dressing up, and looked great either way. Today, however, he would have had to be blind not to notice how long and shapely her legs were in the short skirt and how her snug sweater complimented her slender curves. Her hair hung loose down her back and swung back and forth as she walked. It looked soft and shiny in the sunlight.

"What?" she asked, glancing his way.

"Oh, nothing." He turned to look straight ahead of him. He felt foolish to have been caught staring at her. "I love how your town decorates for the seasons," he said. He needed a distraction from gawking at Char. "The town square looks great."

"It does look charming with the fall garland strung around the gazebo and the hay bales stacked on the lawn. Wait until closer to Halloween, though. The decorations get even better."

They walked toward town, and before they knew it, they were near the center, looking at the very gazebo they'd just been talking about. The town was nearly deserted since the shops were closed and most people went home after church. The café was the only place open, and a couple of people were sipping coffee in a booth by the window.

"Let's sit a while," Joe suggested. They found a bench on the edge of the town square.

"Do you miss living in a big city?" Char asked.

"Not at all. There was always traffic and horns blaring and someone yelling on the street. I love this quiet little town. I dreamt about how peaceful it would be to live here while I was in Vietnam. It's exactly as I'd imagined."

"Because of my letters?"

Joe nodded. The memory of her letters warmed his heart. "Yes. Because of your letters. They gave me something to look forward to. A place to come to and start over."

"I'm glad they helped you," Char said. "But you never really answered my questions in your letters to me."

"I know. I tried to be vague. Talking about the war isn't easy. I simply prefer not to."

"It must make you angry to hear the things Deke says about what happens in Vietnam," she said.

"It's hard hearing him malign the soldiers. Deke likes to point out the worst of the war, but he hasn't been there to see what it's actually like. And how brave the men fighting it are. I've watched good men fight and die honorably. I hate hearing someone say that the soldiers are murderers, because it's simply not true. They're just doing their job." Joe sat silent a moment, thinking about all the men he'd served with and those who hadn't been lucky enough to come home. He was thankful he'd been one of the fortunate ones, and he didn't take his second chance at life for granted.

Glancing over at Char, he saw her staring off across the lawn as if contemplating what he'd said. That was why he didn't like talking about the war. It was too depressing. He gently touched her hand and she looked up.

"Tell me about your brother, Jeremy," he urged softly.

Char smiled. "He was the perfect older brother. He always let me tag along with him and his friends even though I was younger than them. And he wouldn't let anyone pick on me. Once, when I was about eight years old, Deke shoved me out of the way and Jeremy made him leave the yard until he apologized. It's funny, now when I think back on it. But my brother was my hero." She sighed. "He was smart and athletic, too. The total package. He made straight As and loved playing baseball and basketball. He was on the varsity basketball team. Everyone liked him because he was kind, too. He could have been anything he wanted, if he'd only gone to school and not in the army."

"Why didn't he go to college and get a deferment?" Joe asked.

"He said he wanted to serve now and come back to go to college. He never said why, exactly. I think it's because my dad served when he was eighteen, and maybe Jeremy wanted to make my dad proud of him. But Dad was already proud of him. He didn't have to go off to war to prove anything."

Joe nodded. "Our generation grew up believing that going to war for our country was an honor, like our fathers and grandfathers had done. We want to show that we are just as brave and honorable as they were. But their wars weren't anything like Vietnam. And the reasons we're in Nam aren't the same reasons they fought for in World War II."

"Now you sound like Deke."

"Do I?" Joe chuckled. "I hadn't meant to."

"Do you believe in fighting this war, Joe? Do you believe all our young men should be dying over there?" Char asked.

Joe considered her question carefully. "It doesn't matter what I believe. All that matters is I did what I was told to the best of my ability. I served my country, and now, thank God, I'm here."

Char's eyes dropped to her lap. Joe moved closer and placed his arm around her shoulders. "I'm sorry your brother died, Char. I really am."

She raised her eyes to his. "I'm happy you made it home," she said softly.

As late afternoon settled upon them, the air grew cooler and they began to walk back to Char's house.

"Well, I'll see you in class tomorrow," Joe said as Char stepped through the gate.

"Yeah. I'll see you," she said.

Then he slowly made his way down the sidewalk.

* * *

That night, as Joe lay in bed, he thought about the day and how nice it had ended after a rough start.

I'm happy you made it home.

Char's words reverberated over and over in his mind. She'd sounded sincere; he truly believed she'd meant it. He couldn't wait until English class tomorrow morning when he would see her again. And next Saturday, when they'd work together. It had been a long time since he'd looked forward to anything. It made him feel young again, a feeling he hadn't experienced since before he'd enlisted. And it was all because of Char. She brought out feelings in him that had been pushed down since high school.

But she has a boyfriend, you idiot.

Joe sighed. He didn't care that she had a boyfriend. He would enjoy spending time with her whenever he got a chance. Deke could be damned. The jerk didn't deserve her anyway.

Joe chuckled. Yep. He felt like a high school kid all over again.

* * *

Char sat by the window in her bedroom, her fluffy robe wrapped tightly around her. She'd opened the window a little, despite the chilly air. Sitting quietly, she listened, and was rewarded with the first sounds of the night. Crickets chirping, frogs croaking. Off in the distance, an owl called out into the dark.

Night music.

Char smiled, closed her window, and slipped into bed.

Chapter Eight

On a Monday afternoon, two weeks after the lunch-time blow-up, Char, Patty, and Jenny sat in the library, working on their homework. Char noticed Deke at another table and he quickly walked over.

"Char, please don't stay angry with me." He flashed his sweetest smile. Since that terrible Sunday afternoon, Char had avoided spending time alone with Deke. She was furious with him for upsetting her parents and insulting Joe. She respected that he had strong opinions, but he'd purposely done the opposite of what she'd asked him that day. His complete disregard for her feelings had made her think twice about their relationship. But resisting Deke's charm was difficult. It was hard to say no to him.

"I apologized to both of your parents. They've accepted my apology, so why won't you?" He reached for her hand.

Char pulled it away. "You didn't apologize to Joe."

Deke let out a long, drawn-out sigh. "I don't care about him. I only care what you and your parents think of me. I'm sure G.I. Joe will be fine without an apology."

"And stop calling him names," Char insisted. "It's rude. He's never done a thing to you."

"Shh!" A student at the next table hissed.

Deke took Char's hand and pulled her down to the end of a row of bookshelves where they'd have privacy. "Come on, baby. Give me another chance. I hated that you didn't want to see me on your birthday and I miss spending time with you."

Char had quietly celebrated her nineteenth birthday with her parents and had declined Deke's request to take her out or come to the house. He'd left a present for her in the mailbox, and when she'd opened it, her heart had melted. It was a gold heart locket. Inside the small card he'd written: "You have my heart." It was all she could do not to forgive him then and there. But she'd forced herself not to let the gift sway her. Now, he gazed into her eyes with his own deep blue ones, tearing down her resolve.

"But I…" Char began, but Deke bent down and kissed her neck, slowly running his lips up to her ear. Char felt a delicious chill tingle up her spine. She sighed as her anger at him dissolved.

"You're wearing the necklace I gave you," he said. "You can't be too mad at me."

Char felt her skin grow warm as Deke touched the heart locket at her throat, but she kept silent.

"Please, baby," Deke whispered in her ear. "I love you so much. I hate when we're not together."

There was that word, *love*. Deke had told her this before, when they made love, but she'd never said it back. Ever. She always felt guilty that she didn't. She cared about Deke— he made her feel things she'd never felt with any other boy—and she admired him, but did she *love* him? She wasn't sure.

"Sweetie, you're a million miles away," Deke said, tilting her chin with his finger so their eyes met. "I'm professing my love for you and you're staring off into space."

"I'm sorry, Deke. I…I have a lot of school projects to think about. And I'm trying out for the college newspaper, too. I just have so much work to do."

He bent down and kissed her lips. "Tell me you'll give me another chance and I'll let you get back to your homework. If you don't, I'll whisk you away to my chambers and torture you with all your wishes and desires, until you are mine again." He grinned, looking silly and boyish, and extremely charming.

"Okay. I give." Char laughed. "Just promise me you'll be nicer to Joe when you run into him."

"Sure. But just for you, sweetie. Just for you."

He left with a promise they'd meet for dinner that night at the café. Char returned to the table with her friends.

"Well, did he charm the pants off you, again?" Jenny asked.

Char's eyes darted up. "What do you mean by that?"

"Come on, Char. Every time he upsets you, he's able to get back into your good graces with a wink and a smile. You're putty in his hands. Just putty."

"Silly Putty." Patty giggled. "I'd love to be putty in a cute guy's hands. He could play with me all he wanted."

"Patty! Stop it. That sounds awful," Char said. "And I'm not putty in Deke's hands. I stand up to him."

Jenny gave her a side-glance.

"What was that look for?" Char asked, annoyed.

"Deke is handsome, smart, and charming," Jenny told her. "And you're smart too. But to tell you the truth, Char, I think you hide your intelligence when you're around him."

Char was stunned. "You think I play dumb around Deke?"

Jenny sighed. "No. I think you let him overshadow you because it makes him feel superior to you."

Char couldn't believe what she was hearing. She wasn't sure

if she should be angry with Jenny, or take her words to heart.

"Listen, Char. You're my best friend and I love you, so please don't be mad at me. But the girl I know, who is strong and smart, is not the girl I generally see when you're around Deke. His personality shines so bright, you get lost in its glare. And sometimes, well, I think you let it happen. You have opinions, but you don't express them around him."

"I just spent two weeks being angry at him for the way he insulted my parents and Joe. I told him how I felt and made him apologize to my parents. I think I act pretty strong around him," Char argued.

"No, you avoided him until he did what you wanted and then you let him slide back into your good graces. Did you ever really express to him how you felt about his tirade at your parents? Or how he treated Joe?" Jenny asked.

"I just did!" Char insisted. "I told him he had to apologize to Joe and be nice to him."

"Did he apologize?"

Char's shoulders slumped. "No. But he knows how I feel."

Jenny shook her head and went back to her homework.

Char re-played her conversation with Deke in her mind. Then she thought about every conversation she'd ever had with Deke. It was true that she admired him. She thought he was intelligent and loved how he spoke so passionately about his beliefs. It made her wonder if she did hold back her own opinions when she was with him.

"Do you really think I play dumb around Deke?" she asked Jenny.

"I'm sorry, Char. I shouldn't have said anything. I mean, who am I to tell you how to run your relationship when I've never even had one? Just forget I said anything." Jenny gave her a strained smile and went back to her work again.

"Don't worry about it, Char," Patty said. "All girls play a little dumb around their boyfriends. It makes them feel manly. You know that men like feeling smarter than their girl. There's no shame in that."

Char gaped at Patty as her friend returned to her novel. *All girls play a little dumb around their boyfriends.* That statement made Char's skin crawl. Did she really do that?

Then she was reminded about something Joe had asked her that Saturday night at the student union. *Do you believe in what he's saying?* She hadn't answered him because the question had caught her off guard. She usually didn't question Deke's beliefs, and often thought about his words for days after hearing him speak to other students about the war. But she never asked him why he believed that way, or disputed anything he said. She'd stayed quiet out of respect for him, but now she was beginning to feel as if she was doing exactly what Jenny said: playing dumb.

* * *

"Explain to me why you've started talking about revolution instead of peaceful protests against the war," Char asked Deke as they sat in a booth at the Corner Café. She'd decided that she wasn't going to hide her opinions around him any longer. She didn't want to play the dumb girlfriend.

Deke raised his brows. "I didn't know the movement interested you. I thought you were staying neutral about it."

"I've never said that," she told him. "I've listened to your speeches on campus and what you say to people in small groups at the union. But lately, you've been talking more about action than peaceful protests. Don't you feel that 'bringing the war home,' as I've heard you say, would only accelerate the problems without actually ending the war?"

Deke grinned. "You have been listening. Okay. SDS is dead, plain and simple. The philosophy of the Weathermen Underground Organization makes much more sense. I've been to the marches on Washington and the rallies in Chicago. Marching down the street carrying a sign doesn't make a difference anymore. Maybe it never did. We have to hit them where it hurts. We have to fight back. I wish I'd been a part of the 'Days of Rage' in Chicago last October. They didn't have the strong numbers, but they made a dent."

"I don't think I agree," Char said. "Fighting to end fighting. It all seems counter-productive. It makes your group no better than the government that's sending our boys to war."

Deke had been lifting a forkful of hot roast beef sandwich to his mouth but stopped and sat back against the booth, staring at Char in awe. "You amaze me, Char. I figured you weren't interested enough in what I do to have an opinion on it. I'm glad that you are, though. And to answer your question, yes, it may seem counter-productive, but in truth, the government will see us and react if we show them our anger."

"Anger, I understand," Char said. "I'm heartbroken that Jeremy died in Vietnam, but I'm also angry that he had to go in the first place. But I'm not enraged enough to want to blow up a building or hurt anyone. Why are you?"

Deke leaned forward over the table. "I'm angry because our government lies to us. I'm angry that we're sending boys over to a foreign country to fight a war that isn't ours to fight. I'm enraged at the way the cops and National Guard are treating protesters who are peaceful. Look at what happened at Kent State this past May. The cops shot and killed four innocent students. And what about Jackson State College? Two more killed. This can't continue. And yes, I'm angry because Jeremy is dead. So yes, I am furious enough to blow something up."

Char dropped her eyes to her plate, her appetite gone.

Deke continued speaking. "I had just joined the SDS on campus after Jeremy enlisted. I wanted to understand why we were fighting that war, but I wanted the truth, not the crap our government and the news told us. You can say I was enlightened by SDS. Now, I also see why they're falling apart and the national leaders of SDS have transformed into the Weathermen Underground. I was at the national meeting when they decided to pull away and create their own organization. And I agree with them. We have to fight back to make a difference. To stop the bloodshed. To bring our men home."

Char raised her eyes to meet Deke's. "If you're so concerned with the soldiers coming home, why do you accuse them of being murderers? Shouldn't you be welcoming people like Joe home?"

Deke tilted his head. "Is that why you're suddenly interested? Because of Joe?"

"No," Char said quickly. "But you contradict yourself when you say you believe in fighting to bring the men home, but then you turn around and condemn those same men."

He shook his head. "It's not a contradiction, Char. I'm only speaking the truth. The soldiers may not have asked to go to Vietnam, but once they're there, they become just as bad as our politicians who lie to us. They've been taught to kill, and they enjoy it. And they will lie to us about what's going on over there just as our government does."

"What about the veterans who oppose the war? They're on your side. Do you condemn them, too?"

"No. Char, I'm not condemning anyone. All I know is what I see and hear. People like Joe aren't as innocent as you seem to think. Our government is bombing the villages of innocent civilians every day over there. If soldiers are told to go and clean out a village, they do, no questions asked. Women, children, and old men watch their huts being burned to the ground and they're left homeless, because of our soldiers, our government. Many of them are killed for no reason at all. Look at My Lai. The soldiers went on a rampage, raping women and then killing everyone in the village, including children. Then they tried to cover it up. Everyone. The soldiers and our government. We're not protecting the South Vietnamese people from the enemy. We're killing them."

Char shook her head. "Those are isolated events. Joe wouldn't have been a part of such crimes. And I know Jeremy wouldn't have either."

"Oh, sweetie. I'm sorry to disagree, but you don't know what men will do when their lives are on the line. Ask your friend Joe about his box. Every Vietnam soldier who comes home has one. A box of souvenirs from their time there. You'd be horrified to find out what's in it. God only knows what your precious Joe might have a photo, or a piece of, in that box."

She frowned. "How would you know?"

"Because I've known enough vets who've come home to know what they bring back. Many of my high school classmates went to Vietnam. Some returned. Even the nicest guy in the world is changed by war."

Char grabbed her purse and slid to the end of the booth. "I'm going home. I don't want to talk about this anymore."

"Wait," Deke said, reaching for her hand. "Don't go. I'm enjoying discussing this with you. You bring a whole new perspective to it for me. Please stay and at least finish your dinner."

She hesitated, not really wanting to stay. The idea of good men turning into monsters made her stomach churn. But Deke looked at her so hopefully, she gave in and slid back to the middle of the booth.

"Babe, I'm sorry if I upset you. I know it's hard to accept the truth over the lies we've been led to believe. But once your eyes are opened, you'll never see the world the same again. And you'll wonder how you ever missed the truth to begin with."

Deke went back to eating his meal, but all she could do was stare down at hers. Maybe that was what she was afraid of. Seeing the world differently. She liked the world she lived in. Did she really want to see it in the negative, horrific way Deke did?

"Sweetie. I'd love for you to come with me at the end of October to the SDS meeting in Chicago. Groups from colleges all over the four-state-area are going to meet and discuss the future of our local SDS chapters. It's going to be an interesting meeting. It will open you up to a whole new way of thinking."

"I couldn't possibly go," Char said, imagining what her father's face would look like if she suggested such a thing to him. "Even if I wanted to go, my dad would never agree to me going away with you."

"Your dad has to get out of the 1950s. You're nineteen now. You can make your own decisions and he can't tell you what to do," Deke said.

"He can stop paying my tuition and take Jeremy's car away from me," she said, nervously fingering the gold locket at her neck.

Deke waved his arm through the air to brush away her concerns. "They will never do that. Your parents won't risk losing you, too." His eyes lit up. "It would be amazing if you came along. You'd learn so much about the organization and meet new people whose thoughts would blow your mind."

"I can't, Deke. I'm sorry." She thought a moment. "What week is that?"

"The twenty-second through the twenty-fifth. I'll be gone through the weekend."

Char pondered the date while Deke finished his dinner. The fall dance at the college was the same weekend that he'd be gone. She had hoped he would take her. But she didn't want to make a big deal over something that sounded so trivial compared to his dedication to ending the war. Still, she'd so wanted to go to her first college dance.

They cruised around in his car after dinner. Deke asked if she'd come back to his place with him, but she made the excuse that she still had homework to finish. Her excuse was partly true. They'd started reading *The Great Gatsby* in English class and she wanted to read more before going to bed. Mostly, though, she didn't feel like being intimate with Deke tonight. She felt distanced from him, and making love would have left her feeling empty.

That night Char curled up in bed with Fitzgerald's novel and lost herself in a world of wealth and decadence. She'd left her window open just a crack, and every so often, she heard the lullaby of the night music.

Chapter Nine

October arrived with an explosion of red, gold, and orange as the trees hit their peak fall colors. Everywhere Char walked, leaves crunched underfoot, and when the wind picked up, they'd swirl and spin in a dance all their own. She loved the rich colors and the musky smell of the leaves on the ground. They reminded her of carefree days as a child jumping into a huge pile of raked leaves with Jeremy as her father had laughed in the background.

That Friday in English class, the teacher chose to read some of the reports the students had written on *For Whom the Bell Tolls*. They'd been assigned to write about the section of the book that touched them the most, and why. Char had written about the love story, and the contrast of falling in love during war. But much to her disappointment, the teacher didn't read her paper. Instead he read a paper that described the final scene in the book and how the main character, Robert Jordan, must have felt in those last moments, knowing he was dying, yet doing what he'd been sent there to do—fight. The words flowed easily and drew the entire class in, including Char. It was a beautiful and poignant description, and near the end, she glanced over to Joe and saw he was staring at the floor. That was when she realized it was his paper being read, and her admiration for him grew.

She wished she could write even half as lovely as he did.

That Saturday as they worked together in the hardware store, she brought up his paper and how beautifully it had been written.

Joe brushed off her praise. "Thank you," he said. "But it wasn't that good. I only wrote how it made me feel."

"Isn't that what true writing is about? How we feel. Making others feel it too. 'All you have to do is write one true sentence. Write the truest sentence that you know.' Hemingway said that," she told him.

Joe chuckled. "I'm no Hemingway, but I do like to write. I guess we have that in common. Writing, I mean."

She smiled back at him.

"You never said whether you made it on the college newspaper," Joe said.

Char dropped her eyes. This week had been one of disappointments, both minor and major. She'd submitted her best work from her high school paper to the college newspaper but hadn't been chosen. The editor had told her it had more to do with the many juniors and seniors applying and less to do about the quality of her work. He said she should definitely apply next year. But that did nothing to soothe her disappointment. And then there was the fall dance. She had hoped to go with Deke, but that wasn't going to happen either.

"I didn't make the cut at the paper," she admitted to Joe. "But there's always next year."

"I'm sorry, Char," Joe said sincerely. "It's their loss. I'm sure you'll make it next time."

She nodded and headed back to the store's office. She'd begun learning the bookkeeping these past few weeks since Joe had started. Proficient in math, she'd picked it up easily. Now her father was able to take the day off on some Saturdays and left the store in Char and Joe's capable hands. Char felt proud that her father trusted her to make decisions while he was gone. But she did miss working up front with the customers, and working alongside Joe. He was so easy to be around and had a quick sense of humor that kept her laughing. She made excuses throughout the day to go up front just to spend time with him.

Later that afternoon, Joe came to the back room. "Hey? There's a girl out here who wants to ask the manager a question. I guess that makes you the manager." He grinned at her.

"I guess it does," she said. They walked up to the front together where a young girl wearing an incredibly short skirt and tight sweater asked if she could put a poster up in the window.

Char looked at the poster and then nodded. "Sure."

The girl had brought her own tape, so she quickly attached it to the window, waved, and left.

"Sorry I bothered you," Joe said. "I didn't know if you allowed posters."

"It's okay." Char walked over to the front window. The poster was for the college Fall Fling dance coming up on Saturday, October 25th. She gazed across the way, past the lawn and gazebo to Elaine's Dress Shop where an emerald green dress was displayed in the window. It was a frothy chiffon with a satin underskirt and a wide belt made of the same fabric, and a gold buckle. Gold buttons ran down the back. Char had tried it on last week and both Jenny and Patty had told her how lovely it looked. The skirt was short, and when she turned back and forth, it twirled around her legs. She'd fallen in love with the dress, and had hoped to wear it to the dance. But now, she wouldn't have any need to buy it.

"Are you going?" Joe asked, coming up alongside her.

She shook her head. "No. Deke's going to a meeting that weekend."

"Oh. That's too bad," he said, turning away and walking back to the counter.

Char thought she'd seen a flicker of disapproval in Joe's eyes before he turned away. She went to the counter and faced him. "Deke takes these SDS meetings very seriously," she said, crossing her arms.

Joe's eyes met hers. "Does he take his relationship with you just as seriously?"

Her mouth dropped open, but she recovered quickly. "What do you mean by that?"

"Nothing," he said. "Forget I said anything." He picked up the duster and turned to go down the aisle.

Anger replaced her disappointment. She brushed past Joe as she headed for the back room.

"Char?"

She spun on her heel and faced him. "What?"

"It's just a shame that you aren't going is what I meant to say. That dress would look beautiful on you."

Char blinked. "Uh, thanks." She turned and went back to her desk, where she spent the rest of the afternoon wondering how Joe could have known what dress she'd been looking at.

* * *

Joe couldn't believe Deke was stupid enough to miss the first dance of the school year when he had an amazing girlfriend like Char to take. For a full week, Joe let his anger simmer until he finally came to a decision. If Deke was too self-obsessed to take

Char, then maybe he could talk her into going with him.

The next Saturday at work, he tried all day to build up the nerve to ask her to the dance, but each time they spoke, he lost it. *Why would she want to go with me?* he kept asking himself. But then he'd remember the disappointed look on her face and was determined to ask her. By the end of the day he hadn't, though, and as he walked home, he wanted to kick himself.

When he entered the boarding house, Mrs. Bennington was setting the table for dinner.

"There's a letter for you, Joe," she said brightly. "It's on the table there." She pointed to the small table in the entryway just below where a gilt-framed mirror hung.

"Thanks, Mrs. B," he said. He sorted through the pile of letters, found the one addressed to him, and stuffed it into his coat pocket. Then he headed upstairs.

Once he was in his room, he took off his coat and pulled the letter from his pocket. Sitting on the sofa, he studied the envelope. There was no return address, but he recognized the shaky handwriting. It was from Tony "Spaghetti" Funari. Joe sighed. He'd kept in touch with Tony because he'd felt bad for him. Tony had returned from Vietnam a couple of months after Joe and had spent some time in a V.A. hospital for a nervous condition. After that, he'd bounced around from his parents' home in New Jersey to friend's places, guys he'd met in Vietnam. Tony hadn't yet been able to hold down a job or stay in one place for very long. The last Joe had heard from Tony, he was staying in a friend's apartment in Michigan and working at a gas station. Joe had a feeling that this letter was going to say he was on the move again.

He opened it and his suspicions were right. Tony was now in Chicago, staying with a veteran he'd met on his first tour, and was working as a janitor for a department store.

"Can you imagine?" Tony wrote. *"Me, sweeping floors and cleaning toilets. I guess it's not much different than flushing out Viet Cong from tunnels, but it's still rough to think that it's the only job I can get after two tours in Vietnam."*

Joe understood his frustration. Neither of them had been trained to do anything in the service except stay alive under horrendous circumstances. At the end of the letter, Tony suggested they try to meet up since they lived only a few hours away from each other now. Joe wasn't sure he wanted to visit Tony. Joe liked his new life in Grand Falls and wasn't eager to dig up the past. He folded the letter and stuck it in the top drawer of his dresser, hoping that if he ignored it, Tony would forget and move on in a few months.

After school on Monday, Joe gathered up all his courage and stopped at Char's house on his way home. It was a breezy autumn day with a bite to the air. Joe could feel that winter wasn't far behind. A moment after he'd knocked, Char opened the door and stared at him, surprised.

"Hi, Joe. What's up?"

He suddenly felt foolish. He had hoped to find her outside, sitting on the swing, so he could casually sit down and work his way into asking her. But, of course, she wasn't sitting outside on a chilly day.

"Um, I just thought I'd stop by and say hello," he said, realizing how lame he sounded.

"Okay." Char stared at him strangely. "Do you want to come in?"

Joe lost his nerve. He took a step back. "No, that's okay. It's silly, actually. I mean, I see you in class every day. Anyway, I'll be on my way. Bye." He turned and tried to hurry, but his stiff leg and cane made that impossible.

"Joe?" Char called after him. She came out just as he reached the gate and ran up to him. She'd grabbed a sweater and was slipping it on. "Wait. What's on your mind?"

Joe felt ridiculous. Staring down the enemy was easier than asking this beautiful girl to a dance. "It was nothing, really. I don't know what I was thinking, bothering you."

Char grinned. "Come on. Let's go sit in the swing, out of the breeze." She headed back to the porch.

Joe followed. He couldn't believe he'd put himself in this awkward position. Once on the porch, he slipped his pack off and set it down. Then he eased himself slowly into the swing next to Char.

"It's hot chocolate weather," Char said, pulling her sweater closer around her.

"With marshmallows?" Joe asked.

Char's eyes twinkled. "Is there any other kind?"

He laughed, feeling more at ease. "I suppose I'll be trudging through snow pretty soon."

"Not until November. Or if we're lucky, December," she said.

Silence fell over them. The leaves on the trees fluttered in the breeze, making a soft whooshing sound. A gray squirrel sat on the grass, stuffing acorns into his mouth, then scurried up the tree. They both watched him and chuckled at his fat cheeks.

Joe turned to Char. "I was thinking about the fall dance." His heart beat rapidly in his chest.

Char's brows rose. "Oh? Are you going?"

"Well, that's what I was thinking about. I mean, I'm not going, and you're not going, but maybe, if we wanted to, we could go together." There, he'd said it. He searched Char's face for her reaction, but she kept her expression neutral.

"That's nice of you to ask," she said. "But I don't think Deke would like it if I went with someone else."

"I thought of that, too," Joe said. "And I figured that since he wasn't taking you, he really didn't have a say in whether or not you go and with who."

Char looked amused. "I'm not sure he'd agree with you on that."

"Probably not, so I thought of a plan," Joe said. "Let's say I just happen to be going to the dance, and since tickets have to be bought in pairs, I'd happen to have two tickets. Maybe, as I walked to the dance, you could just happen to be wearing a pretty dress, and we would both end up going at the same time." He grinned at her.

"Hmm. I'm not sure," Char said, looking thoughtful.

Joe's heart sank.

"I think it would be too cold to walk. Maybe, you could just happen by and drive me to the dance in my car, you know, so I'd get there safe." Her eyes twinkled mischievously.

His face brightened. "That could be arranged."

"And if anyone asks, we could say that we happened to go to the dance at the same time, so it isn't really a date. It's more like two friends meeting up at the same place," Char said.

Joe would have preferred it to be a date, but he'd take what he could get. "Sounds good to me."

The amusement dropped from Char's face. "I do really want to go to the dance. Is that silly and childish?"

"No, not at all. You should go. I'm not silly and childish and I want to go."

"Well, you can be silly sometimes, but you are definitely not childish," Char said.

They both grinned at each other.

"Then, should I just happen by around seven o'clock that night?" he asked.

"Why don't you make it six forty-five? My mom will want to take pictures." Char rolled her eyes.

"Sounds good."

"A suit is required," Char said. "Do you have one?"

Joe hadn't thought about needing a suit for the dance. "I'll figure something out," he said, feeling determined.

He left after that, even though Char had invited him in for hot chocolate. He didn't want to overstay his welcome and ruin his good luck. He would need to borrow a suit, and he knew he was borrowing Char from Deke for that one night, but that didn't tarnish his mood in the least. He couldn't wait to take her to the dance.

* * *

Char spent that evening working on algebra and history home-work and reading more of *The Great Gatsby*. Even though she did her best to concentrate on her work, she couldn't help but be excited about the upcoming dance. Tomorrow after school, she would go to Elaine's Dress Shop and buy the green dress. Then she needed to buy a pair of shoes to go with it.

For the first time in a long while, it was fun to simply be young and happy.

Char thought about how nervous and unsure Joe had looked when she'd opened the door this afternoon. She'd never seen him act that way before. At the time, she'd been afraid he was going to tell her bad news, like he was quitting his job at the store or leaving town. But when he'd talked about the dance, she was both relieved, and surprised. And flattered. It was so sweet of him to want to take her, despite knowing that she was dating Deke. She knew he'd seen the disappointment in her eyes when she'd told him she couldn't go to the dance, and he was making sure she could go. It warmed her heart just thinking about it. It seemed very much like the type of gesture Jeremy would have made for her.

Except Joe wasn't her brother. This made Char pause.

Did Joe think this was a date?

Char pushed that thought out of her head. She wasn't going to analyze Joe's intentions and ruin going to the dance. She wanted to go, and that was that. All she'd let herself think about was wearing the pretty dress and spending an evening with her friends and Joe.

Chapter Ten

O ver the next two weeks, Char didn't tell Deke that she was planning to attend the dance with Joe. It did annoy her, however, that Deke hadn't even bothered to ask if she was disappointed that she wasn't going. Everyone at the student union was talking about it, so he had to have been aware of it. He was so focused on his upcoming SDS meeting in Chicago that he didn't stop to think about anyone else but himself. That didn't settle well with her.

So she was even happier that Joe had asked her and she wasn't going to let thoughts of Deke ruin the dance.

Char was also thrilled her friends would be attending. Patty had tried working her magic on Justin, but to no avail. Then, Craig Johnson, another of Deke's friends, asked Patty to the dance one night in the student union. Patty accepted, even though she wasn't interested in the short, stocky Craig who wore thick, black glasses. But he was a date, and Patty was glad she didn't have to miss the dance.

Jenny had also been asked, much to her surprise, by Terry Conway, a boy who'd graduated with them from high school. Jenny had been too focused on her school work to notice Terry in her science class. When he'd asked her to the dance, she'd been so flustered that she'd said yes. Both Char and Patty had laughed hysterically when Jenny told them, but they were happy too. Now they would all be at the dance together.

The Wednesday before the big night, Deke took Char out for dinner at a nice restaurant just outside of town. It sat on the bank of the Illinois River and offered quiet dining and delicious food. Deke had brought her here once before, as a special evening, so it made Char wonder why they'd come tonight.

Once they were seated, Deke reached across the table and held Char's hand. "I'm sorry I've been ignoring you these past few weeks. I've been wrapped up in school and all that's going on with SDS. But I hope you understand. Things are changing, and it's an exciting time we live in. I don't want to miss being a part of it."

"I understand, Deke. I know how seriously you take your work against the war." She meant what she said, despite being annoyed with him over missing the dance. She understood that what he was doing was more important than dressing up and going to a dance.

Deke leaned in closer, his eyes bright. "This meeting I'm going to could be a game changer, Char. I can't express how important it is. The national level of SDS is gone, and some of the members have moved on to other ways of expressing their rage against the war. A few of us who've held on to SDS are now talking about disbanding it too. A member of the Weathermen Underground is going to meet with us and discuss what more we can do. It's all very exciting."

Char frowned at the mention of the Weathermen Underground. "You aren't seriously considering joining them, are you? Wouldn't it mean you'd have to disappear?"

Deke shook his head. "They can use people from all walks of life. It's not just about protesting. It's about getting to the center of the problem and breaking it down from the inside. But don't worry, it's only a meeting. We're just going to talk with him and see what we think."

Char didn't say much after that. It was difficult for her to believe that Deke was the same man she'd been dating for over a year. She didn't like his talk about violent protesting. She couldn't understand how that would help bring peace.

Later that night as she lay in bed, she wondered what had happened between her and Deke. She'd always looked up to him, thinking he was mature and wise. But now, she found herself questioning everything he said. A year ago, she was confused about the war. Now, she was beginning to form opinions of her own and no longer looked to him for guidance. She realized that she was the one who was changing.

There was also the issue of love. After dinner, he'd tried to persuade her to come back to his place so they could be alone, but she'd declined. He'd kissed her goodnight in the car and told her he loved her. She'd wanted to say it back, but couldn't make herself do it. She'd always had strong feelings for him, but she wasn't sure if she truly loved him. She wished she could talk to her friends about it. Or anyone, for that matter. But she could never admit to her friends that she'd given herself to a man who she wasn't even sure she loved. They would think badly of her and her parents would be appalled if they ever knew.

So much was changing and she was struggling to understand it all.

* * *

Saturday dawned sunny and surprisingly warm. Char woke
up excited about the day. She had taken off from work and
she, Jenny, and Patty spent the afternoon at the beauty parlor
having their hair and nails done. It was so much fun being silly
and girly for the day, pampering herself and giggling with her
friends. Even serious Jenny was having a good time. Char had
her hair styled in a simple up-do with soft tendrils at her neck
and temples. Her nails were a soft pink in contrast to the dark
purple Patty had chosen to match her purple dress. Patty had
also chosen to have her thick, red hair styled with curls dropping
around her face, but Jenny left her hair down in a no-nonsense
style. She'd bought a new dress, too, in a rich blue color which
magically deepened the color of her eyes.

That evening, Char twirled in front of the full-length
mirror and watched as the skirt lifted and fell around her thighs.
The fabric was filmy and shone in the light. She had bought
black patent-leather shoes with tall, thick heels and a thin strap
so when she danced, she wouldn't have to worry about her shoes
slipping off. At the last minute, she searched through her closet
for the white lace shawl she'd worn to her senior prom and found
it folded up on a high shelf. Wrapping it around her shoulders,
she smiled. It looked lovely against the deep green of her dress.

Char's father whistled softly when she walked down the stairs.

"You look beautiful," he said, smiling proudly. "You'll be the
prettiest girl at the dance."

Char beamed. "Thanks, Dad."

Ellen came in from the kitchen with her Kodak camera in
hand. "Sweetie, you look lovely. Let's take a picture of you before
Joe arrives. Then I want one of the both of you."

Char posed for her mother and that was when the doorbell
rang. Her father went to answer it.

"Joe. Come on in," Ronald said. "Well, don't you clean up nice?"

Joe stepped inside, his cane in his left hand and a small box in the other.

"Joe, you look very handsome." Ellen walked over to greet him. "I'm so happy you and Char are going to the dance together. You'll have such a good time."

"Thank you." Joe turned to Char. "Hi."

Char gazed at Joe. Her mom was right. He looked handsome in a navy suit with a white shirt and a wide, navy and white striped tie. His hair was trimmed shorter than when she'd last seen him. He'd made an effort to look nice tonight. It surprised her that she suddenly felt nervous. "Hi."

Joe stepped closer to Char. "This is for you," he said, handing her the box.

Char opened it and looked inside. It was a corsage made of white roses and baby's breath. "It's beautiful," she exclaimed, elated by his thoughtfulness. She knew this was an expense he couldn't afford, though. "You really didn't have to buy me one."

Joe gave her a small smile. "I wanted to."

"I love it." She turned to her mother for help pinning it on her dress. Char wondered how Joe knew she loved white roses.

After a quick picture of the couple, Joe and Char walked out to her car. She handed him the keys and he held her door open as she stepped inside. When he slid in behind the wheel, he faced her. "You look beautiful tonight."

Char saw his eyes sparkle. "Thank you. You look very handsome."

"Thanks to Mrs. Bennington and Rodney Carson, I had a suit to wear," he said.

"Rodney Carson? Who's he?" she asked.

"He lives at the boarding house. He's a new teacher at the high school this year. We're close to the same size, and when Mrs. Bennington told him I needed a suit, he offered his."

Char smiled. "It fits you perfectly. That was very nice of him."

"Yes, it was. But like Cinderella, I'll probably turn into a pumpkin if you don't get me home by midnight."

She laughed as he started the car and pulled away from the curb. Their light banter put her more at ease about tonight.

"This is an added bonus," Joe said, driving through downtown.

"The car?"

"Yeah. I haven't had a chance to drive in a long time. And luckily, my driving leg wasn't wounded." He winked at her. "I miss driving. As soon as I can save some money, I'm getting a car. Walking everywhere gets tiresome."

"This was Jeremy's car," Char said softly. "My parents let me drive it, but it's not really mine. It will always be his."

Joe glanced over at her, his expression tender. "Then I'll take extra care with it, and his sister tonight."

Char felt herself grow warm and knew a blush colored her face. His words were such a beautiful sentiment. No one had made her blush in a very long time.

They parked near the college gymnasium which doubled as an auditorium. Joe stepped out first and came around to open Char's door. It was very old-fashioned, but she liked it. Deke had done it once or twice when they'd first started dating but hadn't since. It made her feel special.

Joe offered her his bent arm and they walked up the sidewalk. The night air was warm and the moon was nearly full, glowing in the sky. Music drifted out the open gym doors. As they neared the building, Char looked up at Joe and saw the silver flecks in his eyes sparkle. Her heart fluttered.

"There you are!" Patty cried as they entered the gym. She and Jenny stood by the door with their dates hovering nearby. Patty was bubbling with excitement, but Jenny looked like she wanted to bolt out the door.

After everyone had been introduced, they searched for a table for six. On one end of the gym, the band was set up on a tall platform, and a large area was marked off in front of them for the dance floor. Round tables covered in flowing tablecloths sat around the room. Across the other side of the gym was a long table filled with refreshments. As the group sat down, the band began playing the Beatles tune, "Let it Be."

Patty and Craig headed to the dance floor and Jenny reluctantly went to dance with Terry. Char laid her shawl over the back of her chair and watched as the other couples danced slowly around the floor. She suddenly felt awkward around Joe. In her excitement to come to the dance, she'd forgotten about his stiff leg and the cane he needed for walking. Dancing was probably not an easy thing for him to do.

"Would you like to dance?" he asked, standing up and extending his hand to her.

Char hesitated. "We don't have to, if you'd rather not."

He looked at her with an amused expression. "Isn't that what one does at a dance?"

Char took his hand and stood, feeling embarrassed. "I only meant that if it's awkward to dance, I don't expect you to." She felt terrible pointing out his limp.

But Joe only smiled. "I think I can manage the slow dances. It's all the flailing and gyrating I'll have to miss out on. Which is a shame, actually." His eyes twinkled.

Char laughed and her uneasiness melted away. "Then I would love to dance."

Joe set his cane against the table and slowly led Char out to the dance floor. "I hope you don't mind if I lean on you a little," he said as he turned to face her and placed his other hand on her waist.

His hand felt warm through the light fabric of her dress. Warm, and steady. As she gazed up at him, their bodies nearly touching, her face so close to his, a delightful chill ran up her spine.

"I don't mind at all," she said. They began to move slowly to the beat of the song, both in perfect rhythm with each other.

* * *

Joe could hardly believe Char was in his arms. If someone had told him a year ago that he'd be at a dance with her as his date—albeit his borrowed date—he would have said they were crazy. But here they were, moving slowly to the music, so close he could smell the light scent of her perfume and feel her hair softly tickle his neck.

The music changed to a fast song so they walked back to their table. Joe was delighted that Char was still holding his hand. Reluctantly, he let go as she sat down. He offered to bring her a cup of punch. Lifting his cane, he headed to the refreshment table, hoping he could hold both cups without spilling.

Patty bumped into him as he waited in line.

"Oops! Sorry," she said, grinning.

"That's okay," Joe assured her.

She glanced around, as if to make sure no one was listening, before speaking. "I'm so happy you invited Char to the dance.

Between you and me, I don't think Deke would have brought her even if he'd been home. He's a nice guy, but he's too preoccupied with his own stuff to put Char first."

Joe agreed completely but didn't say so. "I'm happy to bring her. She's a sweet girl."

Patty studied him a moment before speaking again. "You really like her, don't you? I mean, more than just as friends."

"What makes you say that?" Joe asked, caught off guard.

"It's the way you look at her. Like she's the only girl in the room. I'd give anything to have a guy look at me that way."

Joe opened his mouth to protest, but then he stopped. What was the point? She was right. He adored Char, despite knowing he could never have her. "Patty. Someday a man will look at you that way. You're a beautiful girl. I'm surprised the boys aren't lining up, begging to date you."

Patty blushed. "You're so sweet. Hopefully sooner rather than later. Otherwise, I'll be in school forever."

Joe chuckled as he came to the front of the line. He handed Patty a cup of punch, then slipped his cane over his arm, and picked up two for him and Char. Walking stiffly, he headed back to the table, careful not to spill on his suit.

Over the next two hours, they had a wonderful time, alternately taking turns on the dance floor and sitting at the table, chatting with the group. Even though Craig was Deke's friend, he didn't seem surprised that Joe was with Char tonight. They talked about their classes and which teachers were good and which to avoid. Craig was a business major although he admitted he wasn't sure how he'd use his degree when he graduated.

"I'll probably be shipped off to Vietnam after graduation anyway," Craig said. "No offense," he told Joe. "I know I have to go, but I'm not looking forward to it."

"No offense taken," Joe said. "I didn't want to go either. But they'll get us one way or another, so I went."

Craig considered his words before nodding. Joe assumed he hadn't expected the answer he'd given him. Craig was used to listening to Deke's rants about Vietnam veterans. Maybe now he'd see veterans in a different light.

Joe thought Jenny's date, Terry, seemed like an okay guy too, after they'd talked a little. He had noticed Jenny seemed more relaxed as the evening wore on and was enjoying dancing with Terry.

"Isn't this great?" Char asked Joe. "I'm glad Jenny is having a good time. She's usually so serious. And Terry seems like a nice guy."

Joe liked how concerned Char was for her friends' happiness. She cared deeply for them, and they, for her. This was what he'd craved all his life. To build relationships and friendships that lasted a lifetime. Tonight, for the first time since coming back from Nam, he felt like he fit in. It felt good.

After one last slow dance, Char and Joe decided it was time to call it a night. Joe's leg felt tight and sore, although he didn't complain to Char about it. But he could tell she knew, just by looking at him. She seemed to understand and said she was tired, too. He was grateful for her thoughtfulness.

They said goodbye to everyone and headed outside. The air had cooled and Char shivered as they walked to the car. Joe slipped his suit jacket over her shoulders. When they got to the car, Char stopped and looked up into the night sky.

"Look at all the stars," she said dreamily. "It's so clear, you can see the constellations tonight."

Standing close beside her, Joe gazed up at the stars. It reminded him of the night Firebase Jack had been attacked in

Nam. The stars had been bright in the sky then, too. He pointed up and moved his finger as if drawing in the air. "There's the Little Dipper, and the Big Dipper, and there's Orion's Belt."

Char watched as he traced out the constellations in the sky. "I see them. Do you know any others?"

"That's all I see," he said, studying the stars. Then he closed his eyes and strained to hear his favorite sounds. He ignored the thumping of the band in the gym and concentrated on the night sounds outside. He smiled.

"What?" Char asked.

"Can you hear it?" he asked. "Close your eyes and concentrate. What do you hear?"

Char closed her eyes and after a time, she grinned. "I hear crickets, and toads. Night music." She opened her eyes and looked up at Joe. "That's become my favorite sound too," she said softly.

In that second, Joe wanted nothing more than to lean down and kiss her. He gazed into her warm, amber-brown eyes and saw her full lips part ever so slightly. She was so beautiful, he couldn't resist. He lowered his head and their lips touched softly in the sweetest kiss.

Chapter Eleven

Char slowly pulled away from Joe's kiss and looked into his eyes. They were dark with desire. Her heart skipped and sweet chills ran up her spine. But after that mere second, when she could read his thoughts in his eyes, he stepped back to give her space to breathe.

"I should take you home," he said huskily, reaching past her for the door handle and opening it.

"Thank you." She felt dazed. What was she thanking him for? Opening the door, or kissing her?

They rode in silence the short distance to her house. Char glanced over at Joe, wondering what he was thinking, but he just looked straight ahead of him as he drove. After he parked the car in front of her house and turned off the engine, he faced her. She wondered for just a moment if he'd kiss her again, and her heart pounded with anticipation.

"I'll walk you to the door," he said.

"You don't have to," Char replied, feeling a little let down.

But he stepped out and walked around the car anyway, opening her door and offering her a hand.

Char accepted it. It felt warm in hers. Together they walked to her front door.

"Thank you for letting me take you tonight," he said.

"I had a wonderful time," she said. "Thank you for inviting me."

He stood so close, Char thought for sure he'd kiss her again. Did she want him to? She wouldn't stop him if he tried. It had felt so good kissing him.

He reached for her hand and lifted it palm up, then gently placed the car keys in it.

Char felt a little flushed and confused. "You keep these," she said, trying to give them back. "Drive home so you don't have to walk. You can always return it tomorrow."

Joe smiled but shook his head. "Thanks, but I can walk. The cool air will clear my head." He walked toward the gate.

Char wasn't sure what to do. Everything seemed so strange and off kilter. Then she realized she was still wearing his suit jacket. "Joe. Wait!" she called, running down the porch steps.

He turned and watched her, looking confused. She stopped close to him, breathless, and slipped the jacket off her shoulders. "You probably shouldn't forget this," she said.

"No, I probably shouldn't. Rodney will want his entire suit back."

They stood there in awkward silence as the breeze shook the leaves still left on the trees and the toads and crickets played their nightly music.

"Good night, Charlotte," Joe finally said.

"Good night, Joe."

He walked slowly down the street.

* * *

Char went inside the house and locked the door behind her. She smiled when she saw her dad asleep in his recliner, the TV on but the sound turned low. Despite trying to step quietly past him, he woke up, startled.

"Charlotte. Are you home already?" he asked, wiping the sleep from his eyes. "I must have fallen asleep while watching a movie."

She came up beside his chair and grinned down at him. "You didn't have to wait up for me, Dad. I was with Joe. You knew I was safe."

"Me? Wait up? Why, I'd never think to do that," Ronald said, winking. "Okay. You caught me. But I wasn't worried."

"I'm safe with Deke, too, you know."

"I'd worry about you no matter who you were out with. It's my job to worry about you." Ronald grinned.

"Oh, Dad." She loved the easy relationship she had with her parents. She knew kids who could barely talk to their parents without arguing. It had never been that way in their household. Her parents had always treated her and Jeremy with respect just as they wished to be treated. It made living at home easy.

"Did Joe go home?" Ronald asked.

She nodded. "I offered him the car, but he declined. I could tell his leg was hurting after dancing tonight. But he wanted to walk home."

Ronald tilted his head as he stared at his daughter. "You know, you really surprised me by going to the dance with Joe."

"We went as friends, Dad," she said, wanting it to be perfectly clear. "Deke was at one of his meetings, and I didn't want to miss the dance. Joe was kind enough to take me."

"And that's all it was? Joe being nice."

"It's nothing more than that."

"Okay. If you say so," Ronald said. He turned off the TV, stood, and stretched. Then he wrapped an arm around his daughter's shoulders and walked with her to the staircase. "I'm glad you went and had a good time. College is supposed to be work, but it should also be fun. Don't take everything too seriously. Enjoy life while you're young."

"I am enjoying it, Dad. I don't mind the work, either." She kissed his cheek and said good night before heading up the stairs. She knew her dad would check the locks on the doors and windows one last time before going to bed. That was what he did. He kept his family safe.

Later, as she lay in bed, Char's thoughts drifted back to the night's events. She'd enjoyed going to the dance with Joe, much more than she'd anticipated. He'd looked handsome in the suit, almost like a completely different man. She'd grown so accustomed to his black tees and fatigues that she'd never thought of him any other way. Joe was a guy-friend. That was how she perceived him. They talked and joked at work, nothing more. But tonight, when he'd slipped his arm around her waist and they'd moved around the dance floor, she'd felt tingly all over.

And then he'd kissed her.

Char touched her lips with her fingertips, remembering how warm Joe's lips had felt on hers. His kiss had felt soft and sweet, just like a first kiss should feel. And it had felt so natural, so familiar, that Char hadn't pulled away. Their lips had fit together as perfectly as they'd danced. Like they'd been doing this forever.

She smiled at the thought.

But what about Deke?

Char rolled over in bed and snuggled deeper under the covers. She wasn't going to compare Deke and Joe. They were two very different people. Besides, Joe's kiss was probably just a random moment, an unconscious reaction as they'd stood in the moonlight with the stars twinkling above.

Romantic. She couldn't stop thinking how romantic it had been.

Deke hadn't done one romantic thing with her in months.

Stop comparing!

Char tried to brush both men from her thoughts as she closed her eyes and drifted off. Yet, it wasn't Deke's face she saw as sleep fell over her. It was Joe's gray eyes sparkling with those delightful silver flecks.

* * *

Joe couldn't sleep. He lay in his bed staring at the ceiling and listening to the sounds of the night through the open window. He wanted to sleep. He tried to fall asleep. But every time he closed his eyes, he saw Char gazing up at him in the moonlight with her amber-brown eyes and her full lips slightly parted, as if wanting to be kissed.

And then he'd kissed her.

Way to go, you idiot!

She hadn't pushed him away, but then, she hadn't said a word to him afterward, either. Or maybe it was he who'd been in such a rush to get into the car and take her home. For that one brief second after they'd kissed, he'd stared into her eyes and thought he'd seen longing in them. Longing for him? Longing to be out of there? He wasn't sure. But he'd never forget the way her eyes looked, those warm, amber pools of desire.

Now I sound like a cheesy dime store novel.

Joe sighed, wondering how he'd face Char on Monday at school. Or work with her next Saturday. Had he ruined their easy friendship by kissing her? Tonight, she'd been polite about it, but how would she feel tomorrow? Had he taken advantage of the moment and laid his feelings bare to her with that one kiss? A beautiful, delicious kiss.

He had only one recourse: apologize to her the minute he saw her and hope she forgave him. He couldn't bear to lose her as a friend. That would break his heart. Sure, he wanted more from her, but he knew it wasn't possible. She was with Deke, despite the guy being a jerk.

Sleep finally came late into the night, but not until he'd memorized every curve of her face and the soft feel of her lips on his.

* * *

Sunday afternoon Char walked down the street toward Mrs. Bennington's carrying a Tupperware container of freshly baked banana bread.

She'd risen early and gone to church with her parents. Once home, they'd eaten lunch as her parents grilled her about the night before. How had Joe enjoyed the dance? Did they have fun? Who was there? Char didn't mind the third degree, but their questions brought it all back to her again. Dancing close to Joe, smelling his musky cologne, walking out into the starry night. It seemed like a dream to her now, but she knew it had all been real.

"Honey, I was thinking of Joe this morning and baked him a loaf of banana bread," Ellen had said after lunch. "Would you mind taking it to him today?"

Char had been trying to think of an excuse to run into Joe today and now she had it handed to her. So here she was, walking up the porch steps to the boarding house and ringing the doorbell.

"Hello, Charlotte." Mrs. Bennington greeted her cheerfully. "What a nice surprise. I was just asking Joe earlier about the dance last night. Did you have a good time?"

"Yes, I did. Thank you for asking," Char said. "Is Joe around?"

"I saw him go up to his room earlier," Mrs. Bennington said. "Is that for him?" She pointed to the Tupperware in Char's hands.

She nodded. "My mom baked him a loaf of banana bread. I think she worries that he doesn't eat enough."

"I worry about that too, dear," Mrs. Bennington said. "Well, I usually don't allow my gentlemen guests to have ladies in their rooms, but I know I can trust you and Joe to act properly. Just go up to the third floor and you'll see the doorway that leads up the steps to the attic." She shook her head. "I can't understand why Joe likes living all the way up there, but if it makes him happy, then who am I to say anything?"

Char grinned. "Thanks, Mrs. Bennington. I won't be up there long." She headed up the stairs and by the time she was on the third floor, Char's legs felt as if they'd run a marathon. How on earth did Joe walk this every day with his stiff leg? She stood at the bottom of the narrow staircase that led to his room and wondered what she should do. She didn't want to walk in on him, so she called up the stairs. "Joe. Joe!"

The door at the top opened and Joe stared down at her. He wore his usual black tee and fatigues, but he was in his stocking feet and his hair looked mussed, like she'd woken him. "Char?"

"Yeah. Can I come up?"

"Uh, sure." He waited with the door open as she climbed the stairs.

When she got to the top, she stopped and smiled. "Hi."

"Hi," he said, looking confused.

His pupils were dilated and Char knew he'd been sleeping.

"My mom wanted me to bring you this." She handed him the Tupperware. "She made two loaves this morning and thought of you. It's banana bread."

Joe stared at the container. His eyes looked like they were finally focusing. "Thanks. That was nice of her. And you."

Char stepped past Joe and looked around the apartment. "Wow. This is bigger than I thought it would be. I love the high ceiling. And that stained-glass window is beautiful." She also noticed the bed was rumpled, as if he'd been lying on it. She had woken him up.

"Yeah. I like it. I don't feel claustrophobic here like I would have in one of the smaller bedrooms." He moved over to the dresser and set the container on it. "Did Mrs. Bennington send you up? She has a rule about women in men's rooms."

Char nodded. "She said I could come up." Her eyes settled on Joe. "She said she trusted us."

A slow smile touched Joe's lips. Char couldn't help but smile back.

"If she only knew." Char waggled her eyebrows.

Joe laughed. "I'm sure I can control myself for a few minutes."

She sat on the arm of the sofa as her smile faded. "How does your leg feel today? I'm worried I made you dance too much."

Joe leaned on the other arm of the sofa. "You didn't force me to do anything. I wanted to dance. But I have to admit, my leg is pretty sore. I rubbed it down and took one of my muscle relaxants so it wouldn't spasm."

Char figured that explained his large pupils. "Sorry. We should have been more careful."

"I'm not sorry at all. I had a wonderful time. A little soreness won't kill me," Joe said.

They sat there in silence a minute until Char started feeling awkward. "So, I guess I should go. I don't want Mrs. Bennington to think anything scandalous is happening up here."

"Are you in a hurry? I was thinking of going to the café for a late lunch. Would you like to go with me?"

"Sure. I'll go along."

Char watched as Joe tied his heavy boots, then go into the bathroom to comb his hair. "Are you sure you want to walk? We can stop at my house and get the car."

"It's not that far. I'll be fine. My doctor at the V.A. said I should walk to loosen up the muscles when my leg is sore."

Char nodded. Joe slipped his coat on, and they walked down the multiple flights of stairs and out of the house. He moved a little slower than usual, but Char didn't mind. She slowed her pace to match his.

It was cooler than yesterday had been, with a crisp breeze, but the sunshine felt warm on her face. As she walked, she slipped her hands in her pockets to keep them warm.

They didn't speak, and from time to time, Char glanced Joe's way. He seemed to be lost in his own thoughts, so she stayed quiet. But she was curious about what he was thinking.

As they reached the town square, Char noticed that several carved pumpkins had been added to the decorations. They were only a week away from Halloween, and the children were already getting the jack-o-lanterns ready for the fall festival held on Halloween night.

"Are you going to carve a pumpkin for the festival?" she asked Joe.

He glanced around, as though noticing the pumpkins for the first time. "No. I'll leave that for the children."

"I carve one every year," she said. "Most everyone does to decorate their porches or the town square. We have a big celebration on the last Saturday of October every year. Many of the businesses have food or game booths and raise money for college scholarships and charities. Halloween is on Saturday this year, so it will be extra special. Everyone will probably dress up."

"Your dad told me about the celebration last week. He said your store always has the apple dunking booth."

"That's right. Dad loves it. He enjoys the kids, although adults dunk for apples too."

They reached the café, and Joe opened the door for Char. After finding a booth to sit in, the waitress, an older woman who'd worked there for years, brought them menus.

"Hey, Char. How are you today?" she asked.

"I'm fine, thanks. I'll just have a Coke," Char said.

"Okay. And what about you, sweetie?" she asked Joe.

"I'll have a bowl of your cream of potato soup and toast," he said.

"I could have guessed that," the waitress said, giving him a wink. "And a Coke, too?"

"Sure. Thanks," Joe said.

Once she'd left, Char stared across the table at Joe. She decided they couldn't ignore what had happened between them any longer. "Do you want to talk about last night?" she asked.

Joe lifted his eyes to meet hers. "We danced and had a good time. What else is there to say?"

"You kissed me, Joe."

Joe nodded. "I did. And at first, I thought I should apologize to you the moment I saw you. But I've thought about it a lot, and I'm not going to apologize for kissing you." His tone was serious.

"I wasn't asking you to apologize. I just thought, if we're going to be friends and work together, then maybe we should sort out a few things."

"There's nothing to sort out, Char. I kissed you because I wanted to in that moment. And if you want the truth, I'd love to kiss you again. Over and over again."

Goosebumps tickled Char's arms. "But I'm with Deke."

"Are you? Really?"

Her eyes widened, but before she could answer, the waitress brought Joe's soup and toast and their Cokes. After she left, Char asked, "What did you mean by that?"

Joe sat there calmly, stirring his soup. "Did you enjoy the kiss?" he asked.

Char's mouth fell open. Who asked that kind of question?

"Come on, Char. It's an easy question. Either you enjoyed the kiss or not," he said quietly.

"It was a nice kiss," she conceded.

Joe smiled. "I thought so too. So, can I ask you another question?"

She nodded.

"Why are you with Deke?"

"What?"

"I just want to know what it is about Deke that makes you want to be with him."

"Why wouldn't I want to be with a guy like Deke?" she asked, her voice rising. "He's smart, he's kind to me, he knows exactly what he believes in and isn't afraid to stand up for his convictions. Any girl would be lucky to be with him."

"But *why* are you with him?" Joe asked.

"I told you."

"No, you didn't. You told me what he's like, but not how he makes *you* feel," Joe said.

Char frowned. "I don't understand what you want me to say."

Joe leaned in closer over the table. "Does he make you feel loved? Does he make you laugh and feel happy? Do you smile to yourself when you think about him or get chills when you kiss him?"

She crossed her arms and sat back against the booth. "Don't be silly. I'm not going to tell you stuff like that."

"You're not going to tell me, or you can't tell me you feel that way with him?"

"I'm not talking about this anymore, Joe. And if you want me to ever talk to you again, you'll drop the subject." She glared at him.

Joe ate a few spoonfuls of his soup and a bite of toast. He chewed slowly, as if he didn't have a care in the world. Just when Char thought he wouldn't speak again, he did.

"I have a theory as to why you're with Deke despite you two being total opposites. Can I tell you what it is without you getting angry?"

Char sighed. "Fine. What's your theory?"

Joe looked at her tenderly. "I think you're with Deke because he's familiar. He reminds you of a better time when your brother was still alive. I think you stay with Deke because you don't want to lose that last connection with Jeremy."

Char scowled at him. "You're totally out of line now. You know nothing about my relationship with Deke, and don't you dare bring my brother into this. Who are *you* to think you know *me*? You've only known me a couple of months, and you hardly know Deke. So, don't go throwing opinions around when you have no information."

He sat very still, looking at her. Char couldn't bear the hurt look in his eyes. She reached into her coat pocket, pulled out a dollar bill, and threw it on the table. "That's for my Coke. I'm leaving."

"Char," Joe said gently as she slid out of the booth. "Don't go."

She ignored him and headed outside and up the street, walking as quickly as she could. Tears formed in her eyes, blurring her vision. She swiped them away as they fell. She didn't even know why she was crying. Anger? Hurt?

Fueled by fury, she pushed on toward home.

Chapter Twelve

Char was halfway home when a car pulled up alongside her and slowed down.

"Char? Hey, what's the hurry?"

She glanced up and slowed her pace when she saw Deke. "You're back."

"Yeah. Get inside the car, babe."

She ran around to the other side and hopped in. Deke reached over and kissed her.

"I missed you," he said when he pulled away. He smiled wide and his eyes sparkled as if seeing her was the best part of his day.

"I missed you, too," she lied, not wanting to ruin his cheerful mood.

Deke studied her face. "Were you crying? Your mascara is running down your cheeks. What's the matter, babe?"

Char turned the rear-view mirror her direction and stared into it. There were trails of black smeared on her face. She grabbed a napkin from the console and tried wiping the mascara away. "The cold was stinging my eyes," she said. "I guess it made them water."

"Oh, okay." Deke didn't sound completely convinced. "Were you headed home?"

"Yeah."

"Let me take you out to eat instead. I can tell you all about my trip," he offered.

Char thought about her parents at home, her mother starting dinner and her father watching television, probably falling asleep in his chair. "I don't know, Deke. My parents like it when we eat Sunday dinner together." She didn't want to invite him to dinner after the last fiasco weeks before.

"Come on, Char. Please? I want to spend the evening with you. We can stop by my place first and you can call and let them know you're going to dinner. Okay?"

In that moment as she gazed up into Deke's deep blue eyes, she thought about what Joe had said. *I think you stay with Deke because you don't want to lose that last connection with Jeremy.* It made her angry all over again. Did Joe really believe she was so needy that she'd date Deke just because he'd been Jeremy's best friend? That she couldn't decide for herself who she cared about. Well, she'd prove him wrong.

"Okay. That sounds fine," she told Deke.

They drove to his place where he stowed away his bag while she called her parents. Her mom seemed to understand, which made Char feel a little better. Then they hopped back in the car.

"Where to?" Deke asked, still in high spirits. "The Corner Café?"

That was the last place she wanted to go right now. "What about that other burger place on the edge of town? Maybe we won't be bothered by anyone so you can tell me all about your trip."

"Sounds good to me."

The little diner was actually a truck stop next to a gas station, the kind of place that only locals knew had good food. They took a booth in the back corner, away from the lone men who sat at the counter and flirted with the young waitress. After ordering their food, Deke reached across the table and took Char's hand in his.

"You wouldn't believe the weekend I had," he told her. "A member from the Weathermen Underground spoke to our group, and it was mind-blowing. Some of the old SDSers didn't get it, but I did. They aren't just trying to stop the war, they're trying to revolutionize the entire country. They imagine a nation where everyone is equal despite their gender or skin color. Where everyone works together to thrive as one unit. Where we all share the wealth, and no one has more than anyone else. It's so exciting, Char. It's a whole new way of thinking. A whole new way to live your life."

Char watched his eyes light up as he spoke. He looked feverish with the energy that flowed from him in his excitement to tell her everything he'd learned.

Their food came and after the waitress left, Deke continued speaking. "A few of us stayed in an apartment owned by a Weatherman but is available for anyone who's working for the cause. They have several places like that around the country. Safe houses, so to speak. But the majority of those who believe in the cause aren't in hiding. They're doing work unbeknownst to the authorities." Deke dropped his elbows on the table and leaned in closer to her. "You should have seen this apartment, Char. There were no doors on any of the rooms, because they believe doors are for hiding secrets. Everyone lives as one family, sharing everything. It felt so freeing to be among people who feel like that."

Char cringed at the idea of no doors. "No privacy? How can they stand that?"

"It's amazing. I know it sounds odd at first, but it makes you feel as if you're a part of a family. Like you're a part of something big, bigger than the little lives we live. More important than just owning the nicest car or living in the biggest house. It's about being the best person you can be internally, and sharing that with the group to lift everyone up."

"But what about the violence? The bombings? Protestors attacking policemen. You don't believe in *that*, do you, Deke?"

"Babe. That's just a small part of it. They believe in helping people, too. They believe in community and working as one for the benefit of the whole."

"But that doesn't change the fact that the leaders of the Weathermen are wanted by the FBI for inciting violence and other crimes," Char said. "I don't know how you can support an organization like that. You've always been about the peaceful protest. What has changed?"

He sighed heavily. "Char, I don't expect you to completely understand what I'm feeling because you haven't been a part of the movement like I have. Since I've become involved, I've seen that peacefully protesting against a violent war doesn't make a difference. We continue to rally against it and our government ignores us. A revolution against the system is the only way to make our leaders take notice. Can't you feel how exhilarating that is?"

Char stared down at her plate of food, her appetite now gone. She wasn't completely sure how she felt about the Vietnam War, but she knew she didn't approve of violence in order to protest violence. No matter what Deke told her, it still made no sense to her.

"I wish you could have been there to hear the Weatherman speak," Deke said, still enthusiastic despite Char's protests. "You would have felt the excitement. Our generation is going to change everything and make this a better world. It's intoxicating just thinking about it."

Deke continued eating his hamburger, but Char gave up on even trying to eat hers. Her mind was a jumble of emotions, contemplating everything Deke had said, then thinking of Joe, too. She couldn't get his question out of her mind. Why was she with Deke? She'd always thought so highly of him, yet what he'd said tonight was hard for her to digest. Then again, maybe it was her small town-upbringing that stood in her way of thinking as Deke did. He'd managed to break out of that safe bubble his parents had raised him in, but she hadn't. Did her ignorance of the world cause her to think his new ideas were strange? Or were his ideas just too radical for her to comprehend as reality?

"Aren't you feeling well?" Deke asked, snitching a french fry from her plate. "You hardly touched your food."

"Sorry, Deke. I have a lot on my mind." She pushed her plate to the middle of the table.

Deke paid the bill and they left the restaurant. Just as they walked through the door, Jenny and Terry were walking up to it.

"Hi, Jenny," Char said, surprised to see her with Terry.

"Hey, guys. Did you two just eat?" Jenny asked.

"Yeah." Deke smiled at Jenny. "Who's your new friend?"

Jenny's face flushed as she introduced Terry to Deke.

"I didn't know you were seeing anyone," Deke said, after saying hello to Terry.

"Oh, well, I'm not really seeing Terry," Jenny said, falling over her words.

"I took Jenny to the dance last night," Terry said. "It took a lot of courage to ask her, but we had a great time."

Char noticed the wide grin on Terry's face. It was obvious that he liked Jenny. She was happy to see that Jenny had enjoyed Terry's company enough to go out again tonight.

"Oh, yeah. Last night was the Fall Fling dance," Deke said. "How was it this year?"

"It was great," Terry said. "We all had a good time. Didn't we, Char?"

Char's eyes widened at Terry's words. She saw Jenny nudge him with her elbow and realization fell over Terry's face that he shouldn't have said anything.

Deke turned to Char, looking confused. "You were at the dance last night?"

"Let's talk in the car," Char said, waving to her friend. Jenny mouthed "sorry" to her, but Char just waved her hand through the air as if to say it was fine. In reality, it wasn't fine at all. She wasn't thrilled about telling Deke she went with Joe. She followed Deke to the car and got in as he started it.

"What's going on?" Deke asked, turning to her. "Wasn't that a couples' dance? I thought you couldn't go without a date."

"I went with someone, but it wasn't a date," Char said. "He knew I wanted to go, so he asked if I'd go with him."

Deke's brows furrowed. "Who did you go with?"

"I went with Joe," she said, watching Deke's frown deepen. "It wasn't a big deal so don't freak out about it. He wanted to go and so did I. Besides, we all sat together as a group."

"Joe." Deke let out a long breath. "Why couldn't it have been anyone but him, Char? You know how I feel about Joe."

His words gnawed at her nerves. "I'm sorry if that bothers you. But I'm not sorry that I went. This is my first year of college and I want to enjoy it. You weren't here to take me, so I didn't see what it would hurt if I went with Joe."

"You never told me you wanted to go to the dance. But you told Joe. You two must be getting pretty chummy." Deke slammed the car into drive and drove down the road.

"We work together and have classes together, too," she said in her defense. "So yes, we talk. He was just being nice. That's all."

"Right."

Deke's tone made her angrier. "Would you have canceled going to your meeting if I'd asked you to take me?"

"No, I wouldn't have. But that doesn't mean I'm happy you went with him."

"I'm not going to argue with you about this," Char said, sitting back in her seat and staring straight ahead of her. "I had a good time and you're not going to ruin it for me. You just got through talking about how that group you admire so much believes in everyone being equal to one another. Yet, you hate Joe. That sounds hypocritical to me."

Deke tightened his jaw. He pulled up in front of her house and parked but left the engine running. "You're right," he said.

"What?" She gawked at him.

Deke sighed. "You're right. It is hypocritical to hate Joe but preach how everyone is equal. But I can't help it, Char. You two have some sort of connection that I don't understand. And it makes me jealous. There. I said it. I'm jealous of G.I. Joe."

She couldn't believe what she was hearing. Deke was strong and self-assured. But he was jealous of Joe? "Joe and I are just friends. I wish you'd believe that."

"Char. You're a beautiful woman. You're smart, and you're sweet. But you're naive to think that Joe isn't looking at you the same way I do. I feel as if I'm losing you, and it scares me. I love you, babe. Don't you know that?"

She nodded, unable to say the words back. "I know you do. But you have to trust me, too."

"I do trust you. It's Joe I'm not as trusting of," he said.

They sat in silence, both staring out the window into the night sky.

"I'm sorry I wasn't here to take you to the dance," Deke finally said. "I forget sometimes that those things are important too. I get so wrapped up in my own interests that I forget to put you first." He reached for her hand. "We'll go to the next one together. Okay?"

Char's heart melted. Every time she began questioning her relationship with Deke, he said something to make her question herself instead. "Okay," she said.

Deke leaned over and kissed her. Char realized for the first time that when she kissed Deke, she didn't feel the same tingling down her spine that she'd felt with Joe.

"I'll see you tomorrow," Deke said.

Char nodded and slid out of the car.

She stood on the porch for a while after Deke had driven off, listening for the sounds of the night. The air grew chilly and damp, like rain was on its way. Still, Char waited for the comforting sounds of the night music. When it didn't come, she finally gave up and went indoors, feeling a little empty inside.

* * *

The dank smell of the jungle assailed Joe's nostrils as he clutched his gun tightly in his hands in the pitch-black night. He could see a light in the distance, coming from Firebase Jack, but he couldn't see anything around him. He looked up at the sky, but there were no stars or moon to guide his way. Closing his eyes, he stood and listened. Silence. Not a sound in the night to tell him everything was going to be all right.

Why was he out here in the jungle so far away from the firebase? Why wasn't he standing in the pit with Clint and Roger? Did he dare call out to see if his unit was with him?

Something rustled in the elephant grass around him. Joe stood absolutely still, his heart beating rapidly in his chest.

Then a twig snapped right in front of him. His blood ran cold.

Sweat rolled down the back of his neck, giving him the chills. He thought he could hear breathing, in and out, in and out, right next to him.

Did he dare shoot? What if it was a fellow soldier?

Suddenly, the sky exploded, raining red fire.

Joe looked up. A Spooky gunship. Relief flooded through him. The good guys.

He heard a footstep in front of him and lowered his gaze to stare right into the eyes of an NVA soldier. Joe raised his weapon, but he was too late. The soldier fired first, and searing pain shot through Joe's left leg. He crumpled to the damp jungle floor, waiting for the next shot that would kill him.

Joe bolted up in bed, his eyes darting around the darkened room. He was breathing heavily and sweat covered his body. He reached for his gun, but all he grabbed was a handful of blanket.

A nightmare he thought. *It was just a nightmare.*

He sat still, trying to calm his breathing. His leg ached, the muscles burning. He reached down and gently rubbed his leg, waiting for relief. When it didn't come, he decided to get up and take an aspirin to dull the pain.

The streetlight outside glowed through the stained-glass window, sending streaks of color across the room. It was enough light for Joe to see to walk into the bathroom and take out the aspirin bottle from the medicine cabinet. He drank down some water with the tablets, then walked stiffly back to bed. Pulling the covers over his chilled body, he thought about the nightmare, trying to remember every detail.

It wasn't the first nightmare of Nam that Joe had experienced, and it wouldn't be the last. But since he'd come to Grand Falls, he'd had fewer nightmares than before. So why did he have one tonight?

Joe thought back to this afternoon and his fight with Char. He hadn't meant to make her angry. He was being honest with her. But Char wasn't ready to face the truth. Now, he felt terrible for upsetting her. She was right—he didn't know her well enough to think he could analyze her reasons for dating Deke. He should have kept his mouth shut, but it was so difficult.

Because I'm falling in love with Char.

Joe could deny that thought all he wanted, but he'd only be lying to himself. He had strong feelings for Char, and that was coloring his opinion of Deke and their relationship.

He knew he had to step back and not push Char too much. When he'd moved here to go to college, he'd never even dreamt he'd meet the beautiful girl who'd written to him in Nam, let alone become her friend. And the fact that he knew her, and was able to spend time with her at work and school, should have been enough for him. She was Deke's girlfriend, and that was that. It wasn't up to Joe to try to take her away from Deke.

But, oh, how he wished he could.

Chapter Thirteen

The next Saturday, Char was organizing the apple dunking booth when Joe walked up. "Hey there." She smiled at him.

"Am I late?" he asked, entering the booth.

"No. Dad and I came early to put water in the washtubs. He just ran to the grocery store for another bag of apples. He thought we didn't have enough."

Joe grinned. "You're a princess!"

"What?" Char was confused a moment, then looked down at the gown she was wearing. She laughed. "Oh, yeah. I wore a costume. I'm Snow White. She's the only dark-haired princess."

"You look cute," he said.

"Thanks. I see you came as yourself," Char said, giving him the once-over. He was wearing his usual fatigues and army jacket. She was certain he also had a black sweater on underneath.

"I wore a costume," he said, looking hurt.

"Really? What are you?"

Joe pointed to the name patch he'd placed over the left-hand pocket of his jacket. It read, "G.I. Joe."

Char broke out laughing. "Really? You're a G.I. Joe doll?"

"Excuse me? A doll? I'm an action figure!"

This made Char laugh harder. "Okay, okay. Action figure. You're funny, you know that?"

Joe shrugged. "Isn't that what Deke calls me all the time? I figured I might as well have fun with it."

Char sobered. "Well, he may mean it as an insult, but I'm glad you turned it around to be fun."

"I'm just happy you're still talking to me," Joe said.

"Friends don't hold grudges against each other. And I like being friends with you."

"Yeah," he said. "Friends."

Ronald came back with two more bags of apples. He was dressed up as an old-time shopkeeper with a red and white striped shirt, garters on his sleeves, his hair slicked back, and a fake mustache that curled up on each end. His costume caused more good-natured teasing from Joe and Char.

Soon the square filled up with townspeople. Char took the money while Ronald and Joe supervised the apple dunking. Kids and adults alike in costumes of superheroes, vampires, monsters, princesses, and cute, little, furry animals took turns trying to grab an apple from the water. The Corner Café had a booth selling hot dogs and french fries, the bakery was selling endless bags of donuts and cookies decorated orange and black, and the gift shop ran a fortune teller's booth where the owner, dressed as a gypsy, stared into a crystal ball and told people their future. Many more food and game booths lined the lawn as local bands took turns playing music in the gazebo.

"Hey," a little girl of about eight years old said to Joe as he stood by the apple bins. "You're a G.I. Joe doll. I'm Barbie!"

Char laughed and Joe shot her a dirty look. But he smiled at the little girl. "You're the prettiest Barbie doll I've ever seen," he told her.

College students came out in droves as well, dressed in costumes and enjoying the food and games. Patty waved as she walked past the booth with Craig. She was dressed as Morticia Addams and he was her Gomez. Char was thrilled to see Patty was still seeing him. Craig was a nice guy. Char searched the crowd for Jenny and Terry, but didn't spot them until they came to the booth. Jenny was too sensible to dress up, but Terry wore a pirate costume.

"Is it silly to dress up at my age?" he asked Char.

She shook her head. "No. You look great." Jenny just rolled her eyes, but she still took his arm as they walked away a few minutes later.

The festival wound down at five o'clock with the judging of the jack-o-lanterns. Char's mother was helping with that, and after the judges picked the finalists, the crowd participated in picking the top three. The little girl in the Barbie costume won third place and was grinning ear-to-ear.

"Your new girlfriend won," Char teased Joe.

"I think I'd better stay in my own age range," Joe said, winking.

Night had fallen, but the street lamps that lined the town square and the Christmas lights that had been strung up around the trees illuminated the night. The parents and children headed out for a night of trick or treating and Char's mother rushed home to hand out candy. Char helped her dad and Joe pack up the items in the booth, and the two men began tearing it down.

"Princesses shouldn't have to work so hard," a voice said, catching Char's attention. Deke stood there, grinning at her.

"Hey, Deke." She noticed he wasn't wearing a costume.

"Our friends are over by the big oak. Come on. Let's go join them," Deke said.

"I will, after I'm finished here," Char said.

"Go ahead," Ronald told his daughter. "We're almost done. You've worked hard enough today."

"Okay." She picked up her cape and slipped it on since the evening air had grown cold. "See you later, Joe." She waved at him.

Joe waved back.

"Yeah. Later, man," Deke said, running his arm possessively around Char's waist.

She stiffened at his touch. She wouldn't have minded if he'd done it out of affection, but she knew he was proving to Joe that she belonged to him. Pulling away from him, Char walked with him to the tree where her friends and their dates were standing.

"What should we do tonight?" Patty asked excitedly. "Is there anything going on at the college? A party? Or is there a place we could go dancing?"

Deke pulled a flask out of his coat pocket and took a drink, then handed it to Char.

She gaped at him. "Since when do you carry a flask?"

"It's Halloween, babe. I'm just adding to the fun," Deke said.

Char shook her head. "No, thanks. My dad would smell liquor on me the moment I walked in the door."

"I'll have some," Patty said, taking a small sip. Craig drank too, but Jenny and Terry declined.

"Justin said he was having a party in his parents' pool house tonight," Craig offered. "That might be fun."

"Or we could go to the student union and hang out," Jenny suggested.

Char figured her friend wasn't too excited about going to a party. She didn't like the idea either.

Deke took another sip from the flask. "Or we could go

around town and play tricks on people. It is Halloween."

"What are we, ten years old?" Char scowled at Deke.

Joe walked slowly past them on the sidewalk. He turned and waved, and Char waved back.

"Night, Joe!" she called out.

Deke's expression turned hard. "Hey, guys. Watch this," he said, pulling something from his pocket. He lit it with a lighter, then threw it in Joe's direction.

Suddenly, there was a loud explosion and several pops went off, sounding like gun shots. Char watched as Joe fell to the ground, curled into a ball, and covered his head as if he were under attack by gunfire. It was then that she realized Deke had thrown firecrackers at him.

She glared at Deke. "What's wrong with you?" Then she ran to where Joe was crouched on the ground.

"Ah, come on, babe. It was a joke," Deke called after her. He laughed at Joe's crumpled form.

The others just stood there, stunned.

Char reached Joe and knelt beside him. "Joe? Are you okay?"

He slowly straightened, seeming to realize what had happened. He reached for his cane, and tried to stand up, but his leg gave out underneath him and he fell again. Deke's laughter could be heard across the lawn.

"Let me help you," Char said, offering her hand.

When Joe turned his face toward her, he was glaring. "I don't need your help," he growled. "Go back to your *friends*."

Char was taken aback by Joe's anger.

"I didn't know he was going to do that," she said.

Joe used his cane to pull himself up and leaned on it heavily. "Just leave me alone," he said. Then he slowly made his way down the sidewalk.

Tears filled Char's eyes. Joe had always been kind to her. He was a good man. Yet, her boyfriend had purposely humiliated him. Joe didn't deserve that. No one deserved it. Anger coursed through her as she stormed toward Deke.

"That was a terrible thing to do!" she yelled at Deke. "You knew he'd react that way."

"Ah, come on, Char. It was funny. He actually thought someone was shooting at him." Deke laughed.

No one was laughing with him.

"We should go," Jenny said, and Patty agreed.

"Yeah. Let's go to the union," Patty said.

"Wait," Deke said. "It was a joke. Don't be a bunch of losers. Let's go to that party you were talking about."

Char clenched her fists. "I'll never forgive you for this," she told Deke. "What you did was cruel and heartless. I'm going home and don't you dare follow me." She turned and walked away.

"Wait! Char! Don't leave!" Deke yelled.

Char kept walking and didn't look back.

* * *

Joe felt humiliated. He walked slowly toward the boarding house, each step painful. He just wanted to get to his room and wait for this night to be over.

Actually, what he really wanted to do was go back and punch Deke in the face. Hard. But he doubted he could stand steady enough to do that.

I hate this damned leg! He hated how inadequate his injury made him feel. If he could walk properly on both legs, without the use of the stupid cane, he could have stood up to Deke. Instead, he was retreating in the opposite direction like a fool.

His leg had already been throbbing from standing on it all day at the festival, but he'd ignored the pain because working alongside Char had made it worth it. But when he'd dropped to the ground because of the firecrackers, he'd twisted his leg, causing pain to shoot all the way up his spine. It was going to take more than a few hours of rest for his leg and back to heal. It was going to take even longer to heal his pride.

Joe finally made it back to the boarding house. Mrs. Bennington was standing in the entryway with a bowl full of candy for the trick or treaters.

"Hello, Joe," she said cheerfully. "Home already? I thought you might go to a college Halloween party with Char."

Joe tried to smile, but he knew it came out as a grimace. "No, it's been a long day. I need to rest my leg," he told her.

Mrs. Bennington studied Joe a minute, then gave him a smile. "Here," she said, stuffing a handful of Tootsie Rolls into his coat pocket. "Happy Halloween."

Joe's face relaxed and his heart warmed. He adored Mrs. Bennington and her thoughtfulness. "Thanks, Mrs. B," he said kindly, returning her smile. Then he limped his way up the many flights of stairs.

Once in his room, Joe undressed and sat heavily on his bed. He pulled the candy out of his coat pocket, unwrapped a piece, and popped it in his mouth. He hadn't had a Tootsie Roll in years. It might not help his leg feel better, but it did cheer him up.

He took a muscle relaxant, then propped himself up on the bed against the pillows. His back ached, and his leg muscles burned. Reaching down, he massaged his calf, hoping it would help.

As he did, he thought again about how badly the night had ended. He felt guilty for yelling at Char when she'd tried to help him up. He'd been so humiliated from dropping to the ground that he couldn't let her help him. It would have made him appear even weaker. He knew that Char and her friends had nothing to do with tossing the firecrackers his way. They had all been nice to him at the dance. It had been Deke who'd done it. Deke had wanted to make Joe look weak, and he'd succeeded. He'd made him look like a fool.

The pill began taking effect and Joe grew drowsy. There was nothing he could do about a jerk like Deke, but there was one thing Joe could do. He could show Char who the better man was by ignoring what Deke had done. She'd figure it out eventually.

But boy, he still wanted to punch that grin off Deke's face.

Joe fell asleep, a smile playing across his lips at the image.

Chapter Fourteen

The next Saturday, Char walked right up to Joe to apologize the minute he entered the shop.

"I know you've been avoiding me all week, and I can't stand it one more minute," she said. "I'm sorry about what Deke did to you on Halloween. He was a jerk. I really didn't know he was going to throw those firecrackers; otherwise, I would have stopped him." Char stared at him expectantly, but he made no reply.

"Please, Joe. Won't you forgive me? I can't stand it that we aren't speaking," she said.

"I'm not mad at you," he finally said. "I know it wasn't your fault. And I owe you an apology. I shouldn't have spoken to you that way when all you were doing was trying to help. I was embarrassed and I just wanted to be left alone."

"Embarrassed? Why? You dropped to the ground out of instinct. We all knew that. You don't have anything to be embarrassed about. Deke is the one who should feel terrible. He knew how the firecrackers would affect you and that's why he threw them. He was being a stupid jerk!"

Joe broke out in laughter.

"What's so funny?" Char insisted.

"You. I love hearing you call Deke a stupid jerk. It's my thoughts exactly."

Char began to laugh, too. She was so relieved that Joe wasn't angry at her. She'd worried all week that he thought she'd been a part of Deke's cruel prank. She was glad to finally clear the air.

After a moment, she grew serious again. "Are you okay? I mean, after you fell, you had trouble getting up again and I was worried you hurt your leg even more. I've noticed that you've been walking slower, too."

"It's nice of you to worry, but I'm fine. My leg was sore, and I twisted my back when I fell, but it's better now," Joe said.

"I'm so sorry, Joe," she said again, feeling terrible that he'd been hurt. "If it makes you feel any better, I broke it off with Deke. I can't be with someone who's cruel to other people. And you know, you were right when you said he and I didn't make sense. We really have nothing in common, except for my brother, Jeremy."

Char had finally realized that was true. She'd had a few days to mull over everything that had happened, and she couldn't come up with one reason why she was still with Deke. They simply had nothing in common, and now, after what he'd done, any warm feelings she'd had for him had disappeared. Deke had come two separate times to her house trying to apologize, bringing flowers and even a gold bracelet. He'd blamed it on the liquor he'd been drinking and his jealously of her friendship with Joe. But Char had stood firm. His prank on Joe hadn't been a silly joke; it had been unusually cruel. They were over.

"I'm sorry it broke you two up," Joe said, looking solemn. "You didn't have to do that because of me."

Char stared at Joe a moment, then raised her brows and smirked. "Really? You're really sorry about our breakup?"

"Okay, maybe not *that* sorry." He grinned back.

"That's what I thought."

The bell over the door rang as the first customer of the day entered.

"Time to work," Char said, turning to go to the back office.

"Char?" Joe said.

She glanced over her shoulder. "Yes?"

"Maybe tonight we could do something together? Like have dinner? I mean, since you're a free woman and all," Joe said.

Char smiled. "Sure. Why not?" She headed to the back room, a smile still on her lips.

* * *

Saturday evening, Char and Joe went to the student union for a burger. Winter had kicked up the crisp, cold winds with a promise of snow, so they drove her car the short distance. When they arrived, Jenny and Patty were also there with Terry and Craig, so the group of six sat down at a big table and ordered. No one in the group seemed to think it was strange that Char was with Joe. They'd all been witness to Deke's awful prank the week before, so it wasn't a surprise that Char preferred Joe's company.

The guys invited Joe to play a game of pool while they waited for their food, and although he seemed reluctant to leave Char, he did at her urging. That left the three girls together, and Patty quickly moved her chair closer to Char and Jenny.

"Does this mean you're dating Joe now?" Patty asked in a hushed voice.

Char laughed. "No. It just means we're two friends having a burger with our other friends."

Patty sat back and rolled her eyes. "Right. Well, you'd better see if that's how Joe feels. Have you seen the way he looks at you? His eyes literally sparkle. This is more than just two friends having a burger to him."

Char turned to Jenny. "Will you please talk some sense into Patty?"

Jenny shook her head. "I hate agreeing with her, but she's right. Joe has a thing for you."

Char protested even though she knew they were right. Hadn't Joe already declared his feelings for her the day they'd talked about the kiss? And, what a kiss! If her friends had known about it, they would be completely convinced that she and Joe were a couple.

But they weren't together. She'd just broken up with Deke. She wasn't ready to jump into another relationship.

Was she?

The conversation flowed throughout the group as they ate their food. Char was surprised that Craig, who'd been Deke's loyal follower, so willingly accepted Joe's friendship. In fact, she hadn't seen Craig hang out with Deke's little group since he'd started dating Patty. She wondered if he'd had enough of Deke too.

As they finished eating their meals and were getting ready to leave, Deke and Justin sauntered into the union. Deke spied them immediately, and his sour expression gave away how he felt about seeing Char and Joe together.

"Let's go," Char said quietly to Joe.

He nodded and they both stood to leave, but as they did, Deke headed straight for their table. He stopped directly in front of Joe and offered his hand.

"I apologize for the prank I played on you last week, Joe," Deke said. "It was immature and insensitive, and I hope you'll forgive me."

Joe stared at Deke's hand, not moving to shake it. But Deke kept his hand extended to him.

"I'll understand if you don't accept my apology," Deke said. "I'm not sure I would either, if I were you."

Char watched as Joe finally lifted his hand and shook Deke's. She was surprised, yet proud of him.

"I appreciate your apology," Joe said.

"Thank you." Deke smiled at Char, then nodded at Joe and headed to the bar.

"Wow," Patty said softly. "I didn't expect that."

"Joe should have punched him," Craig said.

This brought laughter from the rest of the group. They all said goodbye and parted ways.

On the drive back to Char's house, she smiled warmly at Joe. "Do you know that you're just about the nicest guy I've ever met? I can't think of one other person who would have accepted Deke's apology—including Deke."

Joe shrugged as he pulled the car up in front of Char's house. "I'm not that nice," he said. "I still wanted to punch him."

Char laughed, leaning her head back against the seat and gazing at Joe. "I've never met anyone like you. You always make me laugh, and you're so easy to talk to. And you listen to me. It's so refreshing."

The silver flecks in Joe's eyes sparkled, just like Patty had said. In that moment, Char wanted him to kiss her. Just like he'd kissed her the night of the dance. Soft and sweet.

"I'll walk you to the door," he offered instead, and Char sighed. He went around to her side of the car and opened the door for her, then held out his hand for her to hold.

"It's going to snow soon," Joe said. "I can feel the dampness in the air."

"Yeah. It'll be here by Thanksgiving for sure," she said. "You'll have to join us for Thanksgiving dinner. My mom makes the best stuffing in town."

"That sounds delicious," Joe said.

They stopped and stood a moment on the porch. Joe reached up and circled a strand of her hair around his finger, then let it loose.

"I've always wanted to do that," he said. "Your hair is as silky as I've imagined."

Char's heart beat faster as he reached his hand behind her neck and slowly pulled her lips to his. They felt warm and inviting. He ran his tongue along her lips, then pulled away and looked down into her eyes.

"Delicious," he whispered.

Char smiled up at him, wanting to pull him close again but knowing she shouldn't. Joe seemed to understand what she was thinking, because he let his arm drop to his side and took one step away. She missed the warmth of his body close to hers.

"I just broke up with someone," she said. "I shouldn't rush into another relationship right away."

"No, you shouldn't," he agreed.

Char cocked her head, puzzled by his response. "But I don't want to lose you, either."

"We can take things as slowly as you want to," he said, then grinned. "I'm not going anywhere."

With that, he kissed her lightly on the cheek and headed down the porch steps. When he reached the gate, he waved. "See you in school."

Char waved back and watched as he made his way down the sidewalk. The air surrounding her was cold, but all she felt was his warmth still touching her lips.

* * *

"We should have invited Joe over," Ellen said as she, Ronald, and Char sat down to Sunday lunch. "I feel terrible that he's alone on Sundays."

Char smiled at the mention of Joe's name. "I doubt he's alone, although he doesn't mind it," she told her mom. "He's probably at the school library, studying."

"He doesn't walk all that way in the cold, does he?" Ellen frowned.

"He says he likes to walk," Char said. "It's good for his leg."

"Maybe you could offer to drive him to school during the week, now that winter is settling in," Ronald suggested. "He passes our house on the way."

Char eyed her father. She could tell he was trying hard to sound casual, but she could read him like a book. He was playing matchmaker. What he didn't know was he was too late—they were already seeing each other.

"Yes, I should offer to drive him," she said, noting the satisfied grin on her father's face. "If he'll accept. Joe can be very independent. Or just plain stubborn."

"He's a good man," Ellen said.

"Yes, he is," Char agreed. "By the way. I invited him to Thanksgiving dinner. I hope that's okay."

Ellen's eyes lit up. "That's wonderful! It will be nice to have a guest."

"Is Deke coming, too?" Ronald asked.

Char pretended like she was interested in the food on her plate. "No. Just Joe." Out of the corner of her eye, she saw her father share a satisfied look across the table with her mother. Char wanted to laugh but held it in. Her parents probably wanted to jump up and dance on the table because Deke wasn't invited, but they acted as calm as ever.

Later, when she'd met up with Joe at the library, they both had a good laugh when she told him what had transpired during lunch.

"I'm glad they like me," he said.

"Like you? They think you walk on water. But I'm glad they do. It's just so funny watching them try to feel me out for information without asking outright. They think they're so sneaky."

"Your parents love you. They only want what's best for you. You're lucky to have that," Joe said.

"I know I'm lucky." She remembered how different Joe's family was from hers. "Do you think you'll go home for Christmas break to visit your father?"

Joe shook his head. "No. Even if I had the money to go, he doesn't really care to see me. He doesn't understand why I'm bothering to attend college when I could work on the docks like he does. He's never really understood me. I guess I just have to accept that and move on."

Char reached over and took Joe's hand. "That's sad. Maybe someday you and he will be able to connect."

He shrugged. "Maybe. The only thing that ever made him proud of me was my earning a Purple Heart for being injured in Vietnam. He was never proud of my good grades or the fact that I was going to college. But that medal was important to him. He bragged about it to all his friends. So, I gave it to him. He thought it was the best gift anyone had ever given him."

"You gave him your Purple Heart?" Char's eyes widened. She couldn't imagine giving away something like that.

"Why not? He thought it was wonderful. I couldn't have cared less about it. I didn't need a medal to remind me I was injured in that war. I have to live with it every day of my life."

"Oh, Joe. I never thought of it that way," she said sadly.

Joe squeezed her hand. "Don't be sad. I'm not. I'm alive and exactly where I want to be. I consider myself lucky."

She kissed his cheek. "You're amazing, you know that?"

He shook his head. "No. I'm not that amazing. But I am hungry. Let's go to the union."

They strolled across campus, walking outside despite the cold breeze. Char had bundled up in her coat, scarf, and gloves, but she'd taken off one glove to hold hands with Joe as they walked. She liked the feel of her hand in his. It was warm and strong. When they entered the union, Char immediately spied Deke at a table with a group of students. He was holding court, most likely encouraging them to be a part of the anti-war movement.

She chose a table as far away from Deke as possible while Joe went to the counter to order two Cokes, and a sandwich for himself. No sooner had she sat down and taken off her coat, Deke was standing beside her.

"Hey, Char," he said in a quiet voice. "How are you?"

Char looked up at him. "Hi, Deke. I'm fine."

He slid out the chair next to her and sat down, uninvited. "So, is this how it is now? Are you with him?" He jerked his head in Joe's direction.

Annoyance rose inside her. "I'm not *with* anyone," she said. "But yes, I'm spending time with Joe."

Deke's blue eyes gazed tenderly into hers. "I still love you, Char. Won't you give me another chance?"

Studying Deke, Char knew that she didn't feel the same way about him as she had when they'd first started dating. He'd changed over the past year-and-a-half. He'd become less sensitive and more hardened. She'd never really known if she'd felt true love for Deke, but now, she knew for certain that she no longer had feelings for him.

"I'm sorry, Deke. We tried, but it didn't work out. We've both changed. It's time for both of us to move on," she said gently.

"Did it have to be him?" Deke asked, looking hurt.

"This isn't about you," Char said. "I'm not friends with Joe to spite you. And that's all we are right now, friends. But to tell you the truth, I'd be lucky to be with a guy like Joe. He's a good man."

"I just want you to be safe," Deke said. "Remember the things I've told you about returning soldiers. I'd hate for you to find out that he's not the guy you think he is. I don't want to see your heart broken."

"That's not your problem anymore, is it?" Char snapped back, upset that Deke would insinuate that Joe could hurt her.

"Is everything okay here?" Joe asked as he came up beside the table.

Deke stood. "Everything is fine. I was just saying hello to Char." He leveled his gaze at Joe. "I hope you realize how special she is."

Joe beamed at Char and then looked Deke in the eyes. "Yes, I do."

"I guess I'll see you both around then." Deke turned and walked away.

"What was that all about?" Joe asked as he sat down.

"It was nothing. It's just hard for him to let go sometimes. He'll just have to learn."

"I don't blame him for not wanting to let you go," Joe said. "It would be hard losing someone like you."

"You're just too sweet, you know that?" Char's heart warmed

from the tender way he looked at her. "By the way. Don't make any plans for Thanksgiving. I told my mom you're coming to our house and she's thrilled."

"I wouldn't want to go anywhere else," Joe said.

Chapter Fifteen

Char was the happiest she'd ever been. School was going well and she enjoyed spending time with Joe. It was different with him than it had been with Deke. Joe didn't push his ideas and beliefs on her like Deke had, and he was attentive and caring. He also didn't push himself on her, taking their relationship slowly, as he'd promised. She liked that they were getting to know each other as friends first, although she didn't mind the occasional kiss they shared. In fact, she relished it. They were comfortable together and seemed to understand each other. That was what had been missing between her and Deke. He'd been so intense about his fight against the war that Char had felt on edge around him. She still respected Deke's opinions and energy to fight for what he believed in, but she no longer blindly admired him as she had before.

November sped by. Once the snow fell, she was finally able to talk Joe into her driving him to school. Patty and Jenny now had boyfriends who drove them to and from school, so Char and Joe had the car to themselves. They also rode together to the store on Saturdays for work. Char loved the extra time she spent with Joe in the car. She learned that his favorite singing group was The Beatles, that he'd never built a snowman, even as a child, and he hated beets.

"Nobody likes beets, really, do they?" she'd said, laughing.

"Then why do people buy them?" he'd asked, cringing.

It was small details like these that made Char feel closer to Joe.

But she also knew when to give him space. Joe required time alone and she could sense when he needed it. He liked studying in the library after school, so she respected that and went home to do her own school work. He didn't like feeling crowded and she understood that. She enjoyed her own time alone, as well. Char figured his need for space had something to do with his time spent in Vietnam, but she didn't press him on it. She'd given up on asking him to share his experiences with her. He always closed up when she'd talk about the war, and she finally gave up on the subject. She cared about him and didn't want to dredge up bad memories if he didn't want to share them.

Char was also coming to terms with Jeremy's death even though she still didn't understand why U.S. soldiers were fighting in Vietnam. Deke had kept her emotions about Jeremy's death on the surface by constantly talking about the war and how wrong it was. She hadn't realized how Deke's fight for peace had made her feel anything but peaceful. She wanted to move on from her brother's death, not constantly have it thrown in her face. And with Joe, she felt she could finally do that. He was a calming presence in her life. Despite his leg injury, he wasn't angry or resentful. He pushed forward and lived his life rather than blame society for his limitations. He was someone to look up to, and she respected him for his ability to see good in everything, even when life wasn't always perfect.

Char couldn't believe how happy she was and hoped that her life would stay this way.

* * *

Joe couldn't believe the way his life had turned out. As he walked along the freshly shoveled sidewalks to Char's house on Thanksgiving Day, he marveled at how beautiful and peaceful it was outside. It had snowed the night before and the blanket of snow sparkled like glitter in the sunlight. The shimmering landscape reminded him of Char's eyes whenever she smiled at him.

Char, the beautiful girl who he'd never imagined he'd have in his life. He was the boy who'd grown up on the wrong side of the tracks and had hoped to someday find a better life elsewhere. The man who'd gone to war and prayed he'd not only survive it, but be able to live out his days in a picture-perfect town like the one the beautiful girl described in her letters.

Char. The lovely girl who'd seemed like a faraway dream. She was the one who now made each day feel like a dream come true.

Joe arrived at the Parsons' home around noon as Ronald was settling in for the Detroit Lions versus Oakland Raiders game. Char opened the door before her dad could get out of his seat, and gave Joe a quick kiss.

"You should have let me pick you up in the car," she said. "Weren't the sidewalks icy?"

"They were fine. It's beautiful out," he told her, fully understanding that her worry wasn't over his disability. She would have worried about anyone walking the sidewalks in winter.

"Now Char, don't fuss over Joe," Ronald said from his recliner. "He's a big boy. He can take care of himself." He grinned at his daughter with teasing eyes. "Come in, Joe. Get comfortable. Are you a football fan? It's just starting."

Joe wasn't a fan, but he could talk sports as if he were, having learned all the lingo as a child around his sports-loving father. He sat on the sofa and watched with Ronald as Char went off to help her mother in the kitchen.

They sat down to Thanksgiving dinner in the late afternoon as the sun cast long shadows over the snowy yard outside. Ronald said a small prayer, giving thanks, and sending love to Jeremy, who was no longer at the table with them. It was such a warm and loving blessing that Joe's heart went out to this small family that had lost their son.

The turkey was tender and melted in Joe's mouth and the stuffing, with homemade gravy, was as delicious as Char had promised. Joe savored each bite and readily took seconds of everything, including the fluffy mashed potatoes and candied yams.

"I think I've died and gone to heaven," Joe said, grinning at Ellen. "Food heaven."

Ellen beamed. "That's sweet, Joe. But you must have had family dinners like this growing up."

It had been years since Joe had eaten a Thanksgiving dinner as good as this one. He remembered as a child that he'd eaten holiday meals at an aunt's apartment a few times. "I did, but they didn't compare to this," he said, scooping up another spoonful of yams.

Afterward, they all sat in the living room and talked over pumpkin pie and coffee. Night had fallen outside and the clear sky gave a dark backdrop to millions of twinkling stars.

"Tomorrow should be a busy day," Ronald said. "We don't sell much in the way of Christmas gifts, but when people pour into town to shop, they pick up all kinds of supplies as well. I'm glad you both will be there to help out." He smiled over at Char and Joe.

"Don't forget the lighting of the Christmas tree in the

square tomorrow night," Ellen reminded them. "The bakery will have their treats and hot chocolate booth set up. It's always a fun time and I think the weather is going to cooperate."

"Sounds like fun." Joe glanced over at Char. She smiled and rolled her eyes. He supposed she'd been going since she was a child and considered it corny, but he looked forward to the small-town celebration.

"How is college treating you?" Ronald asked Joe. "The semester will be over soon. Are you enjoying school?"

"I am," Joe said. "It's a lot of work, but I don't mind studying and I love learning."

"And he's a natural at writing," Char said. "He's had papers read aloud by the teacher four times. I've only had one read aloud. He should change his major to English."

"That's wonderful," Ronald said. "We have two writers in the family. Maybe you both can graduate and work for the local newspaper. Their writing is terrible!"

Char laughed. "I think I'll pass on that."

"What about you, Joe? Any ideas yet on what you're going to do after college?" Ellen asked.

Joe shrugged. "I'm not sure yet. Teaching, maybe. Or writing, although I'm not sure I'll make much money at that. I still have a few years to figure it out. Until then, I hope to work in the hardware store as long as I'm needed."

Ronald chuckled. "I'm not letting you go anywhere. I haven't had an employee as good as you in years."

"Dad!" Char protested.

"Aside from you, dear, of course." Ronald winked at her.

Later, as Joe was leaving, Char went out on the porch with him. "I wish you'd let me drive you home. I hate thinking of you walking in the cold."

"I don't mind," he told her. "And it's not that far away. I need to exercise my leg to keep it limber."

Char nodded. They stood close together, their hands clasped. "There's no night music in the winter," she said. "Have you noticed?"

"Yeah. Everything is so still. It feels eerie sometimes. But the sky is clear tonight and the stars are bright. There's beauty in that, too." He pulled her close. "Thank you," he whispered in her ear, brushing his lips on her cheek.

"For what?"

"For everything." He faced her, his arms still circling her waist. "For caring about me. For sharing your wonderful family with me. For giving me the life I've always dreamed of."

"Did I do all that?" she asked, grinning.

"And so much more." He moved closer and pressed his lips to hers. Their kiss was warm in the crisp, cold air circling around them.

"I've never been this happy," he said. "I'm almost afraid I've been given too much and it will all be taken away from me at any moment."

"No one is taking anything away from you. I promise."

Joe kissed her again. Maybe it was the frosty air or the stars twinkling above, or maybe it was the beauty of the future that Joe saw in Char's eyes. He'd never know exactly why he chose that exact moment in time, but he wasn't going to take it back after it had left his lips. "I love you, Char. I love you so very much."

Char's mouth opened ever so slightly in surprise but then she pulled him closer and whispered in his ear, "I love you, too."

* * *

Char stood on the porch and watched as Joe made his way slowly down the street. She could still feel the warmth of his body next to hers, his breath close to her ear. The delightful goosebumps on her arms had been caused by his closeness, not the frigid night.

She loved Joe. How special and magical was that? In what seemed like such a short time, he'd become the most important person in her life. She'd never felt this close to anyone else, as if she were a part of him. It felt completely right to tell him she loved him.

A breeze came up and loose snow swirled in the yard. Char glanced up at the stars and studied them. When she was little, she'd believed in fairy tales and magic and places where dreams come true. After her brother had died, she lost the feeling that anything was possible and magic was all around her. But now, as the snow swirled and the stars twinkled above, she believed in magic again. And it felt glorious.

* * *

Friday was as busy as her father had predicted and before they knew it, it was closing time. Joe and Char went to the Corner Café for dinner then bundled up and waited outside in the town square with the rest of the people for the lighting of the Christmas tree.

Everyone was there: business owners, residents, and college students. Jenny, Terry, Patty, and Craig showed up and they stood in a tight group to keep warm. They bought hot cocoa and wrapped their gloved hands around it as they sipped its sweet warmth. The air crackled with excitement as the children ran around them, eager for the tree to display its colors.

As Char snuggled close to Joe, his arms around her, she spied Deke across the lawn, walking with a blond girl she'd never seen before. He looked her way, and their eyes met for a brief moment. Deke gave a little wave then returned his attention to the girl with him.

"That's going to happen a lot in this small town," Joe whispered in her ear.

Char nodded. "I know. It really doesn't bother me. I hope he finds someone he's as happy with as I am with you."

Joe smiled. "You don't know how much that means to me."

"I think I do."

Char's parents joined their group just before the lighting was to take place. The mayor stood in the gazebo and said a few words about the history and traditions of Grand Falls. Then, he started the countdown and everyone joined in. Ten, nine, eight…all the way down to one and the tall blue spruce in the center of the square lit up as everyone cheered and clapped. The holiday season had officially begun.

People milled around the square eating pastries and cupcakes from Berkoff's Bakery's booth. Neighbors visited with neighbors, children had snowball fights, and teens snuck kisses behind the big oak trees.

Ronald and Ellen waved goodbye and headed for home.

"How did you like our small-town celebration? Was it corny?" Char asked Joe.

"I loved it," he said. "It's exactly how I had imagined it and I wouldn't want it to be any other way."

Char shook her head. "You're silly, you know that? You could have chosen to live anywhere when you came back from Nam, but you chose our little town. You must be crazy"

"I think I chose rather well," he said, kissing her.

They said goodbye to their friends and walked to Char's house. They both had to work again tomorrow and were tired from their long day. Joe said goodbye to her at the gate. They kissed, soft and sweet, but as they stood in the crisp air, he drew her closer and their kiss grew deeper, more passionate. When they pulled away, she was breathless.

"Just something to keep you thinking about me tonight," he said.

He'd certainly accomplished that because she thought about that kiss long after she'd crawled into bed and fell asleep.

Chapter Sixteen

The first week of December brought more snow and colder temperatures. Joe was thankful that Char drove him to campus each morning, but he usually walked home in the afternoons. Tonight, he'd come back to the boarding house to drop off his heavy pack of books and was going to meet up with Char at her house. They had plans to meet their friends at the student union for pizza. Just as he was heading out of his room, Mrs. Bennington called up the stairs to him.

"Joe? Can you come down a minute?"

He saw her at the bottom of the stairs, looking worried. Grabbing his cane, he made his way down.

"What's up, Mrs. B?"

"There's a man here who says he's a friend of yours. He's wearing fatigues and an army jacket like yours. I left him in the living room to wait for you."

A man to see him? Joe thought that was strange, but he followed Mrs. B downstairs and into the living area.

"Joe!" the man said as soon as he walked in. "Hey, buddy. It's so good to see you."

"Tony?" Joe's jaw dropped, stunned to see Tony Funari.

"It's been a while, huh, man?" Tony walked over and wrapped his arms around Joe.

Joe let him hug him then pulled away. "Yeah, Tony. It has been a while. I thought you were in Chicago."

"I was, but I had to move on. There was nothing but trouble for a guy like me in that big city." Tony grinned.

Mrs. Bennington was still standing in the room, and Joe turned to her. "I'm sorry, Mrs. B. I should introduce you. This is Tony Funari. We served together in Nam. Tony, this is Mrs. Bennington. She owns this house."

Tony put on a big smile. "So glad to meet you, Mrs. Bennington. Can I call you Mrs. B too? It's a mouthful, isn't it?" He laughed, but no one else did.

"It's nice to meet you, Tony," she said politely. "I'll give you two some privacy."

"She seems nice," Tony said after she left the room.

"She is. So, what's going on, Tony? Why'd you decide to come here? I thought you had a job in Chicago."

"Ah, you know how that is. It was a crappy job anyway. And I was wearing out my welcome with my friend. He was nice and all, but it was time I moved on. You'd talked about this small town so much, I figured I'd give it a try."

"You're staying a while?" Joe asked.

"I thought I could bunk with you for a couple of weeks. I won't be a pain, I promise. I could even try to find a job. I pretty much spent the last of my money on the bus ride to Peoria and then I had to hitch a ride here with a trucker. This town is so small they don't even have a bus coming to it, you know that?"

Joe's mind was spinning. He studied Tony and noticed he looked even thinner than he'd been in Nam. His dark, wavy hair was shaggy and it looked like he hadn't shaved in days. And he was still as jumpy and nervous as ever. He couldn't keep his body still, constantly wringing his hands and moving his feet. It was no wonder Mrs. B looked concerned when she'd come to get him. She probably didn't know if she could trust Tony. Heck, if he hadn't known Tony, he'd be worried about him, too.

"I'm not sure if you can stay in my room," Joe said. "I'll have to run it by Mrs. B. It's not fair that she's only getting rent from one person if two are sharing."

"Hey, I can pay some money, as soon as I find work, man."

"You'd have to sleep on my sofa. It's all I have," Joe said.

"After sleeping on that damned damp ground in Vietnam, do you think I'd complain about a sofa?" Tony said, grinning.

"Wait here a minute," Joe told him. He went to the kitchen to talk to Mrs. Bennington. She said she was fine with Tony staying for a little while and he didn't have to pay extra.

"Maybe he could help me with the shoveling and other chores around here," she offered.

"You're the best, Mrs. B," Joe told her. "I'll make sure he behaves, too."

He went back to the living room. "Okay, Tony. You can stay for a while. But there are rules that have to be followed around here. And Mrs. B thought maybe instead of rent you could help her out a bit."

"Great. Sure. I can do stuff for her. So where are your digs?"

Joe took him up the flight of stairs, telling him the rules about no women in the room and no noise after ten o'clock. Tony kept nodding his head and saying, "Yeah, yeah," but Joe wondered if it was sinking in.

"Wow, man, you've got a lot of stairs for someone with a limp," Tony said as they went up the last flight.

"It's good for me to keep moving," Joe said.

"Sure. Sure. Hey, this is a great room," Tony said as his eyes darted around. "I like the high ceiling." He dropped his heavy pack on the floor then fell onto the sofa. "This will be perfect. Nice and soft."

Joe sighed. He wasn't sure how well this was going to work out. But he didn't want to throw a friend out in the snow with nowhere to stay. "I'm supposed to meet up with Char for dinner," he said. "Do you want to come along?" Joe really hadn't wanted to extend the invitation, but what else could he do?

"Well, look at you, meeting up with your pretty girlfriend." Tony winked. "I couldn't believe it when you wrote that you were dating her. You deserve it, man. I sure wouldn't miss the chance to meet her."

The minute they walked outside, Tony lit a cigarette and offered one to Joe.

"No, thanks. I don't smoke," Joe told him.

"Oh, yeah. I forgot. You were about the only guy in the unit who didn't smoke. Good for you," Tony said. "So, are we walking all the way there?"

"We're walking to Char's house. She has a car. I haven't saved enough money to buy one yet," Joe said.

"Wow. You got the dream girl and she has a car. Good for you, Joe. A guy like you deserves it, you know? You're the nicest guy I've ever met."

"Thanks," Joe said. He was beginning to remember how Tony could rattle on forever and not really say anything. He never knew if he was just talking nonsense or if he meant everything he said. It was all nervous energy fighting to get out.

Char met them out on the porch before they had a chance to knock. She looked surprised to see Tony with Joe.

"Wow! Is this her? My God, Joe. How lucky are you?" Tony

said before Joe could say a word. He dropped his cigarette butt in the snow and walked up to Char. "You don't know me, but I served in Nam with Joe. It's so nice to meet you. I remember Joe carried your picture with him everywhere." He raised his hand to shake Char's.

She accepted but looked a bit startled.

"This is Tony," Joe said. "He just surprised me at the boarding house."

"Oh, well, it's nice to meet you, Tony," Char said, smiling at him.

"My pleasure." Tony pulled out another cigarette and lit it. "Joe is a lucky guy. I always say that. So, so lucky."

"Ah, yeah. He is." Char looked unsure at how to respond to Tony.

"Let's head over to the union to eat," Joe said. "I'm starved."

"Yeah, me too," Tony said.

Char handed Joe the car keys and they all got in, Tony in the back. He cracked the window a little so he could let the smoke from his cigarette out.

"This is a nice car," he said. "I'll be careful not to get ashes in it. We don't want to dirty up the pretty lady's car."

"Thank you," Char said, giving Joe a strange look. "It was my brother's car."

"Really? What happened to him?" Tony asked.

"Tony. Don't ask, okay?" Joe said.

"No, it's fine," Char said. "He died in Vietnam."

"Oh, wow, yeah," Tony said. "So sorry. A lot of good men have died there."

"Thank you," Char said.

"But not me and you, eh, Joe? We made it out. I mean, we both have our problems, but we're still alive, right?" Tony said.

"Yeah, Tony. We did."

Joe parked the car outside of the union and the three of them headed inside. Jenny, Terry, Patty, and Craig were already at a large table waiting for them.

"Hey, guys," Joe said. "This is Tony. He and I served together in Nam." He introduced everyone to Tony.

"Hi, Tony. Nice to meet you," Jenny said. "Did you just get to town?"

"Yeah. I was in Chicago and thought, why not go see my old pal, Joe? So, here I am."

"That's nice," Jenny said.

They ordered three large pizzas and the guys had beer while the girls drank Coke.

"Sure you ladies don't want a beer?" Tony asked.

"We're underage," Char told him. "And the college cards everyone."

"Wow! Really? I figured you were all older. Stupid law, anyway. I mean, if you're old enough to go to war, you should be able to drink a beer," Tony said.

Everyone nodded their agreement and Tony beamed with delight. He waved the waitress over for another beer. By the time the pizza arrived, Tony was on his third bottle.

"Tony. You should slow down on the beers," Joe said, leaning over toward him and speaking quietly. "I thought you said you didn't have much money left."

"I have a little," Tony said. "There's always enough money for beer and cigs, right?"

Joe didn't reply. He glanced at Char next to him and shook his head.

"Everything okay?" she whispered.

"We'll talk later," he said.

"So, I suppose you two guys haven't served yet. Got that college deferment, right?" Tony asked Terry and Craig.

Both nodded. "I wanted to finish college first," Craig said.

"Yeah, right." Tony snorted. "Bet you were hoping we'd be out of Nam by the time you graduated. No luck there, though. The way Nixon is bombing everything in sight, it's not going to end anytime soon."

Craig seemed to bristle at Tony's words. "I'm not planning on running away from my duty. If the war is still on when I graduate, I'll go. But with the war protests going on, you never know what the White House will do. They may still pull us out of Vietnam."

"Don't hold your breath waiting for that to happen," Tony said. "Nixon doesn't give a damn about protesters. The anti-war movement is just a bunch of draft card burners who're afraid to fight. They're not stopping a thing."

"Tony, let's drop it, please. People are allowed their opinion," Joe said, trying to keep things from escalating.

"Yep. That's what we're fighting for. Freedom of speech. But you guys know what? When you're crawling in a tunnel and come face-to-face with a damned Viet Cong guerrilla fighter who'd just as soon see your head up on a stake, no one is thinking about the rights of the guys opposing the war. You're thinking about saving your own skin. You're thinking that it's either him or me, and I don't give a damn what happens to him. You can tell me all about freedom of speech and protesting once you find yourself eye to eye with a man who wants to kill you."

Tony's breath was coming in short gasps as he spoke and sweat beaded his forehead. While the others at the table gaped at him in horror, Joe saw the signs of a man ready to come undone. He stood and patted Tony on the back.

"Let's go get some fresh air," Joe said calmly.

Tony stared at him, his eyes glazed, but nodded and followed Joe outside. Once there, he lit another cigarette and began pacing. "I guess I went overboard in there," he said. "I didn't mean to. Sometimes shit just comes out of my mouth and I don't know how to censor myself."

"Tony, it would be best if you didn't talk about Vietnam. Could you do that for me? Everyone has their own opinion about the war, and it only starts an argument," Joe said.

Tony dropped his cigarette and stomped on it with his boot. "Okay, okay. I can do that." He stopped pacing and stared straight at Joe. "You know, when I flew home from Nam this last time, a man spit on me in the airport. Here, in the U.S. I don't get it. I went to war like I was told and they called me a baby killer. Where's my parade, huh? Where's my confetti and marching band playing the national anthem? You know what I got? Nothing. Yet, I'm the one who has to keep his mouth shut so I don't offend anyone."

Joe was ashamed for asking his friend to keep quiet. He knew exactly how Tony felt. But Joe didn't want to make waves here. He was starting over and things were going well for him. The last thing he needed was Tony spouting off, causing trouble.

"I'm sorry, Tony. I understand how you feel. But for me, please keep it down. This is my life now. I don't want to mess it up," Joe said.

Tony ran his hand through his hair. "I get it, man. I do. I'll do better. I don't want to ruin anything for you here. You live in a nice place and you have a good girl. I'm happy for you. I'll keep my mouth shut, okay?"

Joe patted Tony on the back. "Thanks. Who knows? Maybe you'll like it here, too."

"Yeah. That would be nice. A place to settle down," Tony said.

* * *

Later, they drove back to Char's house and Tony said he'd give them some space. "Three's a crowd. I'll walk back to the boarding house so you guys can be alone. It was nice meeting you, Char." He turned to Joe. "I promise, I'll go directly up to the room and be quiet. It's been a long day. I'll probably be asleep long before you get there."

They said goodnight to Tony then Joe walked Char up to the porch.

"Why don't you come in for a while?" Char said. "It seems like you could use a little time away from Tony."

"Okay." Joe was uneasy about letting Tony go to the boarding house alone, but he decided he couldn't follow him around the entire time he stayed. He'd have to trust him to behave.

They found the living room empty when they went inside. "Dad must have gone up to bed early," Char said. "Would you like a Coke? Or some hot chocolate?"

Joe eased himself down on the sofa. His leg was aching and he couldn't bend it very well. "No thanks. I just want to sit here a while." He grinned and stretched out his arm. "Come sit with me."

Char sat in the crook of his arm, kicked off her shoes, and snuggled in closer.

"This is nice." He sighed happily.

"It was a hard night, huh?" Char said. "Tony is kind of intense."

"Kind of?" Joe chuckled. "He's strung tighter than a guitar string."

"How long do you think he'll stay?"

"I don't know. I'm kind of worried about it. He has nowhere to go, and no money. He's been going through friends since he was let out of the service."

"Let out?" Char asked. "Don't you mean discharged?"

Joe shook his head. "No, he was let out early on a medical discharge. He had some sort of a breakdown. He's been nervous since the day I met him, but I guess it got worse. I feel bad for him, but I'm not sure how long he can live with me. I'm hoping he gets bored of this small town after a couple of weeks and leaves on his own."

"Maybe he'll settle down a bit once he gets used to being here," Char offered.

"I love your optimism. I hope you're right, though." He leaned down and kissed her, enjoying the feel of her soft lips on his. She reached up and wrapped her arms around his neck, pulling him closer. She smelled sweet and tasted even better. Holding her tighter, Joe kissed her deeper as her lips opened. Everything about Char was soft and warm, silky and sweet. He wished he could melt right into her. Instead, he pulled away.

"I'd better leave. Otherwise, it might be hard to get me out of here."

She ran her fingers along the strong line of his jaw, causing delicious chills up his spine. "I wish you didn't have to go," Char whispered.

"Me, too." He kissed her again, then forced himself to stand. "At least we work together tomorrow."

Char sighed as she stood to walk him to the door. "Yeah. Work. Whoopie."

Joe laughed and kissed her one last time. "See you tomorrow." He headed out into the chilly night.

Chapter Seventeen

Char could tell Joe was troubled when he came into work the next morning. He looked tired and irritated, which was unusual for him.

"Bad night?" she asked.

"Yeah." He put away his coat and pulled on the work apron they all wore. Then he gave Char a smile. "But it's better now that I'm with you."

"You don't always have to put on a happy face, you know. I'm here to listen if there's a problem," Char told him.

"It's Tony. He didn't sleep much last night. He got up every few minutes and lit a cigarette, then paced the floor. When he finally did go to sleep, he woke up screaming. It sounds like his nightmares are pretty intense."

"I'm sorry to hear that," Char said. "War nightmares?"

Joe nodded. "It's not his fault. We all have them. But I was afraid he'd wake the entire house with his screams. It took a while to calm him down."

Char hadn't thought about Joe having nightmares. Of course he would. Since he never talked about the war, she had no idea what he'd gone through, or what haunted him.

"Is Tony okay?" she asked.

"Yeah, he's fine. I left as he was waking up. He said he was going to walk around town and look for a job today. Hopefully, he'll find something to make a little money."

Later that afternoon, Char heard a familiar voice up by the cash register. She'd been working on the bank deposit for Monday and her dad and Joe were helping customers. She walked up to the front and saw Tony talking to Joe.

"Hi, Tony," she said. "How are you today?"

"Oh, there she is. The prettiest girl in town. Hey there, Char. I'm doing okay," Tony said, grinning widely.

"Tony was telling me he's applied at a couple of places," Joe offered.

"Yeah," Tony said. "The diner down the street said they need a dishwasher, and there's a job stocking shelves at the grocery store. Not the greatest jobs, but it's money."

"Maybe something else will come along," Char said, trying to sound positive.

"Who's this?" Ronald asked cheerfully, strolling up to the cash register.

"Ronald, this is my friend, Tony," Joe said. "He and I served together in Nam. Tony, this is Ronald Parsons, Char's father. He owns this store."

"Nice to meet you, Tony," Ronald said, extending his hand.

"Happy to meet you, sir." Tony shook his hand. "So, you're Char's dad. She and Joe have been very nice to me even though I made a surprise visit."

"Glad to hear it," Ronald said.

"Tony's been looking for a job while he stays here," Char told her dad.

"Really? Any luck?" Ronald asked.

"There's a couple of jobs I applied for. Menial work, but hey, beggars can't be choosers, right? I don't suppose you have another job opening here at the store?" Tony asked.

"I'm afraid not," Ronald said, then looked thoughtful. "But I might know of a temporary job available. Jackson Contracting is going to do some remodeling and painting at the high school over Christmas break. I talked to Leonard, the owner, the other day and he said he needed a couple more men for the job. It will only be for two weeks, though."

Tony's eyes lit up. "Really? Wow. That would be perfect."

"Give me a few minutes and I'll telephone Leonard and ask if he's still hiring," Ronald said. He headed to the back room to make the call.

"Your dad is the greatest, Char. I hope it works out. Even for two weeks, it would be better than washing dishes," Tony said.

Tony went outside for a cigarette while he waited for Ronald to return.

"I'm not sure if I want him to get that job," Joe said quietly. "I know it sounds awful, but I'm not sure how long I can stand to have him in my room. I'm used to being alone."

"Sorry," Char said. "You know how much my dad enjoys helping others."

"I know. And I appreciate your dad. He's such a great guy. Maybe if Tony's working, it'll keep his mind busy and he'll sleep sounder," Joe said. "I can hope."

By the time Tony came inside, Ronald had returned.

"Leonard said he'd be willing to talk to you about a job," Ronald told Tony. He wrote a phone number and an address on a piece of paper. "Here. Stop by his place on Monday morning at nine. Hopefully, he'll have work for you."

Tony took the paper. "Thank you so much, sir. This is great."

Ronald smiled. "You don't have to call me sir. You can call me Ronald."

"Okay, Ronald. Thank you. You don't know what it means to me to get a chance for a good job. Even a temporary one."

"You're very welcome," Ronald said. "Say? Why don't you and Joe come over for dinner tonight? I think Ellen is roasting a chicken. There should be plenty for everyone." He turned to Char. "Unless you and Joe had other plans, dear."

Char glanced over at Joe, not sure if he wanted to bring Tony to the house. Joe looked uncertain.

"Are you sure Mrs. Parsons won't mind?" Joe asked. "I'd hate to put extra work on her."

"I'm sure she'd love to have company. What do you say?"

"Well, uh, sure. That would be nice," Joe said, looking past Ronald to Char.

Char shrugged but nodded that it was okay. "Dad. You'd better warn Mom so she makes enough food."

"Sure, dear. I will."

"A homemade dinner sounds great," Tony said. "Thank you for inviting me, sir—ah, I mean Ronald."

Ronald smiled. "We'll see you around six." He went back to the office.

"This is a great day." Tony beamed. "A possible job and now dinner. Your dad is amazing, Char."

"Yes, he is," she said. She could see the worry in Joe's eyes. She understood why. She'd known Tony for less than twenty-four hours, yet she already knew how wound up he could be. She hoped he'd be on his best behavior so Joe wouldn't be embarrassed.

Tony left after that, saying he'd promised to do a few chores for Mrs. B. He said he'd meet up with them at Char's house at six.

Later, after they'd closed the store, Char and Joe rode in her car to the house. After they'd parked in front of the house, they both sat there, not moving to get out.

"I hope this goes well," Joe said.

Char reached across the seat and took his hand. "I'm sure Tony will be on his best behavior." She grinned. "It can't possibly be any worse than the lunch with Deke."

Joe chuckled. "I hope not."

They both stared out at the night sky. A few neighbors had put up Christmas lights which brightened the neighborhood. Ronald had outlined their porch with multi-colored lights, too, giving the house some holiday cheer.

"You mentioned that you have nightmares, too," Char said, locking her fingers around his. "Tell me about them, Joe. Maybe it will help to talk about them."

Joe wouldn't look at her. He gazed out the window ahead of him. "I'd rather not."

"Ever? Or not with me?"

Joe sighed and turned her way. "Ever. It's not that I don't want to share my thoughts with you, Char. I promise you that. It's just that my memories of Vietnam, and my nightmares, are so personal that I don't even know what to think about them, let alone talk about them. At least, not yet. Maybe someday."

Char nodded. "Okay. I won't push you. But if they get bad, will you talk to someone? My dad, or another veteran. It's not good to bottle everything up inside, especially bad memories."

"I won't ever let the past come between us," Joe said. "Honestly, if I could wipe those memories from my mind, I would. I want to look toward the future, not back on the past. There's nothing back there for me."

Char drew closer and kissed him. Just as she pulled away, a rapping on the window startled her.

"Hey. You guys going to stay in there all night?" Tony asked, staring at them.

"And now it all begins," Joe said to Char.

She laughed as they left the car.

* * *

Char could see that Tony was a bundle of nerves as he met Ellen then tried making conversation in the living room before dinner. He seemed to be trying hard not to say the wrong thing, but it was difficult for him. Since no one in the house smoked, Tony went outside every few minutes to light up a cigarette. Joe went out to stand with him a couple of times, but it was so often, he gave up.

"I appreciate you not smoking in here, Tony," Ellen said. "Ever since Ron stopped smoking years ago, no one in the house has."

"It's a terrible habit," Tony said. "I wouldn't want to stink up your beautiful house with the smoke. I know I should stop, but it's hard, you know?"

Ellen nodded. "It's a hard habit to quit. Nearly everyone we know smokes. I appreciate your thoughtfulness, Tony."

Her kind words seemed to put Tony a little more at ease.

When they sat down for dinner, Tony piled his plate with chicken, mashed potatoes, and gravy. "This is a treat," he said to Ellen between mouthfuls. "Everything is delicious."

"Thank you. I'm glad you like it," Ellen replied.

They talked about the day at the hardware store and the pretty Christmas decorations that were up all over town. Ellen mentioned that they should get their tree the next day and decorate it.

"I saw they had some nice trees at the nursery on the edge of town," Ronald said. "Charlotte, do you want to go with me to pick one out?"

Char blushed. "You make me feel like I'm ten years old, Dad."

"I'll go." Tony offered. "I haven't picked out a Christmas tree in years."

"Me, too," Joe said, winking at Char. "I don't care if you think I'm ten years old."

Everyone laughed.

"Of course I'll go along, Dad," Char said. "But we're not taking these guys. They'll make fun of me."

After dinner, Char and Ellen served coffee and apple crisp in the living room where the men had gone to sit. Tony and Ronald talked about football since Tony kept up on the sport. Char was just thinking that the night had gone quite well when she heard Tony ask, "Who's that in the picture on the mantel?" He stood up and peered closer at the photo.

"That's our son, Jeremy," Ronald said.

"Oh, yeah," Tony said. "Char told me about him. He died in Vietnam."

Char watched as Joe stood up and made his way over to Tony.

"Yes, he did." Ronald winced.

"Do you know how it happened?" Tony didn't seem to notice the tension building in the room as he lifted the picture off the mantel for a closer look.

"It doesn't matter how it happened," Joe said quietly to Tony. "We don't want to upset the Parsons by discussing it."

Tony looked up and seemed to finally notice Ronald and Ellen's sad faces. "Oh, I'm sorry."

"It's okay, Tony. It's still hurts, though," Ronald said.

"Yeah. I'm sure it does. I just wondered, that's all." Tony gazed at the picture, as if entranced by it.

"Maybe you should put the picture back," Joe suggested.

Tony glanced up, his eyes looking glazed. "Yeah. Yeah. I was just thinking how young he was. It's unfair, isn't it? How some of us make it home and some of us don't? I'm sorry." He lifted the picture and set it on the mantel, but it slipped and fell to the floor. The glass shattered.

Everyone froze, stunned by what had happened.

"Oh, no!" Tony crouched down to retrieve the picture. "I'm so sorry. I thought it was on the mantel. I'm so sorry!"

Ellen rushed over and knelt down. "Don't worry, Tony. I'll pick it up. Be careful. I don't want you to cut yourself."

Char hurried to the kitchen to get a broom and dustpan while Ronald knelt beside his wife, carefully picking glass off the hearth and carpet.

"I'll pay for the frame," Tony said. "Is the picture okay? I'm so sorry." He wrung his hands as he stood there.

Char came back with the broom, and her mother swept the hearth. Char looked over and saw how distraught Tony was. Joe didn't look any happier. She walked over to Tony and placed a hand on his shoulder, which made him jump.

"It's okay, Tony. It was an accident. Don't worry," she said gently.

Tony nodded but didn't seem reassured.

"Maybe we should go," Joe suggested. "It's been a long day."

"Maybe so," Ronald said. He patted Tony on the back. "Don't fret over it, son. It can be fixed. Don't give it another thought."

Tony nodded, but he still looked distraught. He and Joe thanked Ellen again for the wonderful meal, then got their coats and headed outside. Char walked out to the porch with them. Tony lit a cigarette immediately and started pacing the sidewalk in front of the house.

"Maybe you can stop by tomorrow and help with the tree," Char said to Joe.

Joe glanced over at Tony, then back at Char. "Yeah. I don't want to bring Tony, though. I couldn't take another scene like tonight."

"He didn't mean to do it," Char said, "Don't be too hard on him."

"I don't have to be hard on him. He's too hard on himself." Joe kissed her and smiled. "I'll see you tomorrow. Hopefully."

Char watched them leave after waving goodbye to Tony. She felt bad for him. She thought he meant well, but he was so nervous all the time. She hoped he'd find peace soon.

* * *

Joe walked slowly down the sidewalk beside Tony. He was exhausted from not sleeping well the night before, then dealing with Tony tonight. All he wanted was to get back to the boarding house and crawl into bed.

Tony rambled non-stop about what had happened at the house. "Do you think they're mad at me? I was just looking at the picture. I didn't say anything wrong, did I? I hate my mouth. I just blurt crap out. Tell me I didn't insult them. I don't want them to hate me."

Joe sighed. "Stop driving yourself crazy over it. The Parsons are cool. They knew it was an accident. Give yourself a break, okay?"

Tony stopped for a moment to light another cigarette. He looked around like he was lost. "Hey? Are there any bars nearby? I could really use a beer."

Joe stopped walking and turned back to Tony. "Don't you think we've done enough tonight? I just want to hit the sack."

"It's still early, man. Come on. Just one or two beers. It would help me unwind. I may even sleep better if I have a couple."

Joe liked the idea of Tony sleeping better. "Okay. Fine. We have to walk back toward town, though. There's a bar a short distance from here. We'll have a couple of beers and then go home, okay?"

"Yeah. That's great. It'll be fun. You'll see."

Joe wasn't sure it would be fun, but he went anyway.

A few minutes later they walked into the small bar. When they entered, it seemed everyone stopped talking and looked up. Joe felt uncomfortable, like they didn't belong there. He and Tony found a small table in the back corner and sat down. A young waitress in a mini skirt and tight sweater came and took their order.

"She's cute," Tony said, watching the girl as she walked away. "That's what I need. A cute girl, just like you have. Smart, too. I like smart girls."

Joe ignored Tony's ramblings. He glanced around the bar and caught sight of Deke standing across the room at the end of the bar. A tall, pretty blonde was smiling up at him.

Joe groaned inwardly. Of all people, why did Deke have to be here tonight?

The waitress came back with their beers and Tony asked her what her name was.

"Tami," she said.

"That's a cute name," Tony said. "Are you from around here?"

"All my life," she said. "I'm going to the college here. Your friend and I have social studies together."

Joe looked closer at Tami. "Oh, yeah. We do. Sorry I didn't recognize you."

She smiled. "That's okay. It's a big class. So," she turned back to Tony, "are you a student there, too?"

Tony shook his head. "No. I'm just here visiting my friend. We were in Nam together."

"Oh, well, that's nice," the girl said, looking unsure. "I'd better get back to work." She waved and headed back to the bar.

"She likes me," Tony told Joe.

Joe chuckled. "Sure she does."

Tony went over to the jukebox and put change in to play a few tunes. He was four years older than Joe, so his choice of music was from the early sixties. He punched in the song numbers and soon, "Blowin' in the Wind" began playing over the speakers.

"Now we're having fun," Tony told Joe as he waved the waitress over for another beer.

"Just one more, Tony," Joe warned. "Then I'm heading out."

"Sure, sure." Tony said. "A Hard Day's Night" started playing. "This is the good stuff," he told Joe, nodding his head toward the jukebox.

After the waitress brought them each another beer, Deke appeared beside their table.

Crap! Joe thought. *Here we go.*

"Looks like the G.I.s are multiplying around here," Deke said, giving Tony the once over.

"Hello, Deke," Joe said unenthusiastically.

"Who's your friend?" Deke asked.

"This is Tony. Tony, this is Deke. He goes to the college too.

Tony and I served together," Joe said.

"Good to meet you." Tony half stood and raised his hand to shake Deke's, but Deke didn't return the gesture, leaving Tony's hand in mid-air.

"Yeah. Right," Deke said.

Tony frowned. He pulled his hand back and sat down, then wiped it on his pants like it had gotten dirty.

"Where's Char tonight?" Deke asked Joe.

Joe stared hard at him. "Why?"

Deke shrugged. "Just asking. She's usually with you."

The next song, "Up on the Roof," began playing and Deke glanced at the jukebox. "Cripes. Who played this crappy music, anyway?"

Tony glared at Deke. "You got a problem, guy?"

"You being here is a problem," Deke said steadily.

Tony jumped out of his seat so fast the chair skidded back and fell down. His face was red with anger as he stepped up to Deke. He was at least six inches shorter than Deke, but that didn't stop him. Tony had a temper and could fight with the best of them. "I know twenty-five ways to kill a guy with my bare hands," Tony growled. "With you, I only need one."

Joe stood and put his arm out to block Tony from Deke. Instead of being afraid, Deke just looked down at Tony and laughed.

"I'm sure you do," Deke said. "And you just proved my point. Ex-soldiers are dangerous and we don't want them around here."

Joe had to grab Tony's arms to stop him from jumping Deke.

"See you guys later," Deke said, then sauntered off back to the bar.

"Let me go! I'm gonna kill that guy!" Tony yelled, but Joe held on tight.

"Settle down. We're leaving," Joe said through gritted teeth.

The waitress was staring at them wide-eyed as were the rest of the people in the place. The bartender glared at them but didn't move out from behind the bar. Joe dropped a few bills on the table, grabbed his cane, and nearly shoved Tony out of the door.

Once the cold night air hit Tony's face, he began to calm down. He lit a cigarette and paced the sidewalk. "What the hell was that all about? Who was that jerk?"

"Let's go home," Joe said, exhausted. He started walking down the street.

Tony hurried to catch up with him. "You should have let me punch that guy."

"No, Tony. Then you'd be in jail and he'd be laughing his head off. If you know what's good for you, you'll stay away from fighting anyone."

"I don't get it," Tony blurted out. "Why do you let people walk all over you? We were soldiers. We were taught to stand up and fight. What happened to you, man?"

Joe stopped and stared hard at Tony. "I'm not at war anymore. And neither are you. I came to this town to start over and have a nice, peaceful life. I don't want to think about Vietnam, and I don't want to get into fights with guys like Deke who are trying to prove a point. I just want to put the past behind me and move on."

"Okay, okay," Tony said, taking a step back from Joe.

They walked the rest of the way to the boarding house in complete silence.

Chapter Eighteen

Joe was lying in bed in the dark, staring up at the ceiling. Tony lit another cigarette across the room. Joe wished he wouldn't smoke in the room. He hated the smell, but since Mrs. B didn't have a rule against smoking, Joe didn't feel he should say anything.

Sleep eluded Joe. Every time he thought about Deke, he wanted to punch the guy. Joe hated feeling that way. He wanted violence to be gone from his life. He wanted it all behind him.

"I'm sorry about tonight," Tony said.

Joe jumped. It was as if Tony had been reading his thoughts. "Don't worry about it, Tony. It's okay."

"No, man. I mean it. I don't want to do anything to upset you, or mess up your life here. It's just hard, you know? But I'm trying."

"I know you are. Don't get yourself all tied up about it," Joe said.

Silence fell over them again, and Joe heard Tony put out his cigarette in the ashtray Mrs. B had given him. Just when Joe thought Tony was asleep, he spoke up again.

"I didn't want to leave the service," Tony said, sounding sad.

"I liked being in the army. I thought I'd make it my career, you know? But I messed up. I snapped. And they discharged me."

"I'm sorry," Joe said. "You were a good soldier. I know. I saw it first-hand."

"Do you know why they pulled me out of Nam? I shot at a guy in my own unit. It was dark, and I was so nervous and frightened, I shot at a shadow coming toward me. Lucky for me, the guy next to me pushed my gun up at the last second, or else I would have killed the guy. I thought he was Charlie. I really believed the enemy had walked right into our camp."

Joe sat up in bed. He'd known Tony had been discharged but hadn't known the details. "You couldn't help it, Tony. That stuff happens. You were on your second tour, and the first tour had been rough. No one blames you for your nerves snapping."

"They had names for what happened to me." Tony spoke as if Joe hadn't said anything. "Shell shock. War fatigue. It took me a while to stop shaking after being sent home. I spent time in the hospital where the shrinks tried to figure me out. The nightmares were horrible. Still are. I jumped at even the slightest sound, and my temper was short. In the end, they just told me I should forget everything, get a job, and start a new life. But it's easier said than done."

Joe ran his hand over the back of his neck. He'd told Tony that was exactly what he'd wanted to do. "I'm sorry I said that to you earlier. But I meant it about me, not you."

"I know," Tony said. "And for you it'll work because you've got your shit together. I'm not so sure if it will work for me, though. For the last year and a half, I've been trying to do exactly what they said, but I screw it up every time. My parents threw me out because I went nuts on them. All my old friends have told me to hit the road, too. Every one of them has said the same thing. They want to put the war behind them and move on. I wish I could. I really do. But it just keeps going on in my head and I don't know how to make it stop."

"I'm sorry," Joe said again. "Have you thought about going to the V.A. again? Getting more help?"

Tony snorted. "They didn't help me the first time around. I doubt if they will now."

Silence swelled between them. Finally, Tony said, "I want to make it work this time. I really do. Maybe I'll get that job. That would be a good thing, right? I have to try because this is my last shot."

"Don't talk that way, Tony. It's not your last shot. Just take it a day at a time. Things can change," Joe said. But Joe worried about where Tony might go if it didn't work out here. And what would happen to him.

* * *

Joe left the next morning for the library to do homework. He asked Tony if he wanted to go along or hang out in the union and find some guys to play pool with. Tony declined.

"I promised Mrs. B that I'd put up Christmas lights on the house today," he said. "She promised she'd make me a real nice breakfast and lunch for it. Sounded like a fair exchange to me."

"Okay. I'm going to stop by Char's house around one to see if they're decorating the tree. Do you want to meet me there?" Joe asked.

"I'll see how long it takes me here," Tony said.

Joe didn't like the sadness that tinged Tony's voice. He wondered when Mrs. B had asked him to put up lights. He'd been with Tony the past two days and he hadn't heard them talking about it. But he didn't want to press Tony because he'd had another bad night. He'd woken up screaming twice during the night, and had paced the floor the rest of the time.

"Are you okay?" Joe asked as he stood at the door. "I could stay if you want me to."

"Hey, don't worry about old Tony. I'm fine. You go do your thing. I'll try to meet up with you later."

Joe walked downstairs with his pack on his back. He stopped in the kitchen to talk to Mrs. B about Tony putting up the Christmas lights, but she'd already left for church. Shrugging off the feeling of dread that spread over him, Joe headed out into the crisp morning air. He hoped Tony was going to help Mrs. B. It might lift his spirits to work on the Christmas lights and take his mind off his troubles.

Joe spent the next few hours writing an essay for English class and studying for a social studies test. The library was almost empty today. He supposed that most students were either sleeping off a hangover from the night before or going to church. Either way, it left the gothic-style room all to himself. He sat upstairs at a table in a far corner and every so often would look out the window at the white landscape. Joe didn't mind the snow. He'd grown up with it, but where he'd lived the snow turned brown and muddy soon after it fell. Here, it was glaringly white, and sometimes even sparkled in the sunlight. After spending almost a year in Vietnam with its hot, humid temperatures, the snow and cold felt good.

Joe packed up his books around half past noon and made his way to Char's house. By now her family would have arrived home from church and picking out a Christmas tree. As he walked, he thought about shiny glass ornaments, popcorn strings, and colorful lights being strung on a freshly cut tree.

He could picture Ellen making hot chocolate with marshmallows and offering freshly baked cookies as they decorated the tree. It had been a long time since Joe had had a tree at Christmas. He couldn't remember it ever being a joy to decorate one with their broken ornaments and the paper stars he and his brother made. If it hadn't been for their aunts, there probably wouldn't have been presents on Christmas morning either. His father didn't worry about such things. Maybe he'd thought that with his wife gone, there was no reason to celebrate. Joe never knew, because his father wasn't one to share what he was thinking.

Char opened the door before Joe even made it on the porch. She lifted a sprig of mistletoe over his head when he came up to her. "Christmas season is here," she said, grinning, then kissed him.

They went inside where Ronald was lying on the floor, straightening the Christmas tree in its stand by turning the metal screws.

Joe set down his pack and inhaled deeply. The scent of the blue spruce filled the air. "Now, that smells like Christmas," he declared.

"There we go. How does that look?" Ronald asked as he stood up.

"Looks straight to me," Joe told him.

"Oh, Joe. Wonderful! You're just in time for lunch," Ellen said as she came out into the living room.

"I didn't mean to invite myself to lunch," Joe said.

"You're always invited, dear," Ellen told him. "Besides, Char said she'd invited you to decorate the tree, so I planned on you being here for lunch too."

"My day just keeps getting better," Joe said as they all went into the dining room to eat.

After lunch, Ronald brought out the boxes of Christmas decorations. Ellen sorted through them while Ronald and Joe strung lights on the tree. Joe's daydream of hot cocoa and marshmallows came true as they decorated the tree with antique, hand-blown glass ornaments and strings of red and silver glass beads. There was a silver star for the top, and Joe held the ladder while Char placed it. Ellen hung garland and stockings on the fireplace mantel and Ronald played Burl Ives's Christmas album on the stereo. Joe felt as if he'd fallen into one of those old family movies on TV. He loved every minute of it.

"Where is your friend Tony today?" Ellen asked as she worked.

"He's stringing up Christmas lights for Mrs. Bennington," Joe answered. "I invited him to drop by when he was done. It must be taking longer than he thought."

"That's nice of him," Ellen said. "Mrs. Bennington hasn't decorated the outside of her house in years. She'll enjoy having the lights up."

Joe stopped what he was doing and frowned.

"What's the matter?" Char asked.

"I don't know. I'm worried about Tony not being here yet. I hope he's not in a bar in town, or at the union having a few beers. We went out for a couple of beers last night and he almost got into a fight with Deke."

"Deke? Why?"

"You know Deke. He came over and made a few smart remarks. Tony has a temper. He's so wound up, it doesn't take much to make him angry."

"Maybe we should go check on him after we're done here,"

Char suggested. "Then we can go to the union and hang out for a while."

"That's a good idea," Joe said. He glanced around to see if Ronald or Ellen were looking, then kissed Char quickly on the lips. "You're amazing, you know that?" he whispered.

"I do know that," she teased.

They left the house after five and drove to the boarding house. It was dark out, and clouds overhead blocked any view of the moon or stars. After parking, Joe and Char stared at the front of the house. There was no sign of any Christmas lights having been put up.

Char turned to Joe. "Why would Tony lie about that?"

He shook his head. "I don't know. Let's go inside."

They entered the house and Mrs. B met them at the door. The room smelled of pot roast, which she was cooking for dinner.

"Is Tony upstairs?" Joe asked her.

"I think so," Mrs. B said. "I haven't seen him come down all day. Unless he left while I was at church this morning."

Joe's forehead creased with worry. He couldn't figure out what was happening. "Did you ask Tony to put up Christmas lights today?"

"No," Mrs. B said, looking surprised. "I don't even own any. I haven't decorated the house in years."

Joe felt a twist of fear in his gut. "I'll be right back," he told Char, dropping his pack on the floor and ascending the stairs as quickly as his wounded leg would allow.

He stopped at the bottom of the stairs that led to his attic room. It was eerily quiet. *He could be anywhere,* Joe told himself. *He could be sitting at the union, talking to a cute college girl.*

Slowly, Joe moved up the stairs. He turned the doorknob

at the top and swung it open. The room was dark, except for the dim light that filtered through the stained-glass window and dormers. But Joe saw him right away. He caught his breath as his heart beat rapidly in his chest. Tony was hanging motionless from a beam.

Chapter Nineteen

The scream that came down the stairs sounded primal. Char's skin prickled. She knew instantly who had made the sound. Joe.

She flew up the stairs. Rodney was already at the top of the attic staircase by the time Char reached the bottom. He just stood frozen, and fear rushed through Char.

"Joe! Joe!" she cried. She raced up the stairs. From inside the apartment, she heard Joe order Rodney not to let her up there. Rodney grabbed her as she hit the top step and spun her around, but not before she saw Joe doubled over on the floor, Tony's legs dangling in mid-air above him.

Char gasped as her breath caught in her throat. Rodney pulled her down the stairs. Mrs. Bennington was on the landing, looking frightened.

"What is it? What's happened?" the older woman asked.

Rodney handed Char over to her and said softly, "Call the police. Tony is dead." He turned and headed back up the stairs.

Tears spilled down Char's cheeks as she struggled to catch her breath. Mrs. Bennington took her to a bench seat in the hallway and sat her down. "I'll be right back," she said. She headed downstairs to the phone.

Char dropped her head in her hands and let the tears flow.

* * *

Two hours later, the police and ambulance had come and gone along with the local mortician. Char still sat on the bench with her father on one side, Mrs. Bennington on the other. Mrs. Bennington had called Ronald after phoning the police, anticipating that both Char and Joe would need him.

Char had watched as Tony's body was removed from the room in a plastic bag on a stretcher. Joe had walked behind and followed it all the way downstairs to the waiting hearse. Char had gone from sorrow to shock, and just sat there, making no sound, only shaking. The image of Joe bent over on the floor underneath Tony's dangling legs was imprinted on her mind. It was the worst thing she'd ever witnessed, and she was having trouble processing it.

Mrs. Bennington brought Char a blanket and Ronald wrapped it around her. Then he gently guided her off the bench and helped her down the stairs. "Let's go home, honey," he said.

"Joe," she whispered. "I have to see Joe."

"Of course, dear," Ronald said.

* * *

Joe was on the porch when Ronald, Char, and Mrs. Bennington came outside. Char immediately wrapped her arms around him and pulled him close.

"I'm so sorry," she said softly.

"I know," Joe said. "I am too."

They held each other for a long time while the others stood patiently by. Finally, when they separated, Joe turned to Mrs. B. "I'm sorry. I had no idea he would do such a thing."

"Oh, my dear boy. It's not your fault. No one knows what someone else is thinking." She hugged Joe. "I'm so sorry about your friend. I hope he finds peace now."

Ronald patted him on the back. "I want you to come home with us, son," he said. "I won't hear of you staying in that room tonight. Or ever."

Joe was tired and disorientated. He thought about going home with Char and Ronald, but the only room available was Jeremy's, and he just couldn't sleep in there. It would have felt like he was invading Jeremy's space. But Ronald was right. He couldn't sleep in his attic room either. Not tonight. Not ever.

"Mr. Parsons is right, dear," Mrs. Bennington said. "I have an open room on the second floor that you can move into immediately. I won't hear of you going back to that attic room again. I already asked Rodney to pack up your things and put them in there. He was happy to do it for you."

Joe nodded. "Thank you, Mrs. B. Ronald, I appreciate your invitation, but I think I'll stay here."

A worried look crossed Ronald's face. "Are you sure, son?"

"I'll be fine," Joe said.

Char hugged him again and Joe watched as she reluctantly let her father lead her to his car. She stared at him through the car window as they drove off, her face ghostly behind the glass. Joe wished she hadn't witnessed the awful scene. If he could do it all over again, he would have left the room and shut the door before calling out for help. But in the moment, he'd been so overwhelmed with emotion that he'd fallen to the floor in anguish over his friend's death. All sense or reasoning had vanished. All that had been left was pure emotion.

"Let's go inside, Joe," Mrs. B said. He hadn't even realized she was still standing on the porch with him. She ushered him in, steering him toward the kitchen where she made him a cup of coffee and set out a plate of cookies and brownies. Rodney joined them, his job of moving Joe's belongings to the other room complete. They all sat in silence, not touching the treats and barely sipping their coffee.

"I'm exhausted," Joe finally said.

"Of course you are," Mrs. B said. "I'll show you to your room."

It was a small room on the second floor that shared a bathroom with Rodney's room. It was nicely decorated and had a window that overlooked the backyard, but it wasn't nearly as large as his attic room. Joe thanked Mrs. B and gave her another hug before she finally seemed fine about leaving him on his own.

That night, Joe lay in bed staring at the ceiling and re-playing the day's events in his head. He'd felt something was off this morning before he'd left for the library. If only he'd waited until Mrs. B had come home from church to ask her if Tony was hanging lights for her that day. Or he should have insisted Tony come with him to the college. But then what? Would that have just postponed the inevitable one more day? Would Tony have waited until Joe was in class on Monday to do it? Or would it have given Tony more time to think about his actions and decide against it?

How could anyone know what someone else was thinking?

Every time Joe closed his eyes, he saw Tony hanging from a rope tied to the beam. He'd known instantly that Tony was dead. Joe had seen enough death in his lifetime to know when there was no hope left. He imagined Tony tossing the rope over the beam and tying it off. Where had he gotten the rope from? Mrs. B's garage? Then he pictured him pulling the desk chair over to the rope where he'd tied a noose. When he got to the part where Tony stepped off the chair and hung himself, Joe pushed those thoughts aside. It was all too horrible, but he couldn't stop thinking about it.

"You said you wanted to start over again. You told me you wanted to do things right this time. What happened?" Joe whispered into the dark room.

He doubted he'd ever understand.

By the next morning, Joe was so exhausted he didn't even try to get up and go to school. He figured the news would have traveled around town by now, and he didn't want to face anyone. Sympathetic looks and questioning stares would have been too much to bear.

Rodney stopped by his room before heading off to work. Joe thought it might be to check up on him, but Rodney had something to give him.

"I found this on your dresser when I was packing up your things," Rodney said. He handed Joe a folded piece of paper. "I guess the police didn't see it. You should probably give it to them at some point. But I think you need to see it first."

Joe saw his name on the front written in Tony's shaky handwriting.

"Why didn't you give this to me last night?" Joe asked.

"I should have. But you'd been through so much already. I thought it was better to wait a day. I hope you aren't angry with me for making that decision."

"No, I'm not angry," Joe said. "Not after everything you did for me last night. Thank you."

Rodney nodded and left.

Joe sat back on the bed and stared at the paper in his hand. It was common for people to leave suicide notes. He wondered if he even wanted to read it. Would it answer his questions? With a sigh, Joe opened the letter. It was short and to the point.

Joe - I'm sorry. You're a good friend. But I can't take it any longer. The nightmares, the anxiety, the constant shaking. I tried. I really did. Please forgive me.

Tony

Joe folded the letter and set it on the nightstand. He understood how Tony had felt. The nightmares were hellish. The anxiety of always watching your back, even when you knew you didn't have to anymore, took a toll. But was it enough to end your life? What was?

The hard reality was Joe had come home from Vietnam with an injury everyone could see. Tony's injury wasn't as easy to diagnose. Instead of a wounded limb, his mind had become wounded. Joe could still live a relatively normal life with his injury. But Tony's injury? It had been too much for him to live with.

What scared Joe was that he could have easily been like Tony. Any one of them who'd made it home could have been him. So many of the returning vets were as scarred on the inside as they were on the outside. And if it hadn't been for his good fortune of finding Char and her family, who knew how his story might have ended.

* * *

Char was sitting on the sofa trying to concentrate on reading a book for English class when she saw Joe come up the sidewalk.

It was late afternoon, and she'd stayed home from school. After what she'd witnessed the night before, she hadn't slept very well, and she knew she'd never be able to focus on schoolwork or lectures.

As she watched Joe move slowly through the gate, she realized that she'd been waiting for him, without even knowing she had been. She went to the door and opened it before he knocked, reaching out and pulling him into a tight hug. She felt safe in his arms, as if nothing could touch either of them as long as they were together.

Finally, she pulled away and peered up into his gray eyes. There was no teasing sparkle today, no shining flecks. He looked as tired as she felt, and she knew he hadn't slept any better than she had.

"Are you okay?" he asked.

"I'm fine," she said. "But, how are you?"

Joe shook his head as if he wasn't sure how to answer.

"Come in and sit," Char said, taking his arm, but again, Joe shook his head. He turned and stared at the porch swing.

"Okay." Char grabbed the heavy afghan off the sofa and they sat on the swing. She opened it up and wrapped it over their shoulders. It was cold outside, but the sun was shining and there was no wind. Char suddenly understood why Joe wanted to be outside. There were no walls to pen them in. It was wide open, and the air was crisp and clean. It felt good to breath it in, to feel alive on this sad, sad day.

She held his hand and snuggled in close. Joe kissed the top of her head, which warmed her heart.

"I'm sorry you had to see that last night," Joe said. "I was so overwhelmed, I couldn't think straight. I should have protected you."

"It's okay," Char assured him. "I shouldn't have run up the stairs. But I heard you yell and I had to find you. I was so afraid something had happened to you."

Joe sighed and held her close as she dropped her head on his shoulder. "I called his parents today. Tony had a small address book in his pack. His dad didn't sound too surprised. He actually had no emotion at all."

"That must have been terrible," Char said.

"It was. I gave him the phone number of the mortuary. He said they would have him cremated here and the ashes sent home. They're Catholic, but his dad said that since he'd killed himself, it didn't matter how they disposed of the body."

Char lifted her head. "That's awful! Didn't he care that his son was dead?"

"He told me that the last time they saw Tony, he'd been staying with them a few weeks. He was nervous and shaky and couldn't keep a job. One day, Tony flipped out and nearly strangled his younger brother. They told him to leave and not come back until he'd gotten the help he needed."

"God! Poor Tony." Tears filled Char's eyes. How sad to have your own parents give up on you. She wondered about Jeremy. What if he had come home injured or depressed? How would that have affected her family? Would it have ever come to throwing him out? It broke her heart just thinking about it.

"His dad said he didn't want any of Tony's belongings, either. Just to toss them," Joe said. "He only had a duffle bag of belongings, so there can't be much in there. But still, not to want your son's things. It's just terrible."

Char wiped her tears and kissed Joe's cheek. He hadn't shaved and his beard was scratchy. "I'm so sorry, Joe. It's all so heartbreaking."

Joe turned to her, his eyes bloodshot. "I shouldn't be telling you all this. But I have no one else to share it with. No one else who knew Tony and would understand."

Char stroked his cheek with her hand. "I want you to share everything with me. I never want you to hold in anything, no matter how terrible."

They sat there, bundled up on the swing until the sun went down and the night air grew brisk. Ronald came home from the store and patted Joe on the shoulder before going inside. He seemed to understand that the two young people needed privacy.

Char finally asked the question that had been plaguing her thoughts. "You wouldn't ever do what Tony did, would you, Joe? Please tell me you would never let things get so bad that you'd do that."

Joe slowly shook his head. "I've never thought about it before. I always look forward, not back. But who knows what a man will do when he can't handle his demons any longer? We never know for sure what any of us are capable of when pushed too far."

It broke her heart to hear the sadness and uncertainty in Joe's voice, but she didn't press him. She had to trust that she knew Joe well enough to believe he'd never harm himself. They sat there in silence, holding each other, staring up into the night sky, both lost in their own thoughts, until Ellen finally called them in out of the cold to warm up and eat dinner.

* * *

Joe and Char went back to school the next day. They had two weeks left before the semester ended and Christmas vacation began, so neither was able to miss the last days of classes.

Joe was nervous at first, but by the middle of the first day, he relaxed. A few of his classmates expressed their condolences, and some kids on campus stared at him, but that was all. When he and Char went to the union for lunch, Patty and Jenny joined them and told him how sorry they were about Tony. Neither asked questions, much to Joe's relief. If Char had shared any information, they never said. Soon, the talk went back to classes and Christmas break. Joe was thankful for the return to normal. That was what he needed.

By the middle of the week, Joe finally made himself go through Tony's personal belongings. Most of what Tony had brought were clothes, so Joe folded those up and put them in a bag Mrs. B had given him to donate to Goodwill. Wrapped inside a sweatshirt, Joe was surprised to find a small-sized Colt revolver and a box of shells. Tony had made no mention of carrying a gun. But then, it wouldn't be unusual for an ex-soldier to have one. Joe decided to keep it, so he made sure it wasn't loaded then hid it under his socks in his nightstand drawer.

He checked all the pockets of the duffle bag and just when he thought it was empty, he found a small black box with a rubber band secured around it. Joe pulled off the rubber band and opened the lid. Inside, he found Tony's dog tags on top of a pile of pictures. He carefully pulled out the dog tags and laid them on the bed. Lifting out the photos, he thumbed through them, thinking he'd see a few familiar faces from Nam. But these photos weren't from the tour Tony had spent at the firebase. They were from his first tour as a tunnel rat, cleaning out the Viet Cong tunnels.

Joe had heard of Vietnam veterans bringing home mementoes or trophies from the war, and many who kept photos, but he'd never seen any before. These photos didn't show soldiers as they worked, or friends lined up smiling. They showed the horrors of war. One pictured a group of dead Viet Cong guer-rilla fighters piled on the ground with a U.S. soldier standing on top of them holding his M-16, like a hunter would pose with his kill. The others were even more horrifying. Joe's stomach turned. He quickly stuffed them back in the box along with the dog tags and wrapped it tightly with the rubber band.

What was he going to do with these?

Joe had killed men in Vietnam. But he'd never found any joy in it, or a sense of accomplishment. And most of the men Joe had fought beside hadn't boasted about killing the enemy either. Joe hadn't taken photos or brought home any mementoes. He was more than willing to let those memories go if only they'd let him go. But others, like Tony, held on to them.

After seeing the photos, Joe better understood what had snapped Tony's nerves and haunted him in the middle of the night. Tony had talked often of his tunnel rat excursions on hot, humid days as they sat around the firebase waiting for action. Joe couldn't even imagine having enough nerve to drop head-first into a tunnel no wider than a small man and hope you didn't set off a deadly booby-trap or come face-to-face with the enemy. But Tony and his crew had done that day in and day out. If they were lucky, they'd find maps and papers and other intelligence that would give them more insight into what the enemy was doing. They might find medical supplies and ammo. Often, they'd captured and killed the enemy, dragging them out from the tunnels. The toll it took on the soldiers was enormous. They learned how to survive the hard way, and sometimes a man crossed the line of humanity to stay alive. Joe felt lucky that he'd never had to face that line, but he knew now that for Tony, it had been a day-to-day decision. A struggle that had left him broken in the end.

Joe stared at the little box wondering what to do with it. He couldn't send it to Tony's parents. He didn't want to keep it, either. Yet, he didn't feel he had a right to destroy another soldier's property. Unsure, he finally stuck it in the drawer where he'd put the pistol until he decided what to do with it.

Chapter Twenty

A week passed as Joe tried to return to his normal routine. The problem was, nothing felt normal. Tony's death had rattled him. Before Tony had arrived, Joe had been able to push down memories of Nam and focus on school, work, and Char. Despite his injured leg and the nightmares that occasionally plagued him, he'd felt he was successfully moving forward. But since Tony's death, his thoughts kept returning to his time spent in the war. As he lay in bed at night, he found himself re-thinking every battle, every shot fired. He rehashed everything from the day he landed in Vietnam to the day he left. Even when he tried to block out the memories, he couldn't. They flowed through his mind like a faucet he couldn't turn off.

Joe would wake in the middle of the night, sweating, panting, and feeling trapped. His nightmares were strong and vivid, and he'd be exhausted the next day. He wondered if that was how Tony had felt. And he feared that whatever had driven Tony to suicide could also happen to him. That thought made his blood run cold.

The stress of the last week of the semester and finals didn't help. Joe hoped, no, prayed, that after this tense week was over, his state of mind would calm down.

Wednesday night, Joe met Char at the union after he'd studied in the library all evening. She'd been preoccupied with school and finals too, so he thought his anxiety had gone unnoticed by her. As they sat there, sharing a basket of fries and drinking Cokes, he couldn't help but think how lucky he was. No matter how much the past infringed on his thoughts, he still had so much to look forward to. That alone, he hoped, would keep him out of the dark place that had trapped Tony.

Joe noticed Deke sitting across the room with a few students, most likely preaching his anti-war agenda. To his surprise, Deke stood and walked directly to their table. He stretched out his hand in a gesture to shake with Joe.

"I'm sorry about the loss of your friend," Deke said solemnly. "It must have been a terrible shock to lose him that way, and I just wanted you to know how sorry I am about it."

"Thank you," Joe said, stunned by Deke's declaration. He glanced at Char, whose eyes were wide with surprise.

"That's very nice of you, Deke," Char said.

Deke smiled. "Mind if I sit down?" He was already pulling out a chair and moving to sit in it.

Joe didn't think they had much choice in the matter.

Deke folded his arms and leaned on the table. "I'm just going to come out and say what's on my mind. Joe, I'd really like for you to join me in my fight against the war."

Joe couldn't have been more stunned if Deke had slapped his face.

"What?"

"I know I've been nothing but an ass to you since you've come here, and I deeply apologize for that. But I also know that if anyone should be against this awful war, it should be the men who have actually fought in it. More and more veterans are joining the anti-war cause. The Vietnam Veterans Against the War are a strong voice in the movement. You could be a part of that. You could help us end this terrible war by speaking out about it."

Joe had read in the papers about the VVAW and their anti-war work. He'd been impressed by them. But his loyalty lay with his fellow soldiers still fighting in Vietnam. He wanted the war to end, but not by dishonoring those still at war.

"I don't think I'm your man, Deke," Joe said. "I still have friends fighting that war, and I have to respect what they're doing."

Deke clearly wasn't going to give in so easily. He leaned in closer. "Think about it, Joe. Please. I've heard you're good with words. You could speak out on why the war should end. You've seen it first-hand. You know what goes on over there. And you also understand how it feels to come home after serving and try to cope with civilian life again. That's powerful. You could bring so many more people into our college's anti-war movement."

Joe shook his head, but Deke continued. "Don't you want to bring the soldiers you know home? Think about what happened to you there. Think about what happened to Tony. How many more U.S. soldiers' lives do we have to lose to get people to understand it has to end now?"

Joe knew that Deke was an accomplished speaker who could persuade audiences to see things his way, but he had no power over him. "I'm sorry, Deke. I appreciate what you're saying, but it isn't something I can do. I'd feel like I was betraying my fellow soldiers. Like I was spitting on the graves of the men I watched die. My allegiance lies with them."

Deke sat back against the chair and sighed. "At least think

about it, okay? It's important. Probably the most important thing you'll ever do."

"Is it?" Joe asked, eyeing Deke. "Or is it only important I join you so you can build your group's numbers? Is this really about the soldiers or is it more about you?"

"It's for everyone, Joe," Deke said, seemingly undisturbed by Joe questioning his motives. "It's for everyone's younger brother who may find himself on a plane to Vietnam on his eighteenth birthday. It's for the mothers who cry for their dead sons, and the fathers who've worked their entire lives to give their kids a better life, only to lose their sons to war. It's for men like Jeremy. It's for men like Tony. You can think that it's for my own selfish, egotistical needs, but that's not true. It's for all of us affected by this horrible war that we simply can't win."

Joe sat silent. He'd reached for Char's hand and squeezed it at the mention of Jeremy's name. Glancing over at her, he saw her head was bent, and she was staring at her lap. Joe didn't like the way Deke used a person's friends or loved ones against them to get his way.

"At least think about it, okay?" Deke said again. He stood, nodded to them, and left.

"Are you okay?" Joe whispered to Char.

She raised her eyes to his. "He has some solid points."

Joe squeezed her hand again. "I agree. But I have to stick to my own principles, too."

"I understand that."

"Let's head home," Joe said. He was tired and stressed, and just wanted this week to be over with.

* * *

Later, after Char had dropped Joe off at the boarding house, she lay in her bed thinking about everything Deke had said. For over a year while she was dating him, she'd heard all the reasons why he believed in the anti-war movement. Still, she'd hesitated in joining him. She knew how it felt to lose someone you loved in Vietnam. But she hadn't entirely understood the war, or the people who were fighting it.

Char pondered everything Deke had said throughout their time together. Insisting it was an illegal war. Calling our soldiers murders and baby killers. True, there had been incidents of horrendous acts committed, but she believed that most U.S. soldiers were innocent of such crimes. She'd shied away from Deke's view of the war because she didn't entirely believe all of his rhetoric.

Yet, she didn't support the war either. She saw no solid reason why the U.S. should be fighting so far from home. Her history teacher had discussed the war with the class, and her social studies teacher had done so as well. But no one could give good reasons for our boys to be dying in Vietnam.

Char's thoughts returned to the night she saw Tony's legs dangling in mid-air while Joe crouched on the floor beneath him. It was a nightmarish scene she couldn't make disappear. His suicide made it impossible for Char to ignore the horrors of the war any longer. Losing Jeremy had been tough, but seeing the effects of Vietnam first-hand was sobering. She decided it was time she joined in on the fight against the war.

* * *

On Friday night, Char, Joe, and their friends celebrated the end of finals, and the semester, by having dinner at the café then going to the nine o'clock showing of *Love Story* at the indoor theater. After the movie, the boys rolled their eyes while the girls brushed away tears.

"That was a downer," Craig said, and Terry agreed.

Patty slapped Craig's arm. "It was beautiful. I saw you wiping away tears during the movie."

"Me?" Craig said dramatically, then laughed.

Joe chuckled along with the group then they all went their separate ways. Joe and Char took their time walking to her car that was still parked near the café. Fresh snow had fallen earlier that day and the town square sparkled under the streetlights. Joe offered Char his arm and she linked hers through it as they walked.

"I'm happy to see you a little more relaxed," Char said. "I could tell you were stressed these past couple of weeks."

"Yeah, it's been rough, after what happened with Tony and then finals. It was hard for me to focus on school."

"I know," Char said. "I keep re-playing the night Tony died in my mind. I was so scared something had happened to you. It was an awful scene, one I'll never forget."

They stopped at a bench that sat underneath a pool of light from the streetlamp. Joe brushed away the snow with his gloved hand before sitting down. "I'm so sorry you saw that. I wish I could change that night. It's haunted me too. There's so much I wish I could have changed. Maybe Tony would be here today if I'd done more."

She reached for his hand and squeezed it. "It's not your fault, Joe. You couldn't have changed anything. It happened. And maybe I was meant to see it. It's opened my eyes and made me realize that until we all get involved, this war won't end." She looked up into his eyes. "I'm thinking about joining Deke's fight against the war."

Joe's brows rose. "You weren't involved when you were with him. Did Tony's suicide change your mind?"

Char nodded. "That, and also Jeremy's death. I don't believe that soldiers are terrible like Deke does, and I'm not a supporter of violent protesting. But I want to become involved in the peaceful protests. I need to feel that I'm trying to help end this horrific war."

Joe sat back against the bench. It didn't surprise him that Char would want to protest the war. She had a kind heart and would want to help end the suffering. But he wasn't happy about her joining forces with Deke. "Have you told him yet?"

"No. He left today to meet with his friends in the movement in Chicago. I'll talk to him about what I can do when he gets home."

Joe sat silent, gazing at the fresh, untouched snow. He liked how perfect it looked. No footprints, no spots melting into watery puddles. He wished more things in life were this beautiful, left unmarred by man.

"Say something, Joe. Tell me what you think of my joining the movement with Deke."

He turned to her. "I think you're a smart, strong, woman," he said. "You should do what feels right for you, just as I did what I thought was right by going to war. I'll support you no matter what you choose to do."

"Thank you." Char leaned into him, dropping a kiss on his lips. "I love you so much."

He pulled her close. "I love you, too, sweetie."

After a time, they reluctantly rose from the bench and walked back to her car. Joe wished he could spend more time with Char, but it was already midnight and they both had to work in the morning. He kissed her goodnight on her porch, refusing her offer to drive him home. He wanted to walk the short distance and clear his head of the past two weeks. It wasn't easy, but he had to let it go. He wanted to be happy again. Happy with his life, happy with Char. He'd survived the war and been given a second chance at a good life. He refused to lose what he'd worked so hard for.

Chapter Twenty-One

Joe spent Christmas with Char and her family. He attended church with them on Christmas Eve and enjoyed the candle-lit service and singing hymns like he'd done as a child when one of his aunts would bring him to Mass. On Christmas Day, they sat around the tree drinking eggnog and opening presents while holiday music played on the stereo. Joe hadn't expected gifts from Ronald and Ellen, but they surprised him with practical things they knew he needed. Two pairs of Levi jeans, a bag of white undershirts, and new socks. Char laughed at the socks, but Joe was ecstatic over them.

"Sorry," Ellen had said, laughing also. "The mom in me is very practical."

"Mine are so old I'll feel like a new person with bright white socks," Joe said, thanking them for being so thoughtful.

Ronald also gave him a pocketknife that Joe had been eyeing at the store. "I knew you'd never buy it for yourself," he told Joe after it was opened.

Joe loved it and thanked Ronald profusely.

Char had bought Joe a soft denim shirt and a leather wallet.

"I noticed your wallet was falling apart," she told him, suddenly looking shy over the gifts.

"I definitely needed one," he said. Then he gave her his gift. "I hope you like it."

Char opened the small box and her eyes grew wide with delight. "I love it!" She pulled out the silver bracelet with star charms all around it. Slipping it on, she fingered the biggest star in the center as she beamed at Joe. "It's perfect."

Joe was relieved that Char liked it. He had wished he could afford to buy her a gold bracelet instead, but he had to settle for the silver one. Someday he hoped to be able to buy her nice gifts. But for now, he was pleased to see her wear the bracelet.

That night as Joe was leaving, Char walked outside with him to have a few minutes alone. They both craved more time alone together, but it was impossible to find it.

"I love my bracelet," Char said, reaching up to kiss Joe.

"I love my gifts, too," he said. "I feel bad I didn't bring anything for your parents. They were so generous."

"They adore you and wanted to give you gifts. Don't feel bad."

He ran his fingers through her hair, enjoying the soft feel of it as Char snuggled up closer to him. Her hair smelled of strawberry shampoo and he longed for summer days and sunshine and the sounds of crickets and toads humming in the night. Joe sighed. "I should go. But I don't want to. I feel trapped in that small room at the boarding house. I know I could never sleep in the attic room again, but I miss the large, open space."

"Maybe you could find another place," Char suggested.

Joe shrugged. "I doubt I can afford another place. I'll have to make due for now." He kissed her one last time and left. As he reached the corner, he turned and there was Char, still standing in her front yard, staring up at the night sky. He smiled, thanking the very same stars she gazed at that he had her in his life.

* * *

On New Year's Eve, Char, Joe, and their friends all went to the town square where the annual party was held. Lights decorated the trees and gazebo. A string ensemble played soft music in the gazebo while the townspeople milled about buying hot dogs, hamburgers, french fries, and other types of food from venders who had set up around the lawn. The night was brisk, but the sky was clear and everyone was bundled up to ward off the frigid air. Joe bought Char a bag of hot caramel corn and they shared it as they snuggled close on a park bench.

Joe yawned and Char teased him. "Bored of me already?"

He laughed. "No. I'm not sure I'll make it until midnight to see the fireworks. I haven't been sleeping very well."

Char became concerned. "Is there something wrong?"

"No, nothing like that. I think it's that small room. It feels claustrophobic. I spent so many nights in Nam under the stars that I'm not used to small spaces. That's why I liked the attic room so much."

"Is that all?" Char asked, knowing that Joe didn't always reveal his feelings too easily.

"Nothing that important to worry about," he said.

She studied him carefully. "You promised you'd tell me if anything was wrong."

Joe sighed. "You know me too well," he teased. "My nightmares have been getting worse. It's every night, not occasionally like they had been. But I'm sure they'll calm down. Once school starts again, I'll be too busy to think about the past."

"Maybe if you talk about your nightmares, it will help," Char said. "I'd be happy to listen."

Joe shook his head. "I appreciate it, hon, but they aren't something I'd want to share, with anyone."

"Are they that bad? Too terrible to talk about?" Char asked.

"Yes." He bent down and kissed her lips. "Don't worry about me. I'll be fine."

Char couldn't help but worry. She was so afraid that Joe would let his memories and nightmares get the best of him. She wished he'd let her help.

Patty ran over with Craig in tow. "It's five minutes to midnight!" she exclaimed. "Everyone is dancing. Come on!"

Char couldn't help but laugh at her friend's excitement. Patty seemed so happy with Craig. Her reluctant dance date had become her permanent boyfriend, and they seemed to enjoy each other's company. The same was true of Jenny and Terry. Jenny hadn't been looking to find a boyfriend, and unexpectedly did. In only a few short months, all three girls' lives had changed. And they all were happy with their choices.

"Shall we dance?" Joe stood and offered his hand. Char smiled and accepted, following him to the space near the gazebo. Joe wrapped his arms around her and they moved slowly to the music. It felt so good to be in his arms. She felt safe. Happy and safe.

Everyone stopped dancing right before midnight and counted down the last twenty seconds. As the town clock struck midnight, the band began to play "Auld Lang Syne," and the couples danced and kissed and blew horns.

Joe bent down and kissed Char deeply. "Happy New Year," he said after they'd parted.

"Happy 1971," she said, hardly able to believe that the year had gone by so quickly and she'd been lucky enough to find Joe.

Fireworks shot off in the sky in multicolored sunbursts of red, blue, green, pink, and gold. Joe held Char close as they watched them. Char glanced around her and saw her friends each snuggled up with their boyfriends. Her parents, not too far away, were also standing close together. On the lawn were people she'd gone to school with, the couple who owned the bakery, and the woman who owned Elaine's Dress Shop standing with her grown daughter and her grandchildren. Everyone was happy and carefree, enjoying the colors in the sky, forgetting about their troubles or the problems of the world. She knew that some people hated staying in the same small town in which they'd grown up in, but she found it heartwarming. It was comforting knowing everyone's name and feeling safe among friends and family.

"Is everything okay?" Joe asked in her ear.

She leaned closer to him. "Everything is perfect." And she hoped it would stay that way.

* * *

That Saturday, Joe was back at work. The holidays were over and school would start on Monday. He looked forward to starting classes again. It kept his mind busy and he could spend a lot of time in the library and not in his small bedroom.

Char was in the back room working on the bookkeeping while Ronald helped out front. Ronald told Joe that January wasn't very busy but at the first sign of spring, everyone would start thinking of sprucing up their homes or working in their gardens. Until then, people would be tight with their money to make up for holiday spending.

Joe and Ronald moved merchandise around and cleaned. Some extra stock had come in earlier in the week, so they put that out then tried to make space for the leftover in the back room.

"Here. Let's take these old file boxes upstairs and that'll make room for the merchandise down here," Ronald said.

They each carried a box and Ronald opened the downstairs door. At the top of the stairs was another door as well. They stepped into a small entryway which connected to a living room that faced the front of the building. The drapes were pulled shut, so Ronald turned on the lights. To their right was a hallway that led to two bedrooms and a bathroom at the back of the building. Ronald led the way to the smaller of the two bedrooms where boxes were stored.

"This is a big apartment," Joe said, glancing around.

"It is. Did Char tell you we lived up here until after Jeremy was born? It saved us a lot of money. Here, I'll show you around." Ronald took him across the hall to the master bedroom, which was quite large and had big windows that faced the back and side of the building.

"I like all the light in here," Joe said.

"This is a good room," Ronald agreed. He showed Joe the bathroom, then took him out through the living room to the kitchen. An L-shaped counter separated the kitchen and living room. It was a large, open space, which Joe liked.

"Wow, this is nice." Joe thought about his small bedroom at the boarding house and couldn't even compare it to this. He wished he could afford a place even half this size where he'd have room to breathe.

"Char told me you feel claustrophobic in the small bedroom you're in now," Ronald said, as if reading his thoughts. "She said the attic had been roomier for you."

Joe nodded. "Yes. It's pretty small. I don't have much choice, though. And Mrs. B has been so nice about what happened. I doubt she'll ever rent the attic again."

"It was tragic," Ronald agreed.

They both fell silent a moment as they looked around them. There was a layer of dust, but the carpet and walls were clean, even if the colors were a bit dated. There was no furniture, but the old appliances were still in the kitchen.

"Joe. It seems wasteful for this apartment to sit empty. Would you be interested in living up here?" Ronald asked.

Joe's eyes widened. "That's very kind of you to offer, but you could get a good amount for rent on this place. And I could never afford it."

"Well, that's the thing," Ronald said. "I'd never rent this to just anyone because the only entryway is through the store, and I wouldn't trust giving anyone else a key. There is a fire escape ladder, but I doubt if a renter would want to climb that." He chuckled. "I'd trust you, Joe. And think how easy it would be for you to get to work."

"I'd really like to live here, Ronald, but I'm sure I could never afford the rent."

"It's just sitting here empty, and that's a shame. How about this?" Ronald asked. "Everything up here is electric, and it's on its own meter. If you'd pay your own lights and heating bill, you can stay up here, rent free, for as long as you work in the store."

Joe couldn't believe what he was hearing. "But you won't make any money from that."

Ronald placed his hand on Joe's shoulder. "Money isn't everything, son, as I know you are well-aware. It would be the perfect space for you. I'd be happy if you'd take me up on my offer."

"You've done so much for me already. I don't want to take advantage of your kindness," Joe said, overwhelmed by all that Ronald had already done for him.

"I offered, so you aren't taking advantage. And it's not charity, either. You'll be paying your way. You're a good person, and a hard worker. Let me do this for you, Joe."

Joe glanced around the room once more. It would be nice to have all this space to spread out in. And, as much as he appreciated Mrs. B, it would be nice to have privacy. He turned to Ronald. "I'd like to live here. Thank you so much."

Ronald smiled. He put out his hand to shake, but Joe couldn't just shake his hand after all he'd done for him. He reached out and hugged the older man, fighting to hold back tears.

"You've been more like a father to me in these past few months than my own father was my entire life," Joe said, pulling away. "I don't know how I got so lucky, but I appreciate all of it."

Ronald slapped him on the back. "You're very welcome, Joe. Everyone deserves a break every now and then." He scanned the room. "It looks like we'll have to scrounge up some furniture for you. We might have some in the attic, and I'm sure Ellen would gladly let you have some of our older furniture so she can buy new stuff for the house." He laughed. "And I'd bet Mrs. Bennington would be willing to let you borrow a few pieces she has. We'll get you set up in here quite nicely."

"I don't need much," Joe said. "A bed, some sheets, and towels. Maybe a barstool for the counter over there so I can use it as a desk."

"Oh, don't you worry, Joe. The minute the women hear you need things to set up house, you'll be swamped with stuff. Come on. Let's go tell Char. She'll be thrilled for you."

Joe took one last look around him. His own place. A home. He smiled, then followed Ronald downstairs.

* * *

Char was thrilled for Joe when she heard the news. She hoped living in a larger space would help calm his nightmares so he could sleep easier.

It didn't take long for her and Ellen to round up household items for Joe either. At church the next day, they spread the word that gently used kitchen, home necessities, and furniture would be appreciated. Several women immediately handed them lists of items they wanted to give away. Ellen was all too happy to offer up the old dinette set from their kitchen so she could buy a new one. And when Joe had told Mrs. B he'd be moving into the apartment, she'd quickly offered for him to use the bed, sofa, and any other furniture from the attic.

"It's going to waste up there anyway," she'd told Joe, which he'd reported to Char at lunch at the Parsons' home that day.

"Everyone is being so kind," he said. "I can't believe how lucky I am."

Char offered to help him clean the kitchen and vacuum the carpets and drapes. They worked all Sunday afternoon, then went out for pizza at the union, which had opened its doors early for the students returning to the dorms. Patty, Craig, Jenny, and Terry were also there and Char told them Joe's good news.

"A bachelor pad, huh?" Craig said. "Aren't you the lucky guy?"

"Hey. Who says he's a bachelor?" Char piped up, making everyone laugh.

Craig and Terry offered to help Joe move furniture the next Saturday if he supplied a six-pack of beer. He readily agreed. Terry's father had a pick-up truck he could borrow so they could move the larger items.

Everyone except Patty was excited for school to start the next day. "You're all crazy," she said. "Who wants to sit in classes and study? That's no fun at all."

"I'm glad to start school," Craig said. "This is my last semester of college—forever! That makes me happy."

Patty pouted. "Yeah, and then the army will get you."

Craig slipped his arm around her. "I was able to finish college on a deferment, so I'll hopefully go in as an officer. Not everyone gets sent to Vietnam. Maybe I'll be one of the lucky ones."

Terry held up his Coke glass. "Here's to being lucky," he said.

They all clinked their glasses together. "To being lucky."

Afterward, Joe drove Char home in her car and they parked in front of her house.

"You're awfully quiet," she said, placing her hand on his leg.

Joe gave her a half-smile. "I have a lot on my mind. School. The move. I'm looking forward to living in that apartment."

"It'll be a good change for you. You can get your life moving forward again."

"I don't know what I'd do without you and your amazing parents. I knew coming here would be a positive change for my life, but I could never have dreamt it would turn out this good." Joe pulled Char close and kissed her. "You're the best thing that's ever happened to me."

Char's heart filled with love at his touch. Joe was everything she'd dreamt of in a man. He was kind, thoughtful, and intelligent. He'd seen things in Vietnam that she'd never understand, yet he wasn't at all bitter or angry. She was thankful their lives had crossed paths, even if it wasn't completely by accident. Despite everything that was going on in the world around them, they had found each other, and she hoped that nothing would ever change the way she felt at this very moment.

Chapter Twenty-Two

The first week of school went by quickly. Char and Joe still had freshman English together, but no other classes. Char was excited when she heard from the school newspaper. Many of the seniors were taking their last semester off from the paper, so there was an opening for her if she still wanted it. Char readily accepted and was given the "About Town" section. She didn't mind being given the least-liked section of the newspaper. It was a start, and who knew more about the town than she did?

On Saturday, Char worked at the front of the store for Joe while he, Terry, and Craig moved furniture up to the apartment. Ellen dropped by with a carload of items donated by the women from the church, and organized Joe's kitchen and bathroom. She'd bought him a set of new sheets and a blanket, and made up the bed as soon as the men moved it up there. One of the women had given Joe a handmade quilt made from soft pieces of blue and white cotton fabric. It had been a wonderful gift, and Joe told Ellen he'd like to thank all the women personally for what they'd given him as soon as he had a chance.

By the time five o'clock rolled around, all the furniture had been moved, even the dinette set from the Parsons' house. Char closed the shop and ran upstairs to see how it looked. Even though the furniture was used, it all looked nice and fit the space well. Mrs. B had also sent along an old desk that Joe could use. But Ronald had the final touch that he carried upstairs while Char and Joe were admiring the space.

"I figured you could use one of these," Ronald said, carrying a thirteen-inch black-and-white television into the room.

Joe's mouth dropped open. "You didn't have to do that. You've given me so much already."

"It was just sitting in Jeremy's room, collecting dust," Ronald said. "Ellen told me to bring it. It should be used and enjoyed." He set it on a little table in the living room and plugged it in. After pulling up the metal antennas, the picture came in clear. "There. It works just fine."

"Thank you, Ronald," Joe said, clearly overwhelmed by his generosity.

Ronald smiled. "We're happy to do it. Now, enjoy your new space. And don't be a stranger. Ellen said that just because you have a kitchen, it doesn't mean you can't drop by for dinner anymore."

Ronald left after Joe had thanked him one last time, then Joe and Char were finally alone.

"Wow. Do you hear that?" Char asked.

"What?" Joe looked around, confused.

"It's quiet. We're actually alone." She grinned at him.

"We've never been alone, except in the car." Joe smiled mischievously as he drew Char to him and kissed her. Soon, their kiss deepened until Char had to pull away.

"I wouldn't mind continuing this, but I'm starved," she said, feeling a bit awkward at being only steps away from Joe's bedroom. She'd never had to worry about that before. She'd told

Joe at the beginning that she'd like to move slowly, and he'd agreed. Now, it might be hard to resist, knowing they could be completely alone any time they wanted.

Joe laughed. "I can read what you're thinking just by the look on your face. You don't have to worry, though. I wouldn't even think of re-paying your parent's kindness by taking advantage of their daughter."

Char frowned. "Ever? Or just tonight?"

"I don't think I can promise to keep my hands off you forever." He waggled his brows at her.

She laughed. "Whew. I was afraid I'd have to eventually attack you. Let's go grab a burger at the union to celebrate your new place. My treat!"

"I'm a progressive man. I'll let you pay," he teased. He glanced into the kitchen. "It'll be nice to have a place to cook now. I can pick up groceries on Monday and make my own breakfast and dinner. That will save some money."

Char went into the kitchen and opened the refrigerator. She crooked her finger at him to come over and look inside.

"Where did all that come from?" Joe asked, surprised. There was a quart of milk, a dozen eggs, bread, butter, jelly, and apples in the fridge.

"I'm sure my mother was afraid you'd starve to death before the store opened on Monday," Char said.

Joe turned to the cookie jar that sat on the counter. "Do you think she filled this too?" He opened it and found it filled with chocolate-chip cookies.

"Yep. She's officially spoiled you," Char said, grinning.

They drove to the student union and ordered dinner. Joe had a beer to celebrate and Char clinked his glass with her Coke. The place was brimming with students and the juke-box played all the latest hits. The Beatles, Bread, Three Dog Night, and The Guess Who drifted through the room. As they were eating their food, Deke walked over and joined them at their table.

"Hey," he said, making himself comfortable in a chair.

"Hi, Deke," Char said. She noticed that his blond hair was even longer and he had the beginnings of a full beard. But despite his shagginess, he still looked handsome and confident. Looking at him, she realized she had no feelings whatsoever for him, be it nostalgic or romantic. They would always be connected by their mutual love for Jeremy, but not in any other way.

"Have you thought any more about joining forces with me?" Deke asked Joe.

Joe shook his head. "Sorry, Deke. I already told you I can't."

"Such a shame," Deke said. "There are a couple of other vets on campus who said they'd speak out. Your voice would be a much-needed addition to the cause. I wish you'd reconsider."

"I can't speak out against the same war my fellow soldiers are fighting in at this very minute," Joe said. "It's sad enough that the people of this country are turning their backs on returning vets. I can't turn my back on them too."

"I can respect that," Deke said. "I just got back from visiting my friends up in Chicago and there are big plans for this year. They want each smaller college to work on building their list of activists. I'm going to need as much help as I can get to bring students to the cause."

"I'm willing to help," Char spoke up.

Deke stared at her. "Really?"

"Yeah. Don't look so shocked. I know it took me a while to decide, but now I'm ready to speak out against this war. But in a peaceful way. I won't be a part of any violence."

A big grin spread across Deke's face. "Well, what do you

know? I'm impressed, Char." He held out his hand. "Welcome to the cause, sister comrade."

Char shook it. "Thank you. I'm also on the school newspaper now, and I asked if I could write articles about the anti-war movement. They said as long as it's connected to the school, I can submit it. So, maybe we can get the word out that way, too."

"That's great. Wonderful! This is turning out to be a good night after all," Deke said. "I'll let you know what my plans are as soon as I get things put together. I want to have rallies with speakers at least every other Friday throughout the spring. I'll call you as soon as I know more so you can help organize them."

Char agreed and soon Deke left. Joe was quiet as they finished eating.

"Are you mad at me?" Char asked.

"No, of course not. I'm just a little worried about you joining forces with Deke. Remember, you weren't too happy with his ideas of protesting. You hated his talk of revolution and bombings to fight against the war. It bothers me to think of you involved with that kind of stuff."

"You heard me tell him I was only interested in helping with peaceful protests. He agreed. Besides, I won't be blowing up buildings. All I'll be doing is helping him organize rallies and maybe asking people to join," Char said.

Joe leaned in closer to her, gently caressing the side of her face with his hand. "Deke used to be in love with you. What if he still is? Maybe I'm afraid of that more than anything else."

Char placed her hand over his. "*I'm* not still in love with Deke, and that's all that matters. I'm in love with you."

"You promise?" Joe asked.

"I promise." Char gazed into Joe's eyes as The Carpenters sang "Close to You" over the speakers. She kissed him, then pulled back and gave him a devilish grin.

"Uh oh. What's that look for?" Joe asked.

"We'd better get you back to your place so you can get some sleep. You have an early day tomorrow."

"Early day? It's Sunday. I can sleep as long as I want."

Char shook her head. "Not if you're going to church with us tomorrow. Remember? You wanted to thank all the women yourself for giving you things for the apartment."

"Oh, yeah, that's right," Joe said. "Do I get a free lunch after that?"

Char chuckled. "I'm sure you could twist my mother's arm."

"Then off to church I go."

* * *

The next two weeks flew by for Char. Between school work, the newspaper, and helping Deke set up rallies, she barely had a minute to herself. Her classes weren't too difficult, but they were time-consuming because several included extensive reading and studying for tests. Then there was her English class, which she was writing a thesis paper for. She'd chosen the topic, "How America Became Involved in the Vietnam War," and she was spending large amounts of time in the library doing research. Luckily, Joe still preferred studying there, too, so they spent time there together, doing their work. At least they were together.

Joe wouldn't tell Char what his thesis paper was about, which annoyed her. It was so secret that he wouldn't work on his research while she was around him. But she let him have his secret—she'd find out soon enough at the end of the semester.

Char was surprised at how much harder working on a college newspaper was than it had been for her high school paper. Even though the college paper only printed once a week, she had to re-submit articles several times before anything was accepted. At first, it bruised her ego, until she was told by the other writers that it happened to every new writer there. They said she'd eventually learn exactly what the editor would accept.

"And then a new editor will come along and it'll start all over again," Marie, a junior on the paper, said.

Char didn't take her rejections personally after that. She spent a large chunk of her time coming up with ideas and re-writing them until she fell asleep at her home desk late at night.

Although it was still cold outside, Deke planned the first anti-war rally on the last Friday in January on the campus lawn just outside the ROTC building. It was a large, open area lined with old oak trees. A low brick wall ran along one side of the lawn and worked perfectly as a place to set speakers on. Deke acquired the proper permission from the college to hold the rally. An ex-Vietnam soldier, who Deke's friends in Chicago had suggested, was scheduled to speak about his experiences in the war. Deke and Char created posters and placed them all over the college, hoping that a large number of students would attend.

Working alongside Deke felt strange to Char at first. Being friends with someone who she'd been intimate with was new to her. She put all her energy to the task at hand and hoped the awkwardness would go away over time.

Once the word was out about the rally, the ROTC students tried to block it from being held in front of their building. When the school wouldn't cancel it, there was talk that the ROTC students would be there, protesting. Deke's eyes grew bright with excitement when he heard about it.

"This is going to be so much better than I could have ever

anticipated," he told Char the night before the event.

She'd been sitting in the union waiting for Joe to join her when Deke had sat down next to her. "More people than ever are interested now that they've heard about the ROTC students protesting. Imagine that? It's amazing!"

Char wasn't sure it was so amazing. "I hope you aren't planning on causing trouble during the rally. I don't want anything to do with violence. I told you that at the onset."

"I'm not the one causing the uproar," he said, giving his best innocent look. "All I did was organize a speech by a Vietnam veteran. Can I help it that the ROTC is having a fit about it?"

Char wasn't convinced by his innocent act. "You're eating this up and you know it. Promise me, Deke, that you won't go crazy once it starts. If you do, I'm out of there."

"I'm not planning anything radical, I promise. All I need you to do is walk around and ask students to sign the petition against the war. It will give us an idea how many people we might be able to depend on to march in a protest if we have one."

Char hoped all went peacefully the following night. She'd talked Joe into attending and he'd been interested in hearing what a fellow soldier had to say. But if the rally went crazy, she knew Joe wouldn't stay. She didn't want to disappoint him either.

When Joe showed up at the table, Deke left. "What was that all about? Was he bragging about the trouble he's causing tomorrow night?"

Char frowned. "Hey, I'm a part of that too, remember? And it isn't Deke's fault that the ROTC students got upset about the choice of venue."

Joe snorted. "Right. As if Deke hadn't selected that spot just to piss them off."

"Actually, it's the best spot for a gathering in the winter.

The lawn is open enough for a large crowd, but the buildings surrounding it protect it from the wind. He didn't just select that spot to make people angry."

Joe studied Char a moment, then shrugged. "Okay. I don't want to argue with you, especially about Deke. I hardly get to spend any time with you as it is. I don't want to spend our time together angry."

Char took a deep breath and exhaled. He was right. She didn't want to argue either. "You're still coming tomorrow night, aren't you? I'd really like you to be there."

Joe nodded. "I'm coming." He leaned over and gave her a kiss. "Anytime I can see you, I'm there."

She smiled despite being angry moments before. It was hard for her to stay angry at Joe.

"Let's order some food," Joe said. "I'm starving. And then you can tell me about what you've been writing for the newspaper. I love hearing about your article ideas."

Char moved closer to Joe until their legs touched. She liked being close to him and had missed spending time alone with him. "Hopefully, when this rally is over, we can spend a little time together this weekend," she said. "I miss having free time."

"Me, too," he said. "And I am proud of all the work you're doing. You're amazing."

"Thanks. I hope you can say that after tomorrow night."

"Don't worry. If anything goes wrong, I'll just blame Deke."

That did bring a smile to Char's lips.

Chapter Twenty-Three

On Friday, after a long day of classes and working at the newspaper, Char went home quickly to change into warm clothes for the evening ahead. She called out a goodbye to her mother, and bumped into her dad at the door as he walked in.

"You don't even have time for dinner before the big protest?" he asked, a slight tease in his voice.

"Dad," Char said disapprovingly but gave him a quick hug. "It starts at six and I need to be there a little early. You and Mom should come and listen to the speaker. I think he'll be interesting."

Ronald gave his daughter a small smile. "I don't know, sweetie. Protesting war isn't really something I can get used to. But I'm proud of you and everything you do. Will you be reporting this event for the paper?"

"Yes." She showed him the notebook she'd slipped into her coat pocket. "And Joe will be there too."

"Good on both counts. I'll read what happened in your article."

Char ran out to her car and a few minutes later arrived at the rally site. A crowd of people were already milling around the lawn. A few ROTC men stood on the sidelines holding signs.

"Support our Boys in Vietnam" and "We Stand for America" were the prominent slogans. Char had classes with some of these students and could sympathize with how they felt. She'd also been raised to believe in America. Her brother went to Vietnam because he believed it was his patriotic duty. Now, she was no longer sure that duty was a good enough reason to send boys off to war to be killed. At least not *this* war.

Char made her way to the front of the lawn and saw Deke setting up a microphone on a make-shift platform. There were speakers on each side of it.

"Where'd all this come from?" she asked him.

"I begged the music department for it. They said I could use the platform and P.A. system, but I had to swear it wouldn't get ruined."

"I thought you were just going to use the wall," Char said.

"I was, until my speaker arrived. He's missing a leg. There's no way he could stand on the wall."

"Oh." A chill ran through Char. She should have considered that their speaker might be disabled. So many veterans coming home were. Her thoughts turned to Joe. She was so used to his limp and cane that she didn't even notice anymore. Joe seemed the same as everyone else to her. But she remembered the first day she saw him, walking slowly, leaning on his cane, his pack heavy on his back. He had stood out. Now, she knew him as the kind, caring, generous man that he was, and his injury didn't stand out to her. But she of all people should have thought to ask if the speaker was disabled.

"Stop thinking it's your fault," Deke told her with a grin. "I was the one who set it up. I should have asked."

"How'd you know what I was thinking?" Char asked, surprised.

Deke leaned in closer to her. "Because I know you," he said. "I know you very well."

Char felt her cheeks grow hot despite the chill in the air. Deke chuckled and went back to his work. She couldn't deny it—Deke did know her well and it embarrassed her just thinking about it.

She moved over to the small table that Deke had set up with clipboards and sign-up sheets. END THE WAR was printed at the top of each sheet and there were lines underneath for people to sign.

A pretty blond girl in a very short dress, coat, and knee-high white boots came over to the table. "Deke sent me here," she said, giving Char a pink-lipped smile. "I'm helping with the sign-up sheets."

Char looked her over and wondered how she wasn't freezing in that outfit. She figured the college guys would sign anything for a closer view of her. "Okay. Why don't you take a clipboard and pen and walk around the crowd asking for sign-ups? Tell them we need students who are supporting the anti-war movement."

"Okay," the girl readily agreed and disappeared into the fast-growing crowd.

"Cute, right?" Deke asked, walking up to Char. "I have another girl coming, too. The guys will go crazy over them."

Char rolled her eyes. "Chauvinist."

"Hey. I'll do whatever it takes to get people interested," Deke said, his eyes twinkling mischievously. "Seriously, though, the guy who's speaking is waiting over in the English building. If you want any background information from him for your article, you should do it now. He may leave right after he talks."

"Okay, thanks," Char said. "What's his name?"

"Gordon. He doesn't want to use his last name or his rank and such. He wants to stay anonymous," Deke said.

Char sighed. "Okay. That seems strange, but I'll go see what I can get out of him."

"When you're done, send him out and we'll get this thing started."

Char found Gordon waiting just inside the glass doors of the English building. He was tall and slender with a mop of thick brown hair and a heavy beard. He wore a faded denim shirt and jeans and an army coat much like Joe's. He looked no different than any student on campus except for one thing. He was missing the bottom half of his right leg. His pant leg was folded and pinned up and he wore a cowboy boot on his left foot. He leaned on a pair of wooden crutches that looked like they'd seen better days.

Char took a deep breath and headed inside. "Hi. Are you Gordon?"

"Yes."

He stared at her with dark brown eyes. His stare seemed hollow, like he was looking, but not really seeing her.

Char spoke more cheerfully than she felt. "Hi, Gordon. I'm Char. I'm helping Deke with this rally, and I'm also a writer for the school newspaper. I was wondering if I could ask you a few questions before your speech?"

He looked wary but nodded his agreement.

She took out her small notepad and pen. "Deke said you didn't want to use your last name, which is fine. Can you tell me anything about your service in Vietnam? Which part of the country were you stationed in? What type of job were you assigned to there?"

"I'm not going to reveal my unit or where I was stationed,"

he said in a deep voice. "I told Deke I'd only speak about my experiences but without names of places."

"Can I ask why?"

Gordon stared at her with those empty eyes. "What I've seen, and what I'm about to share, won't go over well with many veterans. We were told to go home and forget everything. Kind of hard when you're reminded every day because you're missing a leg. But at least I came home. I know many who didn't. I'll tell my story, that's all. I'll tell what it feels like every time I close my eyes and see it all over again in my head. I'll share that stuff if it will help end this war. But no names, no way to pinpoint exactly who I am and who I fought with."

Char wrote down some of what he'd said even though it wasn't likely she'd forget. "Okay. Thank you. Deke said you can come out now. As soon as we get out there, he'll introduce you."

Gordon nodded, then made his way to the door. He stopped and allowed Char to open it for him. After he stepped through, he turned and looked sadly at Char. "I used to hold doors open for pretty girls, not the other way around."

She smiled at him. "I don't mind holding it."

"Maybe you shouldn't listen to what I'm about to tell the crowd. It's not for a lady's ears," he said.

She was surprised by his words. "I'm sure I'll be fine."

His stare went right through her. "Some sights cannot be unseen. Some words cannot be unheard. Remember that." Then he made his way out to the lawn.

Char couldn't imagine what this man might say that she shouldn't hear. She didn't think of herself as a frail woman. Yet, Joe wouldn't share war experiences with her either, and she'd never heard her father tell a war story from his time in World War II.

Times have changed, she told herself. *Women are strong*. With that in mind, she followed Gordon out to the front of the lawn.

Night had fallen and the area was aglow with lamplights that circled the lawn. Deke was speaking as Char made her way to the table near the stage. The crowd had grown and they were talking noisily to each other, nearly blocking out Deke's voice over the microphone. In the back, the ROTC men could be heard yelling, "Support our boys in Vietnam!" and "Support America!" No one seemed to be paying attention to them.

In the back corner, Char spotted Joe. She waved and smiled. He waved back but stayed in his spot. She turned her attention once more to Deke, straining to block out the noise around her to hear what he was saying.

"We've all heard of the atrocities of the My Lai Massacre in Vietnam, and we were told by top generals that that kind of murderous behavior was not typical there," Deke said. "But I have someone here with us tonight who can attest to the fact that these types of horrors occur on a regular basis, committed by our very own soldiers. So please give our speaker, Gordon, a former army soldier in Vietnam, a welcoming round of applause."

The crowd turned their attention to the man who hobbled onto the stage and balanced himself on his crutches in front of the microphone. Everyone quieted down, even the ROTC protesters. Char had her notebook and pen ready to jot down the important points of Gordon's speech.

Gordon hesitated a moment, staring out into the crowd with those blank eyes. His hands turned white as he squeezed the handholds of his crutches. Finally, he moved closer to the microphone. "Hello. My name is Gordon, and I served in the U.S. Army in Vietnam from 1967 to 1968." He stopped and took a deep breath before continuing. "I was assigned to a unit that did search and destroy missions to flush out the Viet Cong guerrillas in South Vietnam. Every day my fellow soldiers and I walked a fine line between being human and becoming monsters. Some days we succeeded at staying human, while other days we did not."

The crowd stood motionless, their attention on this man willing to tell the truth about Vietnam. Char listened intently to Gordon too, forgetting that she was supposed to be taking notes.

Gordon described a typical day for his unit. They were taken to villages by choppers and dropped off. Their mission was to go through the village, pull out anyone who seemed suspicious, and interrogate them, take them prisoner, or kill them. If any sign of Viet Cong infiltration was detected, they'd torch the huts, kill village animals that could be used for food, and destroy all other food supplies.

"Most of the time, the villagers were sent on their way to a detention facility where they would have food and shelter," Gordon said. "But sometimes, if a villager gave us trouble, or we believed that a family was helping the Viet Cong, they'd be killed immediately. Even if we couldn't prove they'd done anything wrong, they'd be shot."

Goosebumps prickled Char's skin. She surveyed the crowd for their reaction. Many of the young people were frowning. They shifted their feet and crossed their arms. A growing anger seemed to radiate off the people around her. She looked over at Joe, and saw that he, too, was frowning, except he looked more disturbed than angry.

"Often, the people in the village would clear out the moment they heard our choppers coming," Gordon continued. "I was relieved on those days. We only had to contend with destroying their food supply, or burning their huts and crops. No blood would be spilled on those days. It got to where on each day that we set out, I'd pray the villagers would be gone. Unfortunately, prayers aren't always answered in hell.

"Our government doesn't want soldiers to tell you what we've seen and done. They don't want the American people to know the horror going on in Vietnam. I've seen young men, good people who write to their mothers every week, who receive care packages from their grandmothers, or wear a cross underneath their uniform, do atrocious things. I've seen men cut off the enemy's ears for trophies, mutilate dead bodies, or cut off heads and hands for the hell of it. I've watched young children die beside their mothers, and women raped before a gun was put to their head. Don't let our government tell you otherwise: Vietnam is a dirty, nasty war where we can no longer tell the good guy from the bad guy." Gordon took a breath. His eyes scanned the silent crowd.

"Of course, the enemy does nightmarish things to our soldiers too. They set booby-traps that cut off heads in one fell swoop. Landmines that can blow off an entire leg, or tear a man's whole body into tiny pieces. They mutilate bodies of our soldiers, as well. Who started it first? Them? Us? I don't know. What I do know is I see these things every night when I lay down and close my eyes. I can smell the smoke as their huts go up in flames. I can hear the children cry as their mothers beg for their lives. Those memories are imprinted on my mind forever."

Bile rose in Char's throat as her stomach turned at Gordon's words. She'd never wanted to believe Deke when he called returning veterans "baby killers" or other terrible names. But here was a man who had been there, admitting to the very horrors that Deke had always claimed were true.

Gordon's shoulders shook as he broke down in tears.

Deke jumped up on stage and draped an arm around him. "Do you now understand why we must end this war?" Deke asked the crowd, his eyes bright with excitement. "This man was there and saw the atrocities. Do we continue to send our young men there to be turned into murderers? Or to be murdered? Join me now! Join me in the fight to end this war!"

The crowd began chanting, "Hell no! We won't go!"

Deke quickly escorted Gordon off the stage and then returned to chant with the crowd.

"Hell no! We won't go!"

The two young women were running around the crowd getting people to sign the petition to end the war. People began stomping their feet. The noise was so loud, Char was sure the people in the homes that surrounded the college could hear them. And it was then that Char saw the familiar glint in Deke's eyes. The one that said he'd gotten what he'd wanted. The glint that meant something big was going to happen.

She watched Deke scan the crowd until his eyes landed on something, or someone, that Char couldn't see over the hundreds of people crammed together. He grinned wickedly. Whatever he was staring at, it seemed to invigorate Deke even more. He jumped off the stage and grabbed a metal trash can that stood on the sidewalk. Tossing a match into the can, it burst into flames before settling down to a warm glow.

"Let's tell the idiots in Washington that we won't die for their senseless war. Burn your draft cards. Here! Now!" Deke yelled to the crowd.

The crowd grew frenzied with anger. Char stared in shock as men willingly pulled out their wallets and tossed their draft cards into the flames. Everyone was chanting and screaming. Deke was yelling over top of them. Another trash can was pulled onto the lawn and a fire was lit inside it. More men came forward, burning their draft cards.

In a matter of moments, Deke had turned a peaceful protest into a frantic mob. Girls danced around the fires while men threw in their cards. A man had taken ahold of the microphone and started screaming, "Make love, not war!" and others began to chant as well.

Char hurried to the edge of the crowd, desperate to get away from the wild group. She looked toward the back of the lawn for Joe, but she didn't see him. The ROTC protesters were also gone. None of them had been to war yet, and she supposed what Gordon had said had hit them hard.

It had hit her hard as well.

A man grabbed her from behind and began twirling her around in a feverish kind of dance. She pushed at him, but he held on tight. Fear raced through her. The crowd was out of control and anything could happen. As she clawed at the man's arms, Deke appeared and pulled her away from him. He glared at Deke, but let her go.

Deke wrapped a protective arm around her and led her away from the crowd. "Isn't this amazing? I never dreamt we'd have such a crowd. Gordon's speech really got to them." Deke's eyes were ablaze with power.

Char stared at him, aghast. "You promised it would be a peaceful protest! Look at them! They're out of control."

"Our government is out of control, Char," Deke insisted. "It's our time now."

Char broke away from him and ran. She heard Deke calling her name, but she kept running until she found her car and locked herself inside. She could still hear the crowd shouting, still smell the fumes from the garbage cans. The sound echoed around the campus, the smoke billowed up into the night sky. She needed to find Joe. Starting her car, she sped out of the parking lot toward the downtown.

Chapter Twenty-Four

Joe sat on the sofa in his apartment, his bad leg stretched out so he could rub the stiff muscles. Once the rally began to unravel, he'd walked home. The smell of smoke and frenzied chants from the crowd had unnerved him. He'd had a flashback of choppers overhead and gunfire erupting. Sweat had beaded under his shirt and his breathing had grown tight. He'd wanted to put as much space between him and the crowd as he could.

Joe closed his eyes and the words of the soldier reverberated in his mind. Beheadings. Mutilations. The murder of women and children. It was all so heartbreaking, and it turned his stomach at the very thought of it.

Of course, he'd known of such horrors happening in Vietnam. Stories circulated among soldiers, but Joe hadn't been witness to them. He couldn't imagine the men from his unit doing such things, but then again, they'd never been put in the type of situations that drove them to cross the line between humanity and inhumanity. Who was he to judge men who saw the worst of mankind day in and day out? Tony had seen it, and look what had happened to him.

Joe wished the images of war that plagued him would go away.

He'd moved to this small town to start a new life and put the war behind him. Yet, at every turn, the war continued to follow him, haunt him.

He just wanted it all to end.

As the crowd had grown wilder and begun to chant, Joe could have sworn Deke had stared him right in the eyes across the crowded space. He'd looked as if he were daring Joe to come forward. Daring him to fight back. And as he kept his eyes trained on Joe, Deke had called out to the crowd to burn their draft cards. Joe had realized then that it had been for his benefit. Deke had wanted him to see the power he held over the crowd.

Joe had watched the ROTC students drop their signs and walk away, discouraged and defeated. He didn't want to fight either. He'd already fought his war. Deke could have this one. Joe didn't want anything to do with another war.

As he lay there with his eyes closed, Joe heard footsteps on the stairs. The doorknob slowly turned and the door opened quietly. Char walked inside and closed the door as Joe opened his eyes. She looked tired and drawn. He opened his arms, and she came to him and let him hold her close.

"It was awful," Char said, tears falling down her face. "I can't bear to think of the things he said, yet I can't make them go away."

Joe ran his hand through her hair in a soothing gesture and kissed the top of her head. "I know."

She looked up at him. "Was it the truth? Do those things happen?"

Joe gazed into her amber-brown eyes. "I only know what I experienced there," he said truthfully. "I never saw those things happen. But that doesn't mean they didn't. It's war, Char. Men sometimes do horrific things when they live through horrible circumstances. It's not an excuse. It's just a fact."

She pulled away and moved to the corner of the sofa, pulling her legs up and hugging them. She still wore her coat and scarf, but he saw her shiver just the same. "Gordon told me not to listen to his speech. He said some things can never be unseen or unheard. He was right. I'll never be able to get the images of what he described out of my head."

"Some things can never be forgotten," Joe said.

"Is that how it is for you? Will you carry what you've seen with you for the rest of your life?" she asked, looking pained.

"I'm trying not to," he said. "But it isn't as easy as I thought it would be."

Joe moved closer to Char and she curled up against him. He gently brushed the tears from her face, then kissed each damp cheek. She lifted her gloved hands to his face and held it, staring into his eyes.

"I'm sorry," she said. "I'm sorry I made you come tonight. I wanted you there for me, and I didn't stop to think about how it would make you feel."

"Don't be sorry. You had no idea what he would say." Joe kissed her, tracing her lips with his tongue. He wanted to taste her, feel her next to him, feel the closeness of someone he loved and cared about. She responded, their kiss growing deeper. He slowly unbuttoned her coat and reached inside to feel her warmth.

Char slipped off her gloves and ran her hands across his chest and over his back. Her touch made his skin tingle, even through his shirt.

She pulled away and gazed into his eyes. "I don't want to stop," she said breathlessly.

Joe kissed her once more, then forced himself to move away. She watched him, looking confused.

"I don't want to stop either," he said. "But it's been an emotional night, and I don't want that to be what brings us together. I want our first time together to be perfect."

Char took a deep breath and exhaled. "It's late. I should go home. I still have to write about the rally tonight for the paper. That means I'll have to relive what he said. It's going to be painful."

Joe placed a sweet kiss on her forehead. "You can do it. I know you can. It's going to be an incredible article."

She stood and buttoned her coat again, then picked up her gloves. At that moment, sirens blared out into the quiet night. The police had probably been called to the college to shut down the rally.

"Do you want me to drive you home?" he asked. She still looked dazed and the sirens had only made her seem more nervous.

Char shook her head. "No. I'll be okay."

He followed her to the door and gave her one last kiss. "I love you, Char. Remember that."

She smiled. "I love you, too."

Joe watched as she headed down the stairs before closing the door. He walked with great effort to the front window and watched Char get into her car and drive off. In the distance, he could see the smoke rising to the sky from the burning garbage cans. He wondered if Char would still want to help Deke with his rallies after what had happened tonight. He guessed he'd find out soon enough.

Closing the drapes, Joe turned out the living room light and headed for bed, and hopefully, a dreamless sleep.

* * *

Char missed work on Saturday and spent the entire day shut up in her room, struggling to write the article about the rally. Despite the emotions that had welled up inside her over Gordon's descriptions of what he'd experienced, she forced herself to write as objectively as possible. *Just the facts.* She could hear her editor in her head, the line he told her with every story she'd turned in. But writing *just the facts* on such an emotional subject was easier said than done.

Joe called her from the store's phone Sunday night to check on her.

"I'm fine," she told him. "I wanted to make sure the article was perfect. It's too important of a topic to take lightly."

"I completely understand," he told her. "I just wanted to make sure you weren't getting lost in your own thoughts."

Char smiled at this. "Like you?" she teased.

Joe chuckled. "Exactly. See you at school."

Monday morning, she sat with Joe in English class, then headed to the newspaper office to turn in her article.

"Were you here when the police came on Friday night?" Joel, her editor asked. When she shook her head, he added, "Thankfully everyone split peacefully, even Deke, so no one was arrested. I heard the school wasn't going to press charges for his rally spinning out of control, but he's banned from having another one on campus again."

Char knew she shouldn't, but she felt relieved he'd been banned. She'd promised her editor that she'd cover all the rallies throughout the spring, but maybe now there wouldn't be any more. Char wasn't sure she wanted to be a part of any more chaos.

Later that afternoon when she returned to the newspaper again, the editor handed her the article. It had very few red marks on it, which surprised her. Usually, he re-wrote the entire thing.

"This is good work, Char," he said. "Objective, yet respect-ful, and quite interesting. Just fix a few errors on it and hand it in for this week's edition."

Char was elated by his kind words. She'd worked so hard to do exactly what he'd said. She hadn't wanted to sway the readers' opinion about the war or the protesters. It was important for them to decide for themselves. Hearing Joel say she'd accom-plished that made her feel very proud.

When she met Joe in the union for dinner, he asked how the article had turned out.

"Better than I could have ever imagined." She grinned. "My editor loved it and it'll be in this week's paper."

"Congratulations!" Joe said. "I can't wait to read it."

When the paper came out on Friday, there was a buzz in the air over Char's article. People who'd attended the rally agreed she'd captured its essence, while those who hadn't attended now wished they had. Students she didn't know patted her on the back and congratulated her in the hallways. Char felt grati-fied that the students had liked her work. Everyone, of course, except Deke. He met up with her in the parking lot at the end of the day. Jenny was with her to get a ride home since Terry had stayed for a late class.

"Char? What did you do?" Deke asked as the two women stopped and stared at him.

"What do you mean?" Char asked. She'd been feeling good all day because of the article and Deke's negative tone irritated her.

"I thought you were on my side. But your article wasn't slanted one way or the other," he said, looking upset.

"Of course it wasn't slanted. I was covering the protest, not promoting it. I had to stay objective."

"Yeah, but I ended up looking bad. Did you have to mention the police broke it up and the college denied any upcoming rallies on campus?"

"Well, that's what happened, Deke," Char said. "My editor wanted it included."

"But it didn't help the cause. I thought the college newspaper was more liberal."

Char laughed. "Deke, the paper isn't here to benefit your causes. They want the truth reported, and that's what I did. And frankly, I never want to help you organize another rally. You didn't tell me you were going to rile up the crowd and start burning draft cards. That's illegal, Deke! You're lucky the police didn't haul you away."

"Geez, Char. What did you think we'd do? Pass out cookies and punch? Gordon's story got to the crowd and I pounced on the opportunity to use it to inspire everyone. It worked perfectly. I can't wait until the next rally. It will be even bigger than the last."

"You were banned from having them on campus, Deke. How do you plan on having more rallies?"

"The college can't stop a group of students from meeting. They don't need to know it was pre-planned. And if they get huffy about it, I'll find somewhere nearby to hold rallies." Deke grinned wickedly, making Char's stomach turn. The grin she once thought so handsome now looked menacing. Why hadn't she noticed that before?

"I thought you wanted to protest the war," Deke said. "One rally and you're done?"

"I do want to end the war," Char said. "But peacefully. I

believe in the cause, but I don't want to break laws to do it."

"Char, the government is breaking laws just by being in Vietnam. And at this very moment, we're bombing the neighboring countries of Laos and Cambodia. Do you think that's okay?" Deke asked, his voice rising.

Char stood silent. She didn't want to argue with Deke anymore.

"Don't you get it, babe? The tides are turning here in the U.S. Nixon's popularity is way down and so is the support for the war. We're slowly winning. Now is the time to push harder. We *will* stop this war."

Char stood firm. "I'm glad the anti-war movement is winning, Deke. I really am. But I don't want to protest violently. And my articles will always be objective. I refuse to slant them no matter what my feelings are. I have to continue covering your rallies, because I promised my editor I would. But I don't have to help you organize them."

Deke shook his head, looking disappointed. "After all this time, I thought I'd finally gotten to you. I had even hoped you'd dump G.I. Joe and come back to me." He drew closer to her. "I still love you, Char. And because I do, I respect your stance. But just wait and see. I'm going to help sway the tide. I hope you'll be there to see it." He stepped back, gave her a wave, and walked away.

Char stared after him, stunned by what he'd just said.

After Char and Jenny were in the car, the two girls turned and looked at each other.

"I hope you never leave Joe for Deke," Jenny said. "He's getting too radical for my taste."

"Don't worry. It's never going to happen," Char said with great certainty.

Chapter Twenty-Five

February slipped by and the weather slowly warmed up. Deke held two more large rallies with speakers from Chicago who had once been members of SDS. Char was required to attend to write about them but left as soon as the speakers were finished. She didn't ask Joe to go with her. She didn't want to force him to listen to a subject that might upset him or bring back terrible memories. He wanted to forget the war, and the more horror stories she heard about Vietnam, the more she understood his need to put it behind him.

She and Joe were both busy with school that semester, leaving them less free time to spend together. But they grew closer even with their limited time. Char often went to Joe's apartment in the early evenings, staying until she had to force herself to go home. Sometimes Joe surprised her by cooking dinner. They were simple dinners, like hamburgers, spaghetti, or homemade macaroni and cheese, but they tasted good.

She enjoyed eating with him at the little dinette set, then cuddling in front of the small television under a blanket and watching a show or movie. They talked about everything—her articles, the rallies, and their college classes. He told her more about his life growing up in the Bronx, and she talked about her childhood in Grand Falls. They'd had two very different upbringings, yet they connected as if they'd been friends for years.

As their relationship grew, Char found it harder to leave Joe in the evenings to go home. She wondered how it would feel to lie in bed beside him and stay the night. Her heart skipped and her skin tingled just thinking about it. But as long as she lived with her parents, she knew it could never happen. Despite her parents being understanding and easy to talk to, she didn't think they'd appreciate their only daughter living unwed with a man. They weren't that progressive, and she wasn't sure if she was either. But there was no denying that her and Joe's relationship was special. She'd never thought of "forever" when she was dating Deke, but with Joe, it was easy to dream about spending a lifetime with him.

They made love for the first time on a chilly March evening when an unexpected storm blew through, blanketing heavy, wet snow over the town. Char had gone to Joe's apartment while the snow was still light and three hours later, it had piled up. As they stood at the front window, staring out at the mass of white under the pools of light from the streetlamps, a warm feeling came over Char. It was a beautiful sight. The moon shone bright overhead and the snow was perfect and untouched on the sidewalks.

Joe stood behind her with his arms around her waist, and his chin on her shoulder. His hair tickled her ear and his breath felt warm on her neck. It was cozy being here together when it was perfectly still outside.

Char turned in Joe's arms and kissed him, opening her lips to invite his tongue to explore. She ran her hands over his shoulders and back, muscular and strong from lifting heavy boxes in the store. When his lips left her mouth and moved lower to kiss her neck, sweet chills ran through her body. She wanted to hold him close and feel his warm skin against hers.

He was wearing the denim shirt she'd given him for Christmas. She unbuttoned it, then slipped her hands inside to his soft T-shirt underneath. Joe pulled away and gazed at her, his gray eyes dark with desire. He knew what she wanted without words being exchanged.

"Are you sure?" he asked, his voice deep with wanting.

She nodded, then took his hand and they walked together to the bedroom.

He undressed her slowly, kissing her everywhere bare skin appeared. They slipped into his bed and held each other close. Char loved the feel of his body next to hers. She'd never before felt for anyone the way she did for Joe, and this final act of love between them cemented him in her heart. She understood now what had been missing between her and Deke. Love. Pure, sweet love. And as she lay in Joe's arms afterward, she reveled in the beauty of it.

* * *

Joe had never imagined he could feel as blissfully happy as he did now. Who could have known two years ago, when'd he'd accepted that random letter to a soldier, that he would have ended up being with Char? The woman whose photo he'd fallen in love with was now an integral part of his life. Joe had experienced the horror and trauma of war, but it was all worth it if it had brought him here, to her.

He stole a glance at Char as she sat across the table from him in the college library. Her hair was tucked behind her ears and fanned out over her shoulders and her expression was serious as she concentrated on her work. He smiled, thinking how cute she looked, then focused on his work again. They were both writing their thesis papers for English class. Every now and again, she'd try to sneak a peek at his paper, but he'd block it from her. He knew her thesis was about the Vietnam War, but she didn't know that his was too. He didn't want to reveal the topic until they had turned their papers in. Despite his insistence to Char that he wanted to put the war behind him, he'd found it wasn't as easy as he'd thought. Writing this paper, and researching the war thoroughly, was cathartic for him. The more he understood the war, the better he was able to rationalize his participation in it.

After neither one felt they could read another research article or write another line, they decided to call it a night and grab a snack at the union. Char piled her work into her bookbag and Joe did the same in his rucksack. They held hands as they walked through the college buildings and sat in a corner table at the union. It wasn't very busy tonight, so they were able to get a plate of french fries and two Cokes quickly.

"I wish you'd tell me what your thesis paper is about," Char complained. "It's not fair. You know my topic."

Joe laughed. "You sound like a three-year-old."

She lightly hit his arm, then grinned. "Well, it isn't fair."

"You'll see it soon enough," he said.

She stuck her tongue out at him then ate a french fry.

Later, they drove her car back to the shop and went up to his apartment.

"Do you want to watch some TV?" he asked as they took off their coats.

Char grinned at him.

"We could play a game of cards," he said, his eyes twinkling.

"I know a better game." She grabbed his hand and pulled him toward the bedroom.

"Are you taking advantage of me?" he asked, looking shocked.

Char stopped and dropped his hand. "Why? Don't you want me to?"

It was his turn to take her hand and pull her. "I didn't say that," he said, laughing.

* * *

They lay in bed holding each other for a long time afterward, not saying a word, only enjoying their closeness. Finally, Char looked at the alarm clock and sighed.

"I'd better leave or my parents will worry," she said.

Joe brushed her lips with a kiss. "We'll get our chance to be together," he said.

He slipped out of bed and headed into the bathroom while Char picked up her clothes that were scattered on the floor. She reached for her jeans that had disappeared under the bed. A small, black box tumbled out onto the floor in front of her. She stared at it, curious, then she glanced at the closed bathroom door. Bending down, she picked up the box. She knew she should put it back under the bed, but it intrigued her. Besides, what would Joe have that she shouldn't see?

Char's curiosity got the best of her. She sat on the bed and pulled the rubber band off the box. Slipping the lid open, she peered inside. A set of dog tags on a chain lay on top, and she pulled them out and set them on the bed. Then her eyes lit up with excitement. A picture of a soldier standing in the jungle was on top. She thought they were pictures of Joe's time spent in Vietnam. Eager to see them, she dumped the pictures out into her hand and began flipping through them. There was one of a guy who was unfamiliar to Char, and another of a village of huts ablaze with fire. She frowned at that. Joe had said he'd been on a firebase. Why would they be burning a village?

She looked at the next picture, then the next. She couldn't believe what she was seeing. Each photo grew more horrific. The images that Gordon had described in the first rally speech were right here in her hand. Nightmares that someone had photographed and kept. No, not just someone. Joe.

Char dropped the photos and box on the bed and backed away. She suddenly felt like the room was closing in on her. Deke had been right. Some soldiers brought home mementoes of their service. Horrific mementoes. Joe was as guilty as the others. It made her blood run cold to think that she didn't know the real Joe at all.

Joe stepped out of the bathroom and looked at Char curiously. "What's the matter?"

She glared at him, angry now that he'd deceived her about his true character. "How could you do these things?" she asked. "It's no wonder you don't want to talk about the war. The things you did. They're shameful. They're…inhuman."

"What are you talking about?" He glanced down at the bed and his eyes grew wide. "Oh my God! Char. No. It's not what you think."

She didn't wait to hear his excuses. She ran from the room, flew down the stairs, and out of the store. Getting into her car, she sat there a moment, dazed. Had she really seen what she'd thought she had? How could Joe have done those things? Tears burned her eyes. Her heart clenched. She put the car in drive and spun out of there toward home.

* * *

Char avoided Joe. She couldn't face him. The man she'd fallen in love with, the man she'd given herself to, wasn't the man she'd thought he was. He'd known all along about the atrocities in Vietnam—he'd seen them first-hand—and yet he'd denied any participation. He'd lied to her. How could she ever trust him again?

Yet, every time she saw him on campus, every time she thought about him, her heart ached. He'd been so caring, kind, and loving. It was unbearably hard turning her back on him now.

On Friday, when she'd dropped off her latest article at the school newspaper office, she bumped into Deke as she hurried out the door.

"Hey, I was looking for you," Deke said, giving her one of his irresistible smiles.

Fortunately, she was immune to his charm.

"What do you want?" she asked, eager to leave. She knew Joe had come looking for her in here before and she didn't want to risk his coming back and finding her.

"Do you have a moment to talk?" he asked.

Char sighed. "I guess. But not here. Let's go somewhere off campus."

They drove in Deke's car to the café in town and sat in a booth. Char wasn't thrilled that they were sitting in a window seat, but she figured it would be okay. Joe always did his homework at the college library until evening. He wouldn't be walking by here this early in the day.

"What, or who, are you looking for?" Deke asked, following her line of vision out the window.

Char turned back to him. "Nothing. So, what did you want to talk about?"

"Where's G.I. Joe? Isn't he usually your shadow?"

"Is that what you wanted to talk about?" Char asked sharply.

"Hey, don't snap off my head. I just wondered. No skin off my nose. I'd rather talk to you alone anyway."

The waitress came and Deke ordered a piece of apple pie and a Coke. "How about you, Char? Do you want something?"

Char declined. She just wanted to be done here and go home.

"Okay. I can see you don't want to stay long, so I'll get on with it," Deke said. "There's going to be a big march on Washington at the end of April. I'm going because there will be some interesting speakers there. I think you should come along too."

"Me? Why should I go along?" Char asked.

"Because it would give you another perspective of the movement. It would increase your knowledge seeing everything first-hand. This is going to be a big one, Char. The Vietnam Veterans Against the War will be there, and it sounds like they have some intense demonstrations planned. It will be the experience of a lifetime."

"I'm sure it will be interesting, Deke, but I can't just drop everything and leave. I have classes. And the newspaper. There's simply no way I could go even if I wanted to," Char said.

The waitress brought Deke's pie and drink, then left. Deke pushed it aside and leaned on the table, closer to her. "This is worth more than a few days of missed classes. Imagine the articles you could write and the pictures you could bring back. We'll never see anything like it again. It's history being made right in front of us."

She sat back against the booth and crossed her arms. "I appreciate you asking me, and I do understand the historic value of this, but protests aren't my thing. They're your thing."

"Okay." Deke pushed his pie back in front of him and took

a bite. "Ah. This is good." He grinned at Char. "Want some?"

"No, thank you," she said. "Are we done?"

"Wow, you really are in a rush to get out of here. No, it's not all. After the march in Washington, there's a huge protest that's going on in towns all over the country. From San Francisco to New York City, people are going to stand up against the government to protest the war. I've been talking to my contacts in Chicago, and now that I've built up a good number of supporters here, they'll be sending people down here to help us protest. It's going to be a big deal, babe. Big."

She winced at him calling her *babe*. "Is it going to be peaceful?"

"Oh, yeah. Of course it is," Deke said. "We'll start with a couple of speeches at the college, then march down Main Street. The whole point is to show the government that we can shut everything down—businesses, highways, the government itself—if Washington doesn't start listening to us. It's going to be radical. And I had hoped you'd march with us. With me, right at the front of the line."

Char frowned. "Why me? I'm not involved with your group. Not after what you did at that first rally."

He reached across the table and covered her hand with his. "I always hoped when we were together that you'd one day march with me. Washington D.C., here, it doesn't matter where. We'd be marching for our friends who haven't yet gone to Vietnam. And for those we've lost there. For Jeremy," he added softly.

Char pulled her hand away from his and dropped it in her lap. As Deke ate his pie, she thought about everything that had happened since losing Jeremy. She'd looked for answers by writing to a soldier, who'd ended up being Joe. She'd dated Deke, admiring his commitment to the anti-war movement in the name of her brother. Yet, in the three years since Jeremy's death, she still didn't understand this war that raged on. Could these marches and protests really stop it, or were they all futile? She wished she knew. But at least she'd feel she'd done something to stop more young men like her brother from dying.

"I'll march for Jeremy," she finally said. "As long as it's peaceful. When will it be?"

"May first," Deke said, looking pleased that she'd said yes.

"May Day?" she asked.

"Yep. The May Day protests. It has a good ring to it, doesn't it?"

* * *

Joe couldn't get close enough to Char to explain the pictures. For the rest of the week, she sat far away from him in English then hurried out the door at the end of class. He searched for her at the newspaper office, in the student union, and the library, but to no avail. She wouldn't answer his calls to her home, either. Both Ellen and Ronald apologetically told him she didn't want to come to the phone. When Saturday arrived, he had hoped she'd be at work so he could finally talk to her, but she didn't show up.

"Sorry, Joe," Ronald said when he'd asked him about Char. "She asked me to bring the bookkeeping home. She said she was too busy with newspaper articles and schoolwork to come in."

Joe felt terrible. Just when everything in his life was perfect, it suddenly came crashing down around him. All because of those damned pictures! He should have destroyed them. Why had he kept them around? He hadn't wanted to destroy someone else's personal items, yet the pictures were too horrific to keep.

That night, after the store had closed and Joe had eaten

dinner alone in front of the television, he made a decision. He grabbed the box of pictures from under the bed, put on his coat, and headed downstairs. Walking through the dark store, Joe entered the alley and lifted the cover off an empty metal garbage can. Pulling the rubber band off the box, he tossed it and the lid into the can. Then he stood there, staring down at Tony's dog tags. Reverently, he took them out of the box and slipped them into his pocket. He should have sent them to Tony's parents weeks ago. He would now.

Joe pulled out the photos and dropped the box in the can. Then he took a book of matches out of his pocket.

"I'm sorry, Tony," Joe said into the still night. "These are your memories, not mine. This isn't the way I want to remember the war, or you. You were a good soldier who did his duty. I'll remember you that way."

One by one, Joe set fire to each of the pictures before dropping them into the garbage can. He didn't want to risk anyone ever seeing them again.

Chapter Twenty-Six

Saturday evening Char was setting the table for dinner when her father came home from work.

"I brought these home like you asked," he said, setting the bank bag and ledger on the table. "If you don't have time to do the deposits, maybe your mother can."

"Thanks, Dad," Char said. "I'll make time for them. It shouldn't take too long."

Her father left the room to take off his coat and tie. He returned a few minutes later. "Did you get a lot of schoolwork done today?"

"Yes, I did. I was working on my thesis paper. It's taking longer than I thought."

Her father looked at her tenderly. "Joe asked about you. He seemed disappointed that you didn't come to work today."

Char's heart clenched at the mention of Joe. "It couldn't be helped."

Ronald nodded and walked into the living room to relax until dinner. Char followed him.

"Dad?"

"Yes, dear?"

"Why don't you ever talk about your experiences in the war?"

Ronald studied her face a moment before answering. She couldn't tell if he was surprised by the question or not. "Ah, sweetie. What happens in war isn't pretty. It's not something I ever wanted to talk about or dwell on."

Char sighed. "I've been hearing about so many awful things that are going on in Vietnam. It's hard to believe that war could cause men to act so cruelly. How does someone go from being civilized to monstrous?"

Ronald leaned forward in his chair, his elbows on his knees. "Char, unfortunately in war, not everything is good or bad, black or white. The constant stress and fear can change how a man behaves. That's not an excuse by any means, but it happens. Anger also lies under the surface. You see your friends die, the men you've fought with and are closest to, and it can cause even the best of us to do things we wouldn't have imagined possible."

"Do you regret anything you did?"

"Nobody lives a life without regrets," Ronald said, his face softening. "I did what I was told. I served my country. And when I came home, I put it all behind me."

Char stared off in the distance, pondering this. She wondered if Jeremy had to make difficult decisions during his short time in Vietnam. Jeremy had always been such a kind-hearted person. Killing people, or watching others commit horrid acts of violence, would have torn at his soul. But what if he'd been the one to bring home those terrible pictures? Would she be as disappointed in him as she was now in Joe?

"Char, honey," Ronald said, interrupting her thoughts. "Does this have anything to do with your not speaking to Joe?"

She nodded. "I found something disturbing that made me question if I really knew him at all."

"Sweetie. Joe is a good man. I saw it that first night I invited him in for dinner. He's honest and hardworking, and I'm sure he served his country honorably. I don't know what it is you found, but I do know Joe. He survived a terrible war the best way he knew how. Don't judge him too harshly, dear. None of us know how we'd behave until we experience it ourselves."

Char knew her father was right, yet the images she'd seen still made her shudder. "I don't know, Dad. There are some things I'm not sure I can forgive."

"Then the least you can do is let him explain his side," Ronald said.

Later, as Char sat at her desk in her room, she thought about what her father had said. Maybe she was being too judgmental. Or maybe she'd jumped to a conclusion too soon. Still, she felt betrayed by Joe lying to her.

This was all so difficult for her to understand. What was right and what was wrong? Her father had said that not everything could be black or white. She understood that now. Because despite what she'd found at Joe's apartment, and despite feeling betrayed, she couldn't deny one important thing—she still loved Joe.

* * *

Char knew eventually she'd have to talk to Joe, but she still did her best to avoid him all the next week at school. She needed time. Time to figure out exactly how she felt.

March melted into April and with it came longer days and warmer weather. Char realized there were only two months left of school. The year had flown by and so much had happened. Her eyes had been opened in many ways. She was no longer the wide-eyed girl searching for answers from others. She'd transformed from a girl who'd admired someone else's ideals to a woman who formed her own opinions. And she'd experienced what real love felt like.

Sunday evening there was a knock on the Parsons' door. Char was in the kitchen, helping her mother with the dishes, when she heard her father greet a visitor. He poked his head in the kitchen.

"Char. There's someone here to see you."

She walked out through the dining room and stopped. Joe stood in the entryway. Her heart jumped at the sight of him.

"Please talk to me," he said. "I can't go another day with you thinking terrible thoughts about me. Just give me a few minutes."

She nodded, and without saying a word, she took a sweater out of the closet and they stepped outside. The night was mild, but the breeze still had a chill of winter. They sat on the porch swing, a gaping space between them.

"I don't think terrible things about you." Char pulled her sweater around her and crossed her arms. She didn't look him in the eye—she couldn't—otherwise, her resolve to stay strong would fall apart.

"Those pictures were awful. I know that. But they weren't mine. Didn't you see the dog tags in the box? Didn't you read the name on them?" Joe asked.

Char thought back to that night. She remembered pulling them out of the box, but she hadn't read the name. "I assumed they were yours."

He lifted the dog tags out of his coat pocket and handed them to her. They felt cold in her hands. Char fingered one of the tags and read the name. Anthony Funari. She looked up at Joe, her eyes wide. "Those were Tony's pictures?"

Joe nodded. "I found the box in his duffel bag after he died. I was as horrified as you when I saw the pictures. But I didn't know what to do with them. They weren't something I could send his parents, but I'd felt that they weren't something I had the right to destroy. So, I hid them and tried to forget about them."

"Until I found them," Char said.

"Yes. I should have destroyed those pictures when I first saw them. But Tony's death was still a shock and I just couldn't. I burned them after you found them. I don't want anything like that in my possession again."

Char's heart ached. How could she have thought so terribly of Joe? He'd been nothing but kind to her. Tears welled in her eyes. "I'm sorry. I should have let you explain that night. I jumped to conclusions. I thought those photos were your secret mementoes of the war and it sickened me. I've been so immersed in this war, between the articles I'm writing, my thesis paper, and the protests Deke's organized, that seeing those photos put me over the edge. I should have known they weren't yours."

Joe moved closer to Char. "I did bring home a memento from the war." He patted his coat pocket over his heart. Reaching inside, he pulled out a stained envelope, and handed it to Char.

She set Tony's dog tags down in her lap and took it, looking at him curiously. "What's this?"

"It's the only thing from the war that I want to remember. It's the only thing that kept me going even when things got tough. It's what brought me here, to you."

Char opened the envelope as tears streamed down her cheeks. She wiped her eyes so she could focus on what was inside. Pulling it out, she stared at the photo of her and the letters she'd sent him, worn from having been read so often.

"My letters," she whispered.

"Yes. Your letters and your picture. Those were the only things I wanted to bring home from Nam. I kept those close to my heart every day when I was in-country and every day I've been home, too." He took her hand. "Char, I loved you before I ever met you. Your letters told me of a place I didn't think existed anymore. They gave me hope that I had somewhere to go after Vietnam. A place where people smile at you as you pass them on the street, where girls still go to dances with their best guy, and someone like me might just be lucky enough to be with someone like you. I love you, Char. More than anything else in this world. Give me a chance to prove to you that I am the man you believe me to be."

She wrapped her arms around his neck and hugged him tightly as the tears flowed. "I'm so sorry. I'll never doubt you again," she said through her sobs.

He kissed her cheek and brushed away her tears. They sat there as twilight fell over the town. Char's crying subsided and she rested her head on his shoulder.

"Do you hear that?" he asked. "I've waited all winter for that sound."

Char lifted her head and listened. The crickets and toads were singing their nightly tune. A squirrel chattered from a distant tree and small birds twittered on the grass before returning to the safety of their perch.

"Night music." Char sighed. "It means everything is going to be okay."

Joe kissed her then, as the moon rose and the night music sang all around them.

Chapter Twenty-Seven

Joe and Char were inseparable. They went to the egg hunt in the town square on the Saturday before Easter to watch the children search for colorful eggs and prizes. Easter Sunday, Joe accompanied Char and her family to church and spent the day with them at the house. They celebrated Joe's twenty-second birthday on the eighteenth of April with cake and presents at the house, then he and Char went to the union to meet up with Patty, Craig, Jenny, and Terry. Joe felt very lucky to have made so many friends since arriving in Grand Falls. He would have never dared dream his life would turn out so wonderful.

The day after his birthday, they both turned in their thesis papers in English class.

"Now are you going to tell me what your paper is about?" Char asked him as they left the class.

"Nope."

She hit him playfully on the arm. "Well, I really don't care, Joseph Russo," she said, sticking her tongue out at him and hurrying down the hallway.

Joe laughed as he made his way to his next class.

That week, the protests in Washington D.C. were underway.

The Vietnam Veterans Against War staged a five-day, peaceful anti-war demonstration. Vietnam Veteran John Kerry testified on April twenty-second to the Senate Foreign Relations Committee about the atrocities being committed by U.S. soldiers in Vietnam and called for an immediate withdrawal of troops. *"How do you ask a man to be the last man to die in Vietnam? How do you ask a man to be the last man to die for a mistake?"* Kerry asked the committee.

On the twenty-third, nearly nine hundred Vietnam veterans threw their combat medals, ribbons, discharge papers, and other war-related items onto the steps of the Capital building.

Char and Joe read about the events in the paper, not quite knowing if they should be in awe, or shock.

"I don't think I could have done that," Joe said. "Throwing away your medals seems disrespectful toward our country."

"But you did give your medal away," Char said gently. "You said you gave it to your father because you didn't need a medal to prove that you'd served. Isn't that kind of the same thing?"

Joe pondered that a moment. His father had valued the Purple Heart much more than Joe had. "You're right. I didn't value it the same way my dad did. Maybe because my war was different from his. Soldiers from World War II were proud to be decorated, and people thanked them for their service. We didn't come home to parades and accolades. Maybe if I were in Washington D.C. demonstrating, I would have done the same thing."

On the twenty-fourth, nearly half-a-million people converged on Washington D.C. to protest the war. Joe and Char sat in his apartment and watched the news on his small television as it covered the demonstration.

"Isn't that incredible?" Char asked him when they saw the crowd. "Deke is in there somewhere."

"Really? How do you know that?"

"He asked me to go, too. I should have. It would have been an amazing experience. But it's best I didn't go. I didn't want to go with Deke. I would rather have gone with you," she said.

Joe chuckled. "I don't think I'll be marching anywhere, anytime soon. Especially with this leg."

"Or maybe you should be marching because of that leg," Char said.

Her words hit a chord with Joe. He wasn't sure where he stood on the anti-war movement anymore. Over sixty-five percent of Americans no longer supported the war in Vietnam. Yet, as someone who'd fought in it, he felt an allegiance to his fellow soldiers. He had no doubt he wanted the war to end; he just wasn't sure he understood the right way to go about doing that.

* * *

Char was working in the cramped newspaper office on Monday afternoon when Deke came in, bringing photos and notes of the Washington D.C. protest.

"It was incredible, Char. You should have been there. It was like the biggest party in the world, everyone there for one cause: to end the war. I watched the veterans as they threw their medals onto the Capital steps. It was inspiring." He handed her his notes and photos.

"Why are you giving them to me?" she asked, confused.

"I figured you could ask if the paper would let you report on it. You can use my notes to turn them into articles about the protest. You're so much better at that than I am. If the school newspaper won't publish any of it, try the local paper," Deke said.

"I'll try, but I can't promise anything," she said.

Deke's eyes shone with excitement. "Try really hard, okay? We have a week until the May Day protest, and I want to get people excited about it. This is big, Char. It's something that people will remember for a long time. And you'll be a part of it. A part of history!"

Char was flattered that Deke trusted her to write from his notes. Once she began going through them, she realized they were good enough to write a descriptive article and started working on it right away. When she ran the idea past her editor, he agreed that if he liked the article, they'd print it in Friday's paper.

That evening, as she lay beside Joe in his bed, she told him about the upcoming protest on Saturday and the article she was writing for Deke. "He took the most amazing pictures. Thousands of people, young and old, camping right there on the Mall. There were incredible speakers who inspired them, and famous musicians entertained too. John Denver was there! Imagine that. Deke's notes are so specific, you get a real sense of what it felt like being there. I'm really excited about this article."

Joe wrapped his arms around her. "That's wonderful. Of course he would ask you. You're the best writer on the school paper."

"I know that's not true, but I'm happy you think so," she said, kissing his cheek. "Saturday's protest is just one of many in a nation-wide protest, and some of his contacts in Chicago are coming here to speak and march. I told him I'd march with them, so I can write about it for the paper."

Joe frowned as he sat up in bed. "Are you sure you want to do that? Can't you just watch from the side?"

"It'll be okay. Don't worry. Deke promised it would be a peaceful protest. I think he just wants to go out with a bang on his final year of school. You know Deke. He loves the attention."

Joe slid back down in bed. "That's for sure."

"You should march with us," Char said. "Just this one time."

"Sorry. I'll be working at the store with your father. I doubt if he'd pay me to go off protesting," he said with a grin.

Char was disappointed. She'd hoped to persuade Joe to join them. But she didn't push it.

She worked most of Tuesday on her article and turned it in Wednesday morning. Her editor approved it and it was added to the Friday edition.

"This is your best one yet," Joel told her. "I hope you plan on writing for the paper next year, too."

Char wanted to. She enjoyed writing more than anything else. And while writing her thesis paper, she'd been surprised at how much she liked to do research, as well.

On Friday, their English teacher handed back their graded thesis papers. "We had some outstanding papers this year," he told the class. "And some very interesting topics. You should all be proud of the fact that I learned something from each paper."

When her paper was set on the desk, Char stared at it expectantly. She opened it to the first page to see her grade, and then let out a sigh of relief. A big A was at the top of the page. The teacher had also written a note saying that Char was a talented writer and he hoped she'd continue to hone her skills.

Excitedly, she turned to Joe, who was reading his grade. "What did you get?" she asked.

He handed her the paper. "Here. Look for yourself."

She was finally going to see what he'd written about. As she stared at the title, Char's eyes grew wide. It read "Why America Can't Win the Vietnam War." She turned to Joe. "I'm stunned. I never would have thought you'd write a paper against the war."

"It's not against the war, only the truth about Vietnam. If you read the paper, you'll see I'm right," he said.

"But if you believe this, why don't you protest the war?" she asked.

"I can't protest the war the way Deke or the others do. But I'm beginning to believe that I can someday make a contribution to the history of the war. Or, the truth of it. Someday," he reiterated.

Char opened the page and saw the big A in red pen. The teacher had written notes on Joe's page, as well. "Great points. Good writing. If you don't someday write a book about your experience in Vietnam, then it would be a shame."

Char smiled proudly at Joe. "Yes. Maybe someday."

* * *

That evening, Deke found Char and Joe in the student union and sat down at their table. "Oh, my God, Char! Congratulations on your article. It was incredible. I've had dozens of people stop me in the halls and tell me they're going to join us tomorrow."

"That's wonderful," Char said. She'd also had many people stop her to tell her what a great article it was. It felt good to have her work appreciated.

"Some of the people from Chicago are already here. They're all crashing at my house. It's going to be packed there," Deke said. "Tomorrow, we're meeting at nine o'clock on the lawn by the ROTC building. We'll listen to the speakers, then organize the march down Main Street."

"Okay, I'll meet you at the college at nine," Char said.

Deke looked at Joe. "Join us. There will be other veterans there, too."

Joe shook his head. "Thanks, but no. I'll be working at the hardware store."

Deke laughed. "Man, you're a tough nut to crack." He turned back to Char. "I'll see you tomorrow. Be sure to find me. I want you right in front with me when we march." Deke waved and left.

Joe's expression turned serious. "Are you sure you want to participate? Something about this rubs me wrong."

"I have to be there for the paper anyway, so I might as well march," she said. "Stop frowning. He promised it would be peaceful."

"And you trust him?"

"Well, not completely," she admitted. "But he'd never let anything happen to me. Besides, this is our little town. What could possibly happen here?"

Joe didn't look completely sold on it, but Char was growing excited for the next day. If it was going to be as big an event across the country as Deke had said, it would be thrilling to be a part of history.

Chapter Twenty-Eight

Saturday morning Char woke up to a beautiful, sunny day. She was happy it wasn't raining. That would have been miserable. When she went downstairs for breakfast, she caught her dad as he was heading out the door for work.

"So, you're off to end the war, I hear," Ronald said.

"I wish it were that easy," she answered. "This will be my last article for the school newspaper this year, and Deke's last big rally before he graduates and has to start his real life. Might as well end it with a bang."

"Well, don't get arrested and tarnish the family's good name," he said, his eyes twinkling. He kissed her cheek and left.

Char went into the kitchen where her mother was drinking coffee at her new dinette table.

"There're fresh muffins on the counter," Ellen said.

"Thanks, Mom." Char poured a cup of coffee, put one of the still-warm muffins on a plate, then sat down across from her mother.

"Tell me more about this protest today," Ellen said.

"Deke called it the May Day protest. He said that it'll be happening in towns all over the country, and in Washington

D.C. today through Monday. He gave me a pamphlet that was being sent around to movement leaders, but I just glanced at it. I figured when I write my article, I'll look at it closer."

"I hope there won't be any trouble," Ellen said, frown lines gathering across her forehead. "The news on TV says there are still thousands of protestors in Washington D.C. and that something big is being planned."

"Deke told me about that. The plan is for the protestors to try to stop people from going to work on Monday. Their slogan is 'If the government doesn't stop the war, we will stop the government.' The protest today is going to be nothing like they're planning."

"That's good to hear, dear," Ellen said. "Just be careful."

Char found it comical that her parents and Joe were so worried. After all, she'd be around kids she'd gone to school with her entire life. And students from the college. Plus, she'd be with Deke. She didn't feel threatened in any way.

When Char arrived at the college parking lot at eight-thirty, she was surprised to see it was packed full with cars. She had to park down the street and walk back. As she neared the area where the rally was being held, she was stunned. Hundreds of people were crowded in the small area. She'd brought her camera along and took a picture of the mass of protestors. They were made up of mostly younger people, male and female alike, and nearly everyone had long, shaggy hair and wore beat-up jeans. There were several men wearing fatigue pants and army jackets. She wondered if they were veterans or just dressed that way. They were all crammed together, but everyone was talking peacefully amongst themselves as they waited for the rally to begin. Char had never imagined that Deke could bring together such a large crowd.

Walking the perimeter of the group, she made her way to the English building and saw Deke and two other men standing on the steps. Deke glanced up and waved her over.

"Char. I was getting worried about you. Come meet my friends from Chicago," Deke said, meeting her halfway and taking her hand. They walked to the steps and Deke introduced her.

"Guys, this is Char. She's our press for today. Char, this is Marcus and David. They're part of a larger faction of the movement in Chicago. They're going to be our speakers."

Char said hello to each of them. They were both clean-cut and their clothes were newer. They didn't look like they belonged in this crowd, let alone be leaders of it.

"Where did all the people come from?" Char asked Deke. "Are these all students from here? I don't recognize most of them."

"A large group of them are with us," Marcus said. "Ten busloads of protestors came with us this morning. The rest are from around here."

Char calculated that in her head. "You bussed five hundred people here?"

"About that," Marcus answered.

The number didn't seem to impress him as it did Char. She assumed he was used to this.

"And we had close to fifteen-hundred sign up for the rally as of yesterday," Deke said proudly. "They're not all here yet, but people keep streaming in. By the time we march, I'm sure we'll be close to two thousand."

Char was speechless. She'd thought maybe four or five hundred might show up. But this wasn't just a small rally. This was a full-blown protest.

She drew Deke aside. "Are you sure you can control that many people? What if they grow restless and start trouble?"

Deke laughed. "You sound like a parent. Don't worry so much, Char. The May Day protests are supposed to be peaceful disobedience. When we march downtown, it's to show the leaders in Washington that we have the power to shut things down. That's the point of the Main Street march. If we're on the sidewalks and in the streets, no one can shop or go about their business. It's a smaller version of what they're going to do in Washington on Monday. They're going to shut down the government, but we're just going to show we can shut down the town for a short time."

Char hadn't realized that the march would actually stop business today. She had thought it was just symbolic. "It's Saturday. The busiest day in town for shopping."

"Right," Deke said. "That's the point."

"My dad's hardware store is on Main Street."

"Yeah, I know. But so what? He loses a little business on Saturday and he'll make up for it on Monday. It's not a big deal, Char. We need to show the government that we have muscle behind our protests and we're no longer playing games. We mean it. Stop the war!"

"I can't do this, Deke. It's not right. The café. The bakery. They'll all lose business. We've known those people all our lives. It's not fair to them," Char said.

"It's not fair to Jeremy that he died in Vietnam, either," Deke shot back.

Char winced. Jeremy. No, it wasn't fair that he'd died. Or that Joe had been wounded.

Deke's tone softened. "I'm sorry, Char. But honestly, a few dollars lost is not as important as the lives we're losing in

Vietnam. March with us. Write about it. This is important."

She let out a long sigh. "Okay, I'll march," she said, feeling defeated.

Deke gave her his handsome grin. But it no longer had the power to make her feel better. Joe held her heart now, and his smile was the only one that could make her happy.

They returned to Marcus and David as it struck nine o'clock. Deke led Char over to the side of the makeshift stage so she could take pictures and notes. He spoke to the crowd.

"We're here today to show the government that we will not be IGNORED. We will be HEARD. They MUST stop the war, or people will rise up in every town, small and large, and show the government that it is WE THE PEOPLE who make the decisions in this country. Today, we are a part of the biggest national protest this country has ever seen. We are the May Day protestors, and we will be HEARD!"

The crowd cheered and raised their protest signs to show they agreed. STOP THE WAR! PEACE NOT WAR! BRING OUR BOYS HOME! Char took photos of the crowd as Deke's silver tongue drew every emotion out of them that he could manage. She pointed the camera at Deke; his eyes blazing, his face angry, his fist high in the air. He was completely in his element and in that moment, she had to admit, he was powerful. He held the crowd in his hand.

Marcus, and then David, spoke and the crowd grew in both size and energy. More young people streamed in during the speeches. Deke had been right. They would have a huge crowd by the time they marched.

Char was definitely watching history be made.

* * *

Joe and Ronald were busy all morning with customers. Almost everyone who came in mentioned the noise coming from the college on the edge of town.

"It sounds like a mob is being formed," one man said. "They're yelling and chanting. I decided to get what I needed early and go home and lock my doors."

Ronald had chuckled, but the man was dead serious. "It can't be that bad," he said. "They're just college kids."

The man shook his head. "It sure doesn't sound like kids to me."

Ronald and Joe went outside after that and listened. They could hear someone talking into a microphone but couldn't make out the words. Every so often, the crowd roared. It echoed down Main Street.

"It does sound like a lot of people," Ronald said, frowning. "I hate to think of Char in the middle of all that."

Joe secretly agreed but didn't want Ronald to worry. "I'm sure she'll be fine. Deke said she'd be with him the entire time. It's supposed to be a peaceful protest."

"Supposed to be," the older man said, obviously unconvinced.

As the morning wore on, they noticed there were fewer and fewer customers coming in. Ronald mentioned he thought that was strange for a Saturday, especially on the first of the month when sales were usually higher. Joe once again felt uneasy about the protest but kept quiet.

A short time after noon, a police officer entered the shop. "Are you the owner?" he asked Ronald.

Ronald nodded. "Is there a problem, Officer?"

"I'm advising businesses to close up for the day. There's going to be a large protest march coming down this street in the next hour or so, and I don't think you'll want to be here when it happens," the officer said.

Joe had come up to the front when he heard what the policeman was saying.

Ronald gave a little laugh. "It's just the kids from the college, Officer. I've known the leader of that march since he was five years old. I highly doubt it will be dangerous."

The policeman didn't look amused. "It's more than just a few locals, sir. Several busloads of protestors came here from Chicago. We've been told by good authority that it's possible for violence to erupt. It would be best if you and your employee lock up and leave. Otherwise, once the march starts, you might get caught in the middle."

"The middle of what?" Joe asked, alarmed.

"Just close up and go home," the policeman said. Then he left the store.

The two men stared at each other.

"Was he a local policeman?" Joe asked.

Ronald shook his head. "I've never seen him before."

Fear washed over Joe. He and Ronald went outside to see what was going on. They were shocked when they looked up the street that led out of the business district to the neighborhoods. Thirty police officers in riot gear stood there. Behind them, army trucks were parked in the distance with National Guard soldiers jumping out of them.

"They called in the National Guard? For this?" Ronald asked.

"They must know something we don't," Joe said. "There's more going on with this protest than we were led to believe." Anger replaced Joe's fear. Anger at Deke for placing Char in harm's way.

Ronald turned to him, and Joe knew immediately what he was thinking.

"I have to get Charlotte." Ronald pulled off his work apron and headed back into the store.

"Wait, Ronald." Joe followed him inside. "Let me get her. I know where they are at the college. Maybe I can get to her before they march. Or catch her as they hit Main Street. She's supposed to be right in front with Deke."

Ronald glanced at Joe's cane, then back up to his eyes. The deep creases in his forehead said it all.

"I realize you could walk faster than me," Joe said. "But I'd fit in with that crowd better. Please. Go home so you're safe and Ellen doesn't worry. I'll get Char and if we can't get past the police to bring her home, we can hide out up in the apartment until it's over."

"All right," Ronald conceded reluctantly. "I'll trust you to get her. I know you can protect her. Call the house as soon as you're safe if you aren't able to come home."

Joe nodded. He took off his apron and went upstairs for his coat. He figured if the protestors saw him in his army jacket, they would think he was a veteran protesting the war with them.

When he came down, he walked with Ronald out the back door into the alley.

"Be safe," Ronald said, squeezing his arm. He headed down the street toward home.

Joe went back inside and picked up the extra key for the back door. He walked into the alley and locked up, then turned toward the college. Joe hoped they hadn't started marching yet. He had to get Char before anything terrible happened.

* * *

Char glanced at her watch as she waited for the large crowd to assemble behind her and Deke. He yelled out instructions through a megaphone so the people in the very back could hear. Several other local college students had been chosen to walk in the front too, as well as David and Marcus.

"Please keep in formation!" Deke instructed. "Remember, this is a peaceful protest march. We are only attempting to disrupt business for the day. There will be no violence."

He turned to Char, who'd covered her ears from the blaring sound coming from the megaphone. "Too loud?" He chuckled.

"A little," she said, rolling her eyes. She just wanted the march to be over with. The crowd had been worked up all morning from the speakers and now they were restless. Char wanted to start marching before the others walked right over top of them.

Deke waved his arm in a sign to get moving. "Let's march!" he yelled.

They started walking at a slow pace, side-by-side, ten across. Char glanced back to see how long the line was, but she couldn't see its end. Protest signs were raised proudly in the air and several people were chanting, "Peace, not war!"

She looked over at Deke and saw his face was flushed with excitement and his eyes were bright. He was definitely in his element today. He turned to her and smiled wide. Then he linked his arm through hers as they marched on.

* * *

Joe made his way down the alley for two blocks until he was behind the grocery store then he turned and walked over to Main Street. He heard the protestors chanting before he saw them. About three blocks down, they were headed in his direction.

Joe looked in the opposite direction. The Corner Café and all the shops up Main Street were closed with their lights off. At the end stood the police, lined up ten across. National Guardsmen stood behind them.

Joe continued toward the protestors. As he drew nearer, he saw Char on the very end, with Deke next to her, her arm linked with his. Char's brows rose when she saw Joe.

Much to Joe's surprise, Deke turned with a megaphone in hand and called out to the protestors, "Stop walking! Stay where you are!"

There stood Joe, one man with a cane standing in the street facing a crowd of two thousand.

Char dropped Deke's arm and walked over to Joe. "What's going on? Why are you here?"

"I came to get you," he said. "There's going to be trouble. Look." He pointed to where the police and National Guardsmen stood.

Char squinted, the sun in her eyes, and stared in the direction he was pointing. "Why are there cops here?" she asked, looking confused.

"They're expecting violence. A policeman came into the store and told your dad to close for the day. All the stores have closed. It's just your group, the police, and the National Guard out here."

Deke came up to them. "Are you joining the march, Joe?" He seemed unconcerned by the situation.

"No!" Joe said, frustrated. "Take a look down the street. They're waiting for your group to start something."

Deke shaded his eyes and stared ahead. "We're not doing anything wrong. We have a permit to march downtown. They can't touch us unless we do something."

Joe ignored Deke and turned back to Char. "Please come with me. I promised your dad I'd bring you home."

"Char, don't leave," Deke said. "March with us. Nothing bad is going to happen."

Her eyes darted between Deke and Joe, looking unsure. "We're not doing anything wrong," she told Joe. "They wouldn't dare touch us if we're peaceful."

"Char, please," Joe pleaded.

"It's going to be fine, Joe," she said.

He could tell by the look on her face that she didn't completely believe that.

Deke broke out into a smile. "Looks like I win, soldier. You're welcome to walk along with us." He turned to the crowd. "Remember. We march for peace!" he yelled over the megaphone. "Let's go!"

The large crowd began moving again. The chanting grew to a roar. Joe had no choice but to walk along next to Char. He'd promised Ronald he'd keep her safe, and he meant to keep his promise.

They passed the Corner Café. Then the bakery. Each step brought them closer to the line of policemen in riot gear.

"Please, Char. Let's get out of here," Joe pleaded.

She looked at him, and her eyes showed her resolve was wavering. Yet, she marched on.

Suddenly, a loud crash echoed down the street. Char and Joe both spun around and saw that someone had broken the big glass window at the café. Immediately, a rock sailed through the air and shattered the window of Annie's Gift Shop. Chaos erupted. Joe looked in the direction of the police. They were no longer standing still—they were running toward them.

Chapter Twenty-Nine

Joe grabbed Char's hand and pulled her away from the crowd. They slipped into the narrow space that separated the hardware store from the bakery. Once they were in the shadows, Char stopped and let go of Joe. She watched the scene before her. Several protestors were abandoning the cause and running across the town square. Other protestors were still chanting, and above that, she heard more glass shattering. Deke still stood at the front of the line, looking dazed.

"Come on, Char. Let's go!" Joe pulled her hand once more and she followed him. They made their way to the back alley then stopped behind the hardware store.

"The police cars are blocking the alley. We can't leave the area," Joe said. Pulling the key from his pocket, he unlocked the back door and they ran inside, securing it behind them.

Char headed for the front windows to see what was happening, but Joe stopped her. "We have to get upstairs. We're not safe down here."

She frowned at him. "What do you mean?"

Suddenly, one of the hardware store's windows shattered. Char screamed.

Joe yanked her to the staircase that led up to the apartment. He locked the downstairs door behind them, then told her to run up while he followed as fast as his hurt leg would allow. Once upstairs, Joe locked that door and jammed a chair under it.

Char had run to the window to look down at the street. The line between the police and protestors had vanished. They were intermingled in mass confusion. Some of the police had their batons out and were using them to push the people away from the buildings. But the crowd seemed endless. Below, more glass exploded, and Char jumped at the sound.

"Back away from the window!" Joe yelled. "Don't let them see you're up here."

She moved away slowly as the drama outside hit her fully. "My dad's shop. They're breaking into my dad's shop. Why?" Nothing seemed real. She felt like she was in the middle of a nightmare.

Joe came up behind her and wrapped his arms around her. "It's what the police were waiting for. Somehow, they knew something would happen."

Char turned to face him. "Or maybe something happened because the cops were there, waiting. It fueled the protestors' rage."

"I don't know, Char. Maybe."

Noise came from below. Footsteps inside the store, items being tossed around.

A chill crept through Char. "They're in the building," she whispered.

"We need to secure our space," Joe said. "Go get a large towel to jam under the door. I'm going to make sure the windows are locked up tight."

Char froze, paralyzed by fear.

"Go Char!"

His command brought her back to her senses. She ran to get a towel from the bathroom and when she came out, he was checking the window locks.

"Shove the towel against the bottom of the door as tight as you can," Joe said, heading to the bedroom.

"Why?" Her hands were shaking and she felt cold all over.

"Tear gas. The police will start using it soon. We don't want it to seep in up here."

Char did what she was told. When she was finished, she saw Joe coming from the bedroom with a pistol in his hand. Her eyes grew wide. "Why do you have that?"

"Just a precaution." He set it on the dining table. "If the crowd down there starts looting, and if they break down the door to come up here, we'll need protection."

"You'd actually shoot someone?" Char asked.

He moved over to her. "Only if we're threatened. We need to be prepared for anything."

Char wrapped her arms around her. Fear gripped her. It was all so surreal. One minute, she was walking peacefully down the street, the next, she felt like she was in a war zone.

"Where did you get that gun?" she asked.

"It was Tony's. I found it in his bag." Joe said, his voice calm.

She just stared at him. Joe had never mentioned he owned a gun. It shouldn't have surprised her. Her father had a pistol hidden in a drawer near the bed. If she'd known about it earlier, it wouldn't have bothered her. But seeing it now, with chaos down in the streets, intensified the situation.

Joe pulled her close and held her tight. "I'm sorry if it scared you, sweetie. My first thought, my only thought, is your safety."

She nodded, still feeling dazed. They moved closer to the

windows to see what was happening outside. People were running all about. Many were trying to get away. Others stood there, stoic, holding their signs and chanting while insanity swirled around them. The police were trying to stop the people who were throwing rocks through windows. Char saw several people running down the street with boxes under their arms and items in their hands.

"They're stealing," she said, horrified. "They're taking stuff from our store."

Something flew through the sky and hit the ground. In seconds, smoke filled the air.

"Tear gas," Joe said. "I hope these windows are tight. I don't want to have to leave the apartment."

Char stared down at the street again. She couldn't believe what she was seeing. This happened in big cities, not quiet little towns where the biggest excitement was fireworks on the Fourth of July.

Tears filled her eyes. She thought of all the damage being done to the stores up and down the block. To her father's store. The shop owners had never done anything bad to anyone to deserve such treatment. They had all worked hard to earn a living. And look what only a few minutes could do to a lifetime of work.

Joe kept his arms tight around her. "I'm sorry, Char. It's awful, I know."

"I don't understand," she said softly. "It was supposed to be peaceful. This shouldn't have happened. Why are they acting that way?"

"Deke wanted a revolution," Joe said. "That's what he got. It's easy to toss that word around, but living it is ugly."

They went to the sofa and sat, huddled together. Joe pulled

the afghan from the back of the sofa and wrapped it around them. Downstairs, they still heard noise, like someone throwing merchandise around. Her heart pounded as she prayed they wouldn't try to come upstairs. She felt trapped and terrified. She'd never have believed she'd feel that way in her hometown.

"Is this what war feels like?" she whispered. "Being scared, waiting to see what will happen next? Hoping that nothing will happen?"

"This times a thousand," he said. He kissed her cheek tenderly. "I'm here, Char. You'll always be safe with me."

She curled in closer to him, laying her head on his shoulder. She believed him when he said she'd be safe. That was how much she trusted him.

* * *

Hours went by as Joe and Char huddled together on the sofa. The noise outside faded, and soon disappeared. Luckily, the tear gas didn't seep inside the apartment. Char fell asleep with her head on Joe's shoulder. When she woke, it was dark outside and everything was deathly quiet. She sat up, realizing that she'd been lying down on the sofa.

Joe was gone.

Panic flooded through her as she glanced around the dark room. Then, she heard footsteps on the stairs and her heart pounded. Did she dare call out for Joe? Should she hide?

The door opened and a beam of light proceeded the man behind it. From the dull glow coming in the windows, she could tell it was Joe. Char exhaled a sigh of relief.

"Sorry if I scared you," Joe said, coming over to the sofa. "I tried to be quiet."

"Where were you?"

"I went downstairs to call your parents. I figured they'd be in a state of panic by now. They were, but at least they were smart enough not to come downtown. I told them you were safe and with me."

"Is it all over? Was anyone down there?" Char asked, fear still lurking inside her. She hated how it felt. It made her feel weak.

"Everyone is gone. The police are patrolling the streets, and your dad said the whole town is on curfew tonight, so no one is supposed to be out walking around. He said you should stay here instead of going home. He'll come first thing in the morning to assess the damage."

Char pulled the afghan to her and wrapped it tightly around her to ward off the chill that still ran through her. "How is it downstairs? Is it as bad as it had sounded?"

Joe sat next to her. "The front windows are broken, but luckily the side windows weren't touched. There's merchandise all over the floor, and racks are knocked down. I didn't stay down there too long. I just made the call to your parents and came back up."

She shook her head sadly. "My poor dad. He didn't deserve this. I should never have been a part of this protest. I should have known better." Tears threatened to fall again. "Do you think Deke knew it would erupt in violence? Did he lie to me—again?"

"I don't know, hon. He may not have known it was going to happen. Maybe he did believe it was going to be peaceful. The police had known something would happen; otherwise, they wouldn't have been there with the National Guard."

Char no longer knew what to believe. She'd trusted Deke.

But maybe he'd trusted his colleagues from Chicago and been lied to. All she knew was her father's store, and all the other stores, were damaged, and she had been a willing participant in the march. It made her sick just thinking about it.

"It's almost midnight," Joe said. "Let's go to bed and get some sleep. There's nothing that can be done until tomorrow."

She nodded and stood up with Joe's arm around her. They walked to the bedroom and Char slipped between the covers without even getting undressed. She was exhausted.

Joe kissed her cheek before leaving the room. He returned a minute later and placed something in the drawer beside the bed. Char knew it was the pistol. Thankfully, he hadn't needed to use it.

"Goodnight, sweetie," Joe whispered into her ear as he curled himself around her.

She was so tired, she couldn't even answer. But she felt comforted and safe knowing that he was right beside her.

* * *

Sunlight streamed in through the bedroom window the next morning. Char slowly stretched, thinking how wonderful it felt to wake up next to Joe. It took a moment for her to remember why she was there, and suddenly, her heart sank. Today they'd have to face the reality of what had happened yesterday.

They both got out of bed and Char quickly cleaned up in the bathroom. Joe offered to make her breakfast, but she declined. She just wanted to go downstairs and assess the damage to the store.

It was almost nine o'clock by the time they both went downstairs. Stepping out the door, into the shop, Char stopped. Brisk morning air filled the room through the broken windows, but the chill Char felt came from deep inside. Shards of glass were scattered all over the floor. The display counter where the register had sat was also shattered. Merchandise lay strewn about, up and down the aisles. Wall shelves had fallen to the floor, and cans of paint had burst open and sprayed color everywhere. Destruction was everywhere and it brought Char to tears.

"Charlotte." Her father walked over the glass and kicked away the items on the floor to reach her. He pulled her into a hug. "I'm so relieved you're okay. Thank God for Joe."

Tears trailed down her cheeks as she pulled away. "I'm so sorry, Dad. I shouldn't have been a part of that march. Look at what they did. Your store is ruined!"

Ronald hugged her again. "It's okay, dear. All this can be fixed and replaced. But you? If anything had happened to you, that would have been a tragedy. All I cared about was your safety."

He held her close until her tears slowed. Char had often taken her parents' love for granted, as if it were her right. But today, she felt that love intensely. It showed in the way her father held her, and how he looked at her so tenderly. After the fear she'd experienced last night, her father's strength and love were a great comfort.

After a time, Ronald stepped back and assessed the damage. Char watched him walk through the store he'd worked in and owned all his adult life. The store his father had opened and Ronald had worked in as a boy. Everything was destroyed. When he turned, she saw the weariness in his eyes. From worry? Disappointment? She didn't know. It broke her heart to see her father's disheartened expression.

"I never in my life thought I'd see anything like this in our little town," Ronald said, shaking his head. "Do these young people really believe they can stop a war by turning our towns into war zones?"

Char had wondered the same thing every time Deke talked about a revolution.

Joe walked up from the back. "The storage room doesn't look too bad," he told Ronald. "It looks like they tried prying open a locked file cabinet. Probably searching for money."

"It's a good thing I brought the weekly deposit home yesterday," Ronald said. "At least they didn't get any cash." He looked Joe in the eyes and placed his hand on his shoulder. "Thank you for finding Char and keeping her safe. She means more to me than all of this. You're a good man, Joe."

Joe nodded. "You're welcome, sir. But to be honest, I did it for me, too." He grinned at Char. "I'm getting used to her being around."

Ronald laughed and Char rolled her eyes.

"I can take care of myself," she said. But in truth, she was relieved that Joe had been with her.

Ronald put his hand on his hips. "Well, it looks like we have a lot of work ahead of us. The insurance adjustor is coming by this morning to assess the damage then we can start cleaning this place up. I need to get a few sheets of plywood to cover those broken windows until they can be replaced. But first, I'm going to check on the other businesses and see what they need. Maybe the lumber mill can deliver the plywood for everyone all at once to save them a trip."

Char, Joe, and Ronald went outside into the bright May sunshine. Already, the other shop owners were working on their stores. They had all sustained similar types of damage as the hardware store had.

As Char walked up the street, her heart went out to the people she'd known her whole life. Despite it all, everyone seemed to take it in stride. They would clean up and continue on. Yet, Char couldn't help but feel something had shifted. The innocence of the small town had vanished. Doors would be locked tight from now on, and strangers would be watched warily before handing out welcoming smiles. Everyone would be suspect, just because one beautiful day in May, things got out of hand and their tiny place in the world changed.

Chapter Thirty

As Deke had predicted, the May Day protest had been the largest ever around the country. From Washington D.C. to San Francisco, demonstrators did their best to show America that the people ruled. That Monday, Washington D.C. had become a war zone with helicopters landing on the Mall to drop off Marines and tanks on Dupont Circle. More than seven-thousand of the twenty-five thousand protestors were arrested as they tried to shut down the government by blocking streets, bridges, and entrances into government buildings. Over the three-day period, six thousand more protestors were arrested. Their numbers were so large, they had to be held at the practice fields near RFK Stadium. And while the bigger cities got all the news coverage, the protest in Grand Falls only made it into the school newspaper. Deke and his friends weren't rewarded with national headlines for their efforts. Basically, it had all been for nothing.

* * *

In the last week of school, Char turned in her final article to the school newspaper. It detailed the protest, how it had started out as an uplifting event then turned violent. She tried to be as objective as possible, but it had been difficult. After spending all day Sunday and several nights that week helping her father clean up the store, her anger at the protestors and looters had deepened. But Joel liked the article and reiterated that he hoped to see her next term.

Char learned more about what had happened during the protest after the police had intervened. Roughly one hundred and fifty people had been arrested, Deke included. Marcus and David had fled as soon as the rioting began. Many of the others who'd come from Chicago had headed for the buses and left immediately before anyone could stop them. A few were detained, but then released on bail. Char heard that Deke's father had bailed him out of jail Sunday morning. Since the authorities couldn't prove who'd thrown the rocks and broken the windows, they couldn't hold the protestors they'd arrested. However, the ones they'd caught carrying merchandise from the stores were charged with theft.

On Friday afternoon, as Char and Joe were walking out to the school's parking lot to her car, Deke appeared.

"Hey, Char. Joe," he called, casually walking up to them as if he didn't have a care in the world.

"Deke? Where have you been all week?" Char asked.

"Tying up a few loose ends," he said. "I'm sorry I didn't contact you sooner. It's been kind of crazy since the protest."

"I'll say." She crossed her arms.

"Char, I'm sorry about Saturday. I truly am. And what happened to your father's store and all the stores on the block. You have to believe that I never had any intention of causing violence that day. When I promised you a peaceful protest, I'd meant it," Deke told her.

"And I'm supposed to believe that?" Char asked angrily.

Deke sighed and ran his hand through his long hair. "I hope you will. I went around to all the stores, including your father's, and apologized to the owners. It wasn't supposed to happen."

"Then why were the police and National Guard here? They suspected something," Char said.

"I was just as surprised as you to see them there. I talked to Marcus on the phone the other day and asked him what had happened. He suspects that there was an informant in their group. It happens more than people realize. An undercover FBI agent joins a group to learn their plans about protests. Then they inform the police. Marcus and David admitted they were responsible for the rioting. They had placed a few people in the crowd to start trouble. They wanted this small-town protest to make the national headlines and show the country that the anti-war movement is everywhere, not just in the big cities. I had no idea he was planning such a thing."

Char shook her head in disgust. "I'm glad they didn't make the news. They shouldn't be rewarded for what they did. But it's good that you apologized to all the store owners."

Deke's face softened. "I've lived here all my life, too. I've eaten at the café countless times and bought treats from the bakery since I was a child. I care about these people."

She nodded, but she was still angry with him for what had happened.

"Anyway," Deke said. "I came to thank you, Joe, for making Char leave the protest and taking care of her. It was mayhem after the first window was broken. I would have felt terrible if she'd been hurt or arrested. I appreciate your good sense to make her leave."

"You're welcome," Joe said. "Although, I'm sure she would

have figured out what to do even without my help."

Deke turned to Char. "I also came to tell you that I'm leaving. Now that I'm finished with school, my college deferment is over. Vietnam is calling my name and I refuse to go. I'm heading up to Chicago to join the anti-war group there, and then, who knows? I can go underground if necessary. Or go to Canada."

Char's mouth dropped open. "You're dodging the draft? But that's illegal!"

"So is this war," Deke said. "I can't make myself go over there and kill people. I'll put my talents elsewhere."

"But don't you have to stay here? You were charged with disorderly conduct and inciting a riot. You can't just leave," Char said.

Deke grinned. "Just watch me."

Char was speechless. She never thought Deke would go so far as to become a fugitive to protest the war.

Deke reached out and hugged her. "Goodbye, Char," he said tenderly. "I wish things between us had turned out differently. I'll always have a soft spot in my heart for you."

She hugged him back. "Goodbye, Deke. Please take care of yourself."

He pulled away and faced Joe with his hand raised. "You're a good man, Joe. I really believe that even though I didn't always treat you very well. Take good care of Char. She deserves only the best."

Joe shook his hand. "I will."

"I suppose you think I'm a traitor, leaving like this," Deke said.

"That's not my call," Joe told him. "I don't condone what you're doing, Deke, but I can't condemn it either. We all have to do what's right for us."

"Thank you," Deke said. After one more long look and smile at Char, he spun on his heel and left.

Char drew closer to Joe and he draped his arm around her waist as they watched Deke walk away. "What do you think will happen to him?" she asked.

"I think he'll find his way, eventually," Joe said.

Char thought that they all would—eventually.

Epilogue

2018

C har and Joe sat in the dining room eating dinner as the nightly news played quietly on their television.

"So much going on in the world," Joe said, shaking his head. "It never ends. The faces change but the topics never do."

"But the world keeps spinning anyway," Char said, taking a bite out of her grilled chicken. "How was the first day of classes?"

Joe chuckled. "The same as always. A lot of moans and groans over the syllabus. Apparently, kids don't enjoy reading American history. Luckily, my other class has older students who want to be in it. The class on the Vietnam War is always an interesting one to teach."

Char nodded. Joe had been teaching that class for years, ever since he'd written books about the Vietnam War. His non-fiction book, *The Rise and Fall of the Vietnam War*, had been a popular one, and the college granted him permission to base a class off the subject. He'd also written a memoir of his war experiences in Vietnam.

After his first year of college, Joe had changed his major from political science to history with a minor in creative writing. He'd felt it was important to preserve and teach history. Maybe it would teach the younger generation not to repeat it. By the look of today's events on the news, so far that objective hadn't been successful.

Char had received her degree in English and teaching then had gone additional years to earn her Master's. She'd taught English literature and creative writing at the college for years, and had also been the teacher in charge of the school newspaper. Her desire to write, though, finally got the best of her and after her first women's fiction novel had been published in 1986, she quit teaching and pursued a career as a novelist. To date she'd written twenty-five novels and at sixty-seven years old, she had no plans of quitting.

The summer after college graduation, Char and Joe had married and lived in the apartment above the hardware store while they both worked and pursued their Master degrees. Joe had continued to work for Ronald in the store part-time, and also student-taught until he was hired as a full-time professor. After that, they'd bought a nice home in a quiet neighborhood where the trees were mature and white picket fences lined the yards. Joe had insisted on having a front porch swing where he and Char could sit in the evenings and enjoy the cool breezes.

They still lived in that house today, and had also been able to afford a summer home on a lake in Wisconsin. They loved their summer retreat where they could walk the wooded trails and take their boat out on the water on sunny days.

Grand Falls no longer resembled the small town it had been in 1971. The downtown was tired-looking, although the town square still had the lovely lawn and gazebo. Unfortunately, a July storm had knocked down many of the old oak trees, but new ones had been planted. Main Street had changed greatly. Her father retired in 1992 and sold the building to a florist shop. Since then, it had been a craft shop, a tattoo parlor, and a wedding boutique. Currently, it sat empty, waiting for its next reincarnation. Every shop on the street, including the Corner Café, had changed hands. The bakery had been gutted and turned into a second-hand clothing shop and the café was now an antique store. When Char walked by it, the few times a year she was downtown, she'd see toys from her youth and smile. Well, she guessed they would be antiques to children today.

The college had re-built a few of the dormitory buildings, but other than that, it was very much the same. Out past the college a Walmart and Target store had been built, and beyond that was the Grand Falls Mall, which, since 2008, had been hurting for business.

Other things had changed, as well. Mrs. Bennington sold her house when she'd grown too old to run it and had moved into an assisted living facility until she'd passed away. The large house had been renovated with an elevator added and had been used first as a group home for disabled individuals, then as a home for the elderly. Rumors spread over the years that footsteps could be heard in the attic late at night, and sometimes an orange glow, like a lit cigarette, could be seen in the attic window. Some said it was haunted by the soldier who'd hung himself. Because of that, the house had stood empty, for sale, for years now. Char and Joe hoped that the rumors weren't true. They didn't like to think of Tony spending eternity pacing in the attic. They hoped he'd found peace.

Char's father and mother had lived long, happy lives. After Ronald had retired, they traveled a little, and enjoyed life. In 2010, her father became ill and passed away at the age of eighty-five. Her mother passed three years later in 2013. It had been hard on both Char and Joe. Ronald and Ellen had always treated Joe like a son, and had been wonderful parents.

After the first year of college, Char's friend Patty quit school and married Craig. He'd been spared the draft since his lottery number was low and they'd moved to Chicago where he worked for a large finance company. They had three children and Patty loved being a stay-at-home mom. For many years, the two couples would get together in the summer and it would be just like old times. Patty and Craig also visited at their lake home in later years. In 2013, Patty was diagnosed with an aggressive breast cancer and died two years later. Char missed her friend dearly.

Jenny had finished college and had recently retired from working as a college librarian. She and Terry had broken off their relationship in her junior year and she concentrated on school instead. Jenny had worked as the grade school librarian for a couple of years after graduation, but when her parents decided to move to Florida, it only took her one visit to decide to move there too. A few years later, she'd met a science professor where she worked, and they eventually married and had one child. Char never saw her old friend, but they still exchanged Christmas and birthday cards every year.

The Vietnam War ended when the last U.S. soldiers left in April 1975. Whether it ended because of the pressure put on by protestors for years, or because the politicians finally admitted it could not be won, Char had no idea. The years of protesting had changed the public's perception of the war, and perhaps that of the politicians, as well. No matter why it ended, she and Joe celebrated when the last of the Vietnam veterans came home.

Through the years, Char had heard tidbits of Deke's where-abouts from Craig, who occasionally heard from him. Deke disappeared for several years, and re-surfaced after President Jimmy Carter pardoned draft dodgers in 1977. She never saw him again, not even when first his father, then his mother, died. She supposed that the rift between him and his parents over his running from the draft had been too wide to mend. She'd found that sad, considering the wonderful relationship she'd always had with her parents. The last she'd heard of Deke, he was living in San Francisco, teaching at Berkeley. He had married a beautiful woman, had two children, and lived a good, prosperous life.

Char and Joe had never been blessed with children, and had long ago accepted that one disappointment. Instead, they lived for their work, and through the years, they'd traveled the world. Char volunteered weekly at the local food shelf and with the reading program at a local grade school. Besides teaching, Joe was in the process of writing another book. At the age of sixty-nine, he still enjoyed teaching. He and Char talked about his retiring every year, and every September he said: "Just one more year." As long as he continued to enjoy his work, he didn't want to give it up.

Char never completely understood the reason for the Viet-nam War and the deaths of so many young men, including her brother, Jeremy. After years of searching for answers, she real-ized there were none. Her brother died an honorable death while serving his country. She could live with that.

After dinner, Joe switched off the television and helped Char clear the table.

"Are you ready to go for a walk?" he asked after she'd placed the dishes in the dishwasher.

"Ready in a minute." She grabbed a sweater and slipped it on.

They headed outside into the cool autumn evening. Joe's leg had grown stiffer through the years, but he continued to walk to keep it from becoming completely useless. He leaned heavier on his cane these days, but that was to be expected. As they strolled around the neighborhood, they waved to children playing in their yards and stopped a moment to exchange greetings with several neighbors. They felt lucky to have so many friends after living in the same place all these years. Sometimes, it felt like they knew everyone, either from being associated with the college or volunteering. But that was fine with them. That was one of the things they loved about small-town living.

After they'd circled the block, the couple walked up their front steps and sat on the wooden porch swing. Joe wrapped his arm around Char's waist as she moved in closer against him. They watched as the sun set in the sky and the first of the stars began to shimmer above.

"Do you hear that?" Joe asked, his gray eyes twinkling as they had the first time she'd ever shared a porch swing with him decades ago.

"Yes, I do," she answered. All around them were the sounds of the night. The crickets chirping and toads croaking.

"Night music," he said.

"It means we're going to be just fine," she said.

And they sat there and listened to their favorite music of all.

The End

Acknowledgments

Writing a novel is a solitary job, but preparing it for publication takes a team of talented people. I'm lucky in that I have the most amazing team to help me polish and package my work.

A big thank you to my editor, Samantha Stroh Bailey, for her incredible ability to take my rough draft and help me turn it into a polished story. Her heartfelt encouragement throughout the project is so greatly appreciated.

Huge appreciation goes to my enormously talented book cover designer and formatter, Deborah Bradseth of Tugboat Design. She's been with me since my very first book and I can't even imagine working with any other cover designer. We work so well together: I drive her crazy and she produces the perfect cover for me every time.

My novels would never find readers if it weren't for a large group of book bloggers who spread the word about their favorite books and authors. I appreciate them all and the time they spend supporting authors. I'm especially grateful to Susan Deuel Schleicher of The Book Bag who has been reading my books since the very beginning and has been wonderfully supportive.

Most of all, I thank the readers who've supported me since

the very beginning. Your heartfelt reviews and constant encouragement has made writing a joy.

Night Music is the book that no one wanted to publish. Let's hope it's the novel that everyone will want to read.

About the Author

Deanna Lynn Sletten is the author of *Maggie's Turn, Finding Libbie, One Wrong Turn,* and several other titles. She writes heart-warming women's fiction and romance novels with unforgettable characters. She has also written one middle-grade novel that takes you on the adventure of a lifetime. Deanna believes in fate, destiny, love at first sight, soul mates, second chances, and happily ever after, and her novels reflect that.

Deanna is married and has two grown children. When not writing, she enjoys walking the wooded trails around her home with her beautiful Australian Shepherd, traveling, and relaxing on the lake.

Deanna loves hearing from her readers.
Connect with her at:
Her website: http://www.deannalsletten.com
Blog: http://www.deannalynnsletten.com
Facebook: http://www.facebook.com/deannalynnsletten
Twitter: http://www.twitter.com/deannalsletten

Made in United States
Orlando, FL
27 July 2022

20243735R00173